THE BURYING
GROUND

Thaddeus Lewis Mysteries

On the Head of a Pin
Sowing Poison
47 Sorrows

THE BURYING GROUND

A Thaddeus Lewis Mystery

Janet Kellough

DUNDURN
TORONTO

Editor: Allison Hirst
Design: Laura Boyle
Cover Design: Laura Boyle
Front Cover Image: © Shutterstock/Suppakij1017
Printer: Webcom

Library and Archives Canada Cataloguing in Publication

Kellough, Janet
    The burying ground : a Thaddeus Lewis mystery / Janet Kellough.

Issued in print and electronic formats.
ISBN 978-1-4597-2470-9 (pbk.).--ISBN 978-1-4597-2471-6 (pdf).--
ISBN 978-1-4597-2472-3 (epub)

    I. Title.

PS8621.E558B87 2015   C813'.6   C2014-907097-
                                              C2014-907098-5

1   2   3   4   5   19   18   17   16   15

 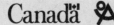

Conseil des Arts du Canada   Canada Council for the Arts   Canada   ONTARIO ARTS COUNCIL CONSEIL DES ARTS DE L'ONTARIO an Ontario government agency un organisme du gouvernement de l'Ontario

We acknowledge the support of the Canada Council for the Arts and the Ontario Arts Council for our publishing program. We also acknowledge the financial support of the Government of Canada through the Canada Book Fund and Livres Canada Books, and the Government of Ontario through the Ontario Book Publishing Tax Credit and the Ontario Media Development Corporation.

Care has been taken to trace the ownership of copyright material used in this book. The author and the publisher welcome any information enabling them to rectify any references or credits in subsequent editions.

                                                          J. Kirk Howard, President

Printed and bound in Canada.

VISIT US AT
Dundurn.com | @dundurnpress | Facebook.com/dundurnpress | Pinterest.com/dundurnpress

Dundurn
3 Church Street, Suite 500
Toronto, Ontario, Canada
M5E 1M2

For Autumn and Heili
because I promised to put their names in a book

Chapter 1

Morgan Spicer had just locked his back door and turned toward the hallway that led to his bedroom when he happened to glance through the tiny kitchen window that looked out over the rows of graves behind the Keeper's Lodge. Inky shadows chased across the ground as light from the gibbous moon streamed through swaying branches and spilled past marble markers and granite headstones. The distortion made it difficult to decipher the true nature of anything that stood in the burying ground, but Morgan was sure that he had glimpsed something odd — a glint of metal, a reflection of moonlight. Or maybe it was just the tail of a shooting star.

And then, as he squinted into the darkness, one of the shadows suddenly shifted sideways and was caught in silhouette by the moonlight breaking past a cloud.

It was a man in a John Bull hat.

Again Morgan saw a small flash of light. A man in a black hat with a dark lantern, shuttered to shield his presence. Morgan fumbled to unlock the back door. Then he rushed down the path that led past the stone chapel that stood in the centre of the graveyard.

As his eyes adjusted to the darkness, he realized that it was not one man, but two, halfway down the length of the grounds, in the middle of the right-hand rows of graves. The man in the hat turned and saw Morgan thundering down the path. With a shout he dropped the lantern. The second man tossed a spade to the ground and they both ran toward the back of the cemetery, where they scrambled over the fence and dropped to the other side. Both men disappeared into the alleyway that wound its way through the surrounding blocks of buildings.

Morgan was tempted to climb the fence and follow them, but he was winded from his run, and the men had far too great a head start for him to ever catch up. He stopped for a moment to get his breath, then he walked back through the Burying Ground to where he'd first seen the intruders.

A mound of soil was heaped beside an open grave, the granite marker knocked to the ground. The lid of the wooden coffin was pried open and the body tossed up against a corner of the hole as if to get it out of the way. One arm was draped along the edge of the hole, the bone shining eerily white as it poked through its winding sheet. The rest of the corpse slumped back into the pit, as if longing to slide back into the earth.

With a sigh, Morgan retrieved the discarded lantern and opened its shutters to cast some light to work by, and then he gently lifted the shrouded body back into its coffin. He used the spade the intruders had left behind to shovel the dirt back into the hole. Only when the earth was mounded over the grave again did he trudge back toward the cottage. The stone could wait until morning.

* * *

The local constable was unconcerned when Morgan reported the incident the next day.

"Grave robbers, most likely," he said. "Resurrectionists. Wouldn't be the first time."

"But they didn't take the body," Morgan pointed out.

"I expect you surprised them before they had time to grab it."

"I suppose." But he was doubtful about this premise. "Then why wouldn't they be more careful with the marker? It would have been one less thing to put back."

Grave robbers had targeted the Toronto Strangers' Burying Ground before. Usually the culprits tried to leave the site as undisturbed as possible in an attempt to disguise their activities. Any items buried with the body were removed and left in the empty coffin. Should the bone diggers be discovered, they would not then be open to charges of theft, as, in that peculiar way of the law, clothing and jewellery were property — a body was not. Once the cadaver was secured, the culprits would replace the earth and rake the surface level in the hope that no one would notice that it had been dug up. No such care had been taken this time. There was no point, Morgan realized. An attempt to restore the appearance of the gravesite only made sense if the burial was recent. This corpse had been in the ground long enough for the dirt to settle and the grass to grow over it. There was no disguising the fact that it had been tampered with.

"Medical students, mark my word," the constable grumbled. "Students, or those that supply them. Why else would someone want to dig up a grave?"

"But it was such an *old* body," Morgan protested. "It was little more than bone. There's nothing there to dissect. Resurrectionists take bodies that have been dead for only a day or two."

"Well, if it wasn't them, then it must have been hooligans," the constable said, sounding annoyed by Morgan's persistence. "In any case, there's no harm done, is there? The body is back where it belongs. I don't see what you expect me to do."

In all honesty, neither did Morgan. Even if the constable was right, and the body was the object of plunder, once the culprits had secured it all they had to do was take it to one of the medical schools and sell it. There would be no way to prove where it had come from.

"I wonder why you bothered burying it again, what with the talk going around," the constable said. "They're all going to be moved anyway, from the sounds of it."

The Toronto Strangers' Burying Ground was nearly full, its six acres crowded with those no church would bury. Strangers, as its name indicated — those who had no nearby family to see to a fitting burial: indigents, suicides, madmen, alcoholics, murderers. By 1826 there were enough of these in York County that their interment became a civic issue. It was the little rebel, William Lyon Mackenzie, who wrote fiery editorials in the *Colonial Advocate*, calling for a section of land to be set aside as a Potter's Field. The corner of Yonge Street and the first concession line north of Lot Street was chosen as the site for this non-denominational graveyard, the land purchased with donations from the public. It was in "The Woods," far from the city at the time. Over the years it became the final resting place not only of outcasts, but also of those unaffiliated with any of the established Toronto churches, which disdained the burial of anyone not their own.

But no one could have foreseen how fast the area would grow. Now, in 1851, the bustling village of Yorkville crowded in on the Burying Ground. It was swelling to envelop the cemetery, and its citizens were calling for the bodies to be moved to the newly established Necropolis, farther still from the growing city. There, the park-like setting along the bank of the Don River could easily accommodate the unmourned of Potter's Field. If the colonial government could be persuaded to agree, this stumbling block to future growth would be conveniently removed. But no one seemed to know how long this might take.

Morgan's midnight labour in reinterring the body was no wasted effort as far as he was concerned. He'd found it such a sad sight, the body ripped from the earth, the arm bone wrenched from the comforting folds of its shroud. He had wanted to restore it to what, after all, was supposed to be everlasting rest.

He thanked the constable for his time and left the man to fret over the wayward pigs and tavern licensing that comprised the normal concerns of a village policeman. And then, as he walked home, he realized that he would also have to make a written report to the Board of Trustees. This august body seldom met, consisting as it did of a number of prominent Toronto gentlemen who had far more important things to do with their time than to concern themselves with the day-to-day routine of the Strangers' Burying Ground. Still, they would have to be informed.

Morgan wanted to put his sense of outrage into words, to make the board understand that he, too, felt violated by the desecration. That, as Keeper of the Burying Ground, the crime had been committed as much against his office as against the body. But words had never come easily to him, especially when they had to be written down. As he struggled to put the report to paper, scratching and crossing out, leaving blots of ink along the edges, he kept wishing that he could have simply escorted the gentlemen through the graveyard and shown them white bone against dark brown earth.

Chapter 2

The skeleton in Dr. Christie's office was giving Luke Lewis a bad case of the collywobbles. The problem wasn't so much that the bones represented all that remained of a human being. He had seen plenty of dead human beings in 1847 when he'd helped bury typhus victims in Kingston. He'd also dissected two bloated and foul-smelling cadavers during his medical training at McGill University. The act of plunging a scalpel into a gelatinous, putrefying body hadn't sickened him at all. He had been too eager to see what lay underneath the flesh, to discover firsthand the hidden organs and systems that coursed beneath the flesh of a person. He knew that as far as Dr. Christie's skeleton was concerned, his agitation didn't stem from squeamishness.

It was more, he thought, the way the bones were wired together. The skeleton hung on a stand in an upright position with one hand resting rakishly on a jutting hip. The other arm was outstretched, the index finger pointing in admonition from an otherwise clenched fist. This accusatory finger seemed to follow him wherever he moved, whether he was seated at the oak desk in the middle of the room or standing at the cabinet that served as a dispensary. Combined with the slightly opened jaw, wired to give a good view of the teeth, the overall effect was a bony caricature of mocking, sneering contempt. But it was the finger, Luke decided, that bothered him the most.

He had read of pictures that were so well-painted that they unsettled observers in the same manner — ancestral portraits hung in dining rooms or depictions of public figures in civic halls that drove people mad by the way the painted eyes followed them around the room. Likenesses of ancient forebears come to life to cast disapproving glares at the antics of their descendants. Murdered wives seeking revenge. Bygone martinets outraged that history had passed them by. But that was the stuff of novels, allegory, he supposed, for the wrath of God. And he had certainly never heard of a skeleton that could have the same effect.

Dr. Christie was quite proud of the bones that graced his office.

"Boiled him down myself," he told Luke during the initial tour of the premises. "Back in '11 in Edinburgh. Made a devil of a smell."

"Where did you get the body?" Luke asked.

"From the university," the doctor replied. "They were finished with him. He'd been sliced and diced by seven or eight of us and there wasn't a lot left for anyone else to see, so I took him. They were glad enough to be rid of him. Saved the disposal fee."

"Were cadavers hard to come by in Edinburgh?" An adequate supply of bodies for the purposes of dissection was a chronic problem for the medical school at McGill. Sometimes a whole crowd of students would be assigned to the same corpse, making it difficult to see the component parts as they were coaxed into the open, and one careless slice on the part of one of them could spoil the exercise for everyone else. Some of the students had taken matters into their own hands, extricating newly buried bodies from nearby churches and fattening their purses by selling the corpses to unscrupulous lecturers.

Christie shrugged. "There are never enough. Most of ours were criminals, hanged for their sins. This fellow probably came straight from the gibbet. I don't really know what his crime was, but I've named him Mul-Sack, after the famous highwayman."

Luke had never heard of Mul-Sack, although he knew what a highwayman was. Travel was dangerous anywhere, road agents and pickpockets could lie in wait for the unwary even in Upper Canada.

He had given the skeleton no more thought at the time. It was only later that his disquiet surfaced. Christie introduced him to the housekeeper, Mrs. Dunphy, and then he'd been shown the parlour and the dining room and the two small rooms on the second floor that had been set aside for Luke's use. He had been given a small bedroom and an adjoining sitting room at the front of the house, "so that there's room," Christie said, "for your father when he visits."

After the tour he was left to cool his heels in the office while Dr. Christie went off to do heaven only knew what in the nether regions of the house. Whatever it was, it seemed to entail a great deal of shouting at Mrs. Dunphy, and a rather obnoxious smell that seeped under the door by the dispensary.

Luke's eye would catch the bony, pointing finger no matter where he stood in the room. He'd told himself that he would get used to the skeleton after a time. Familiarity would dull the effect. But the next day his unease grew worse.

He wondered if his nerves were getting the better of him again, as they had in Montreal when he'd first arrived there. He'd had difficulty getting settled at first. Lodging was scarce.

The cheapest accommodation in the city was in the St. Anne's suburb, but all the rooms there seemed to be taken by the Irish emigrants who had made it no farther than Montreal in their desperate flight from famine. After two days of searching, Luke finally found a tiny, unheated attic room at the southeast end of the Récollets Faubourg. The landlady was willing to rent it to him, she said, only because he wasn't an Irishman. The accommodation seemed fine in October when he first arrived, but as the weather turned colder its shortcomings became far too apparent. The roof leaked and the wind rattled the glass in the window as it blew through the gap between the sill and the sash.

He resolved to spend every evening studying the notes he had taken each day, but when he returned to his cheerless closet of a room after a full slate of lectures, he found that he was exhausted. He seemed unable to do anything but throw himself on the narrow cot that had been provided and fall into a disturbed sleep tormented by loneliness, bedbugs, and fear of failure. He began to have difficulty concentrating on what his professors were saying, and he knew he was falling behind in his studies.

The amount of information he was expected to process was overwhelming, his ignorance laid bare by off-hand references to classical works he had never heard of and by the assumption that he already had a thorough grounding in Latin and Greek. Materia Medica and Therapeutics proved particularly troublesome, the potions and elixirs referenced by exotic-sounding names, when all too often he would subsequently discover that the lecturer was talking about some common garden-variety ingredient.

Hardest of all had been the attitude of his fellow students. Many of them appeared to know each other already and shared notes and knowledge. Luke knew no one. There were a few others in the class who appeared to be as much an outsider as he was, but although they were civil enough when he spoke to them they seemed little inclined to establish a relationship that went any further than a nod of acknowledgement when he met them in the halls.

To add to his worries, he realized that his money was disappearing far faster than he had anticipated. He had to get through two years of lectures and two years of walking the wards of Montreal General Hospital before he could be licensed. He needed to find an odd job for evenings and weekends and full employment when classes ended for the year, but every menial position in the city appeared to be firmly held down by the desperate Irish.

Only after he'd found a better place to live and a job of sorts, had he settled down and started to enjoy his studies. He was sure that it was this same reaction to the unfamiliar that was affecting him here in Yorkville. It was the novelty of his new circumstances that made him over-imaginative. After all, he had only just joined the practice. He had no routine yet, and was still taking the measure of Dr. Christie. Besides, he could scarcely ask that the offending object be removed. The older man would think him strange indeed, and Luke couldn't afford to do anything that would jeopardize this welcome partnership with an established physician.

Having completed his medical studies, Luke could have gone anywhere that was without a doctor and simply hung out his shingle. In fact, his original intention was to return to the Huron Tract, where his brothers both had farms and where doctors were scarce. Later on he had imagined that he would stay in Montreal. Then everything had changed, and he realized that upon graduation he would have no money for necessary instruments, nor a stake that would see him through the first lean months of a fledgling practice.

And then, an aging doctor who lived at the northern edges of Toronto wrote to the medical department at McGill asking for help in finding an assistant. He had himself, Stewart Christie said, trained at the University of Edinburgh, but "failing to entice anyone from that august institution to the wilds of colonial Canada," he was willing to settle for a recent graduate from McGill who had been thoroughly schooled in the Scottish method, provided he was able to engage one who was "fit and able to shoulder the more onerous duties attendant on the practice." The doctor was offering a small salary, a fully-equipped office, and free living quarters on the second floor of his house.

One of the surgeons, Professor Brown, had duly brought the letter to the attention of the graduating class, to a less than enthusiastic response. Luke's fellow students had never heard of Yorkville and scorned the prospect of a village practice.

"Middle of nowhere," one of them scoffed as they trailed down the ward in the surgeon's wake.

"Farmers and ploughboys," said another. "Not very interesting."

But what they really meant, Luke knew, was "not lucrative." Many of Luke's classmates had family money that would help them get started or family connections that would guarantee them a place with a prosperous city practice. Their futures had been assured almost as soon as they had been accepted at medical school.

After rounds finished, Luke approached Professor Brown and indicated that he might be interested in applying for the position. And then he promptly wrote to his father seeking his opinion on the matter.

"Able to shoulder the more onerous duties?" Thaddeus had written back. "In other words, you'd be a drudge. On the other hand, I can think of no more expeditious way for you to enter the profession you have chosen. You might be wise to consider this."

His father was also familiar with the village called Yorkville, as Luke had known he would be.

"Although it's true that it's a small place right now, it can't be any more than two or three miles to Toronto," Thaddeus wrote. "In a few years, it's entirely likely that the city's limits will have stretched to encompass the entire area. By the time your elderly doctor is ready to hand over the reins, you could well find yourself with a city practice after all."

Armed with this knowledge, Luke wrote to offer his services.

When he arrived in Yorkville, he found a sleepy little village on Yonge Street, which — according to Christie, who seemed to have an extensive knowledge of the history and events of the area — had sprung up around a tollgate and a tavern, The Red Lion Inn. This public house was famous as a rallying point for the rebels of 1837.

"Brigands, all of them," the doctor said. "Should have been sent straight off to the hangman."

A small stream to the northeast had attracted the attention of Joseph Bloor, who built a brewery beside it in the early '30s, and then of John Severn, who did the same. The two breweries, along with the brickworks that produced a distinctive yellow product from local clay, were, Christie said, the major industries of the village.

"You won't see many grand estates here. It's mostly small houses and cottages for the local workers, more's the pity. I could do with a few clients who don't have to be hounded for payment."

To Luke, it seemed like a very self-sufficient little community, but he could see signs that his father might well be correct about Yorkville's future. Just south of the village, the area between the Tollgate Road and Queen Street was designated by Toronto as part of its liberties — not really city, not really county — but a legislative distinction that cleared the legalities for future annexation. City factories, once too far away for the workers of Yorkville to reach every day on foot, were now serviced by omnibuses. And the Strangers' Burying Ground, a cemetery on the corner of Yonge Street and the concession line, once considered on the verge of wilderness, now formed a barrier to the ever-expanding sprawl of houses in the village. Yorkville would probably always be a small town, Luke figured, but by the time Dr. Christie finally packed it in, its fresher air and slower pace might well have attracted a more well-heeled population.

In the meantime, as junior partner, Luke was relegated to the tasks that entailed the most work. This arrangement meant that he handled the cases that required walking any great distance. Dr. Christie's definition of "any great distance" was narrow in the extreme, as the older man was disinclined to indulge in any sort of effort and much preferred that his patients come to him. Few patients ever did this. As a rule they attended to their gumboils and bunions themselves, and when a more serious ailment presented itself, they expected a physician to treat them in their own homes. This meant that Luke would be handling virtually all of the calls. That was fine, as far as he was concerned — every time he was called out it meant that he could leave the office and the sneering skeleton behind.

When a small boy pounded on the door the day after his arrival, Luke eagerly grabbed the scuffed leather satchel that contained his potions and instruments and followed the child down Yonge Street and into a side alley that led through a cluster of modest cottages.

"Hurry," the boy said, "Pa's bleeding something fierce."

Luke's patient was still in his back dooryard where he had been splitting firewood. The axe had sliced through the man's boot and embedded itself in the big toe of his left foot. The man had not attempted to remove either the axe or the boot, instead slumping to the ground to await the doctor's arrival.

He was not suffering in silence, however, and his yells and moans had drawn a crowd of his neighbours, who hung over the garden fence to watch the drama.

"You'll be all right now, Holden," one of them said when he saw Luke. "The doctor's here."

"He'll probably have to remove the leg, you know," another offered, resulting in a further, and louder, round of moaning from the injured man.

"Shush!" a woman said to the man who had spoken. "You're scaring him!"

"That was what I was hoping to do."

"Well, stop!"

Luke ignored them all and lowered himself to one knee in order to assess the injury. Sometimes these wounds could be nasty, the laceration rarely clean, the edges of the wound ragged and shredded, depending on the sharpness of the axe.

After a moment, he turned to the boy. "Can you find me some clean rags?" he asked. "Freshly washed ones, that haven't been used for anything else?"

The boy nodded and disappeared into the house.

Luke untied the boot, removing the laces entirely in preparation for taking it off. There was a great deal of blood spilling out from the slash in the toe. He would have to move quickly once he'd withdrawn the axe.

The boy returned, wordlessly holding out a wad of rags. They looked reasonably unstained. *They will have to do*, Luke thought. *I can only hope they're truly clean.*

He looked around at the gaggle of onlookers at the fence.

"Could you give me a hand?" he asked. "You," he said pointing at the man who was hoping for an amputation. The woman who had shushed him pushed him toward the garden gate. The man approached Luke reluctantly.

"I need you to pull the axe out while I take his boot off."

The man paled, his jokes forgotten, but he reached for the wooden handle.

"Not until I tell you, mind. And pull it straight up and out."

Luke grasped the edges of the boot, then said "Now."

As soon as the axe head was freed, he slid the boot off in one smooth motion, then grabbed the bundle of rags and jammed a wad of them into the wound as blood spurted out. His patient screamed.

It had only taken a few seconds to accomplish, but it had been long enough for Luke to see that the toe was almost entirely severed, attached to the foot by only a small piece of bone and a flap of skin. He would have to remove it.

He would have preferred to get the man inside and away from the prying eyes of the onlookers, but that would take too long — the sooner the severed digit was out the way, the sooner Luke could stop the bleeding.

He looked up at the man who was still standing with the axe in his hands.

"The toe's gone," he said. "It's hanging by a shred. I need to finish the job, but I'll need you to hold while I cut. Do you think you can manage that?"

"What? Oh, my toe, my toe," the injured man wailed.

Luke ignored him.

The standing man gulped. "All right, I guess."

"Put the axe down and kneel down, on the other side of the foot."

The man complied.

"Now, when I take the rags away, you need to grab the toe by the end and pull it taut so I can see where I have to cut."

"Nooooooo!" screamed the injured man.

"I haven't actually done anything yet," Luke pointed out to him. "Save your screams for when I do." And then he looked at the other man. "Now."

He held his scalpel ready with one hand and pulled the cloth away with the other. His unwilling helper gingerly grabbed the toe and lifted it away from the foot. Luke sliced. The toe detached and both his patient and his helper fainted, the latter still holding the severed digit like a purple, blood-spattered trophy.

The bleeding was easing off a bit, Luke could see, the wound starting to clot on its own. There was enough skin left, he judged, that he could suture it closed around the jutting piece of bone. He fished a needle and a length of catgut out of his bag and began coaxing the skin up around the wound, sewing it in place wherever he could find undamaged flesh.

He was halfway through the task when the man holding the toe came to again. He took one look at the grisly relic in his hand and promptly fainted again.

When he was satisfied with his handiwork, Luke enlisted the aid of a beefy neighbour, and together they carried the patient into his kitchen, where they laid him on the small bed in the corner. Luke sluiced himself off at the kitchen pump.

When he emerged into the dooryard again, the swooning assistant was gone. He had left the toe where it fell, in the middle of the yard. Luke retrieved it, wrapped it in an unused rag, and handed it to the boy.

"Bury this under a bush somewhere," he said. "That way your Pa's foot won't itch so badly. I'll check on him tomorrow."

Satisfied with his morning's work, he tipped his hat and left by the garden gate, suddenly feeling quite optimistic about his decision to come to Yorkville. The village was still small enough that word of his backyard surgery would spread, especially since no account of the operation would fail to include a grisly description of the toe, or the information that a grown man had fainted at the sight of it. The next time a mishap occurred, few would insist on waiting for "the old doctor" instead of accepting Luke's attendance. The fees he brought in to the practice wouldn't be exactly *lucrative*, as his old schoolmates so seemed to desire, but they would be steady and help to solidify his position as the junior partner. In spite of Dr. Christie's unsettling office skeleton, Luke was starting to feel quite cheerful about his future prospects.

He was lost in these pleasant thoughts as he made his way back to the Christie house, so it took him a moment to realize that a voice from somewhere behind him was calling his name.

"Mr. Lewis?" the voice said again. "Is that you?"

Luke turned to discover that he had been hailed by a scrawny little man whom he was quite sure he had never seen before.

"Yes, I'm Mr. Lewis. Well … *Doctor* Lewis, actually." It still seemed odd to use the title. "Could I help you?"

But the little man had a puzzled expression on his face. "I'm sorry, I've mistaken you for someone else. I was sure you were someone I once knew, but now that I'm closer I can see that you couldn't possibly be him." His brow wrinkled. "And yet you say your name is Lewis?"

"Yes. Luke Lewis. And you are…?"

"Morgan Spicer. Pleased to meet you." Then the worry lines on his brow cleared away. "*Luke* Lewis? You're Thaddeus's son then."

Luke sincerely hoped that his father's reputation as a solver of crimes had not reached Yorkville. He had been forced to recount the stories of Thaddeus's adventures far too many times. It had all happened a long time ago, though, and with any luck the memory of them had faded. His own adventure with his father, on the other hand, was known to only a handful of people. There had been none of the public acclaim that had attended the other two crimes. And then, from somewhere deep down in his mind, something stirred in his memory. Morgan Spicer. Where did he know that name from?

"I met you once," Morgan said. "A long time ago. In Demorestville. You were about to travel west with your brother."

And then it came to him. Spicer was a sorry little stray who had tagged along with Thaddeus on the Hallowell Circuit, in Prince Edward County. He had wanted to be a preacher, Luke recalled, but Thaddeus determined that he needed to learn how to read and write first, and offered to teach him as they rode. It was a propitious decision on his father's part — Spicer had been instrumental in the apprehension of the murderer Isaac Simms.

"Mr. Spicer. Of course." Luke held his hand out for Morgan to shake. "I do recall our meeting."

"I'm sorry about the mistaken identity, but you must realize how much you look like your father."

"Not so much these days, I'm afraid. My father has aged since my mother died."

Spicer's face fell. "She's dead? Oh dear. I didn't know. I'm so sorry. She was a nice lady."

"She was. We all miss her sorely. But what about you? Are you a minister here?"

"No. I'm not a minister. My application was never approved." It was obviously a sore subject, Luke realized, for Spicer quickly went on. "So where is your father now?"

"Here as well. More or less. He's gone back to the preaching business, at least on a temporary basis."

Spicer seemed excited by this intelligence. "Here? On Yonge Street? I would like very much to see him, and not only to renew our acquaintance. I have a difficulty I would appreciate his advice on."

"I'll tell him I met you," Luke said. "He will have completed his circuit in a few days, I expect and then he'll come back here. Could I give him any indication of the nature of your difficulty?"

He had no idea if his father would be happy to see Morgan Spicer or not, especially if the man required advice. Although, he supposed, that was what a preacher was for, really.

"It's to do with the Strangers' Burying Ground," Spicer said. "There has been a very odd occurrence there, and I can make no sense of it. I'd like to ask Mr. Lewis what he thinks. Tell him he can find me at the Keeper's Lodge by the front gates."

Luke's first thought was that Spicer must be referring to ghosts or hauntings or some other nonsense that people associate with graveyards. He knew that his father would be quick to dismiss anything of this nature as a trick of the imagination, but then Spicer peered up at him anxiously. "Tell him it's important. Tell him it's a *puzzle*."

No request would bring his father running faster, Luke figured, whether he was personally interested in seeing Spicer again or not. Thaddeus loved a puzzle.

"I'll tell him," Luke said, and then he tipped his hat and went on his way, wondering if anything that happened in a graveyard could possibly be any stranger than a skeleton whose finger followed you around the room.

Chapter 3

Thaddeus Lewis had given up horseback riding, and now made his rounds in a hired trap pulled by a rib-thin pony. The provision of a horse and cart was one of the conditions that he had insisted upon when he'd been approached by Philander Smith to take temporary charge of the Yonge Street Circuit. He was too old to ride, he pointed out to the bishop, and his aching joints plagued him too badly.

He was reluctant at first to agree to do even that much. He was settled into a comfortable routine in Wellington, after he'd got over the initial shock of his wife Betsy's death. His son Luke kept him distracted for a while. Luke called upon him to unravel a mystery that had arrived on Canada's shores with the great influx of sick and starving Irish three or so years before. They chased up and down the shore of Lake Ontario from Kingston to Toronto and back again and eventually found the truth of the affair. But at the conclusion of the excitement, Luke went on to Montreal to study medicine, and Thaddeus was faced with the unappealing prospect of returning to his small cabin behind the Temperance Hotel where he spent his days alternately helping out with the routine drudgery of looking after guests and assisting one of Wellington's leading citizens, Archibald McFaul, with his complicated business affairs.

It was enough — only just enough — to keep his loneliness at bay, although he still felt a pang of loss every time he returned to the cabin at the end of the day. He never really became used to the idea of Betsy's death, but he seldom let this be known. He kept his sorrow to himself and mumbled over it late at night when he had nothing else to distract him. It became a treasure of sorts that he guarded jealously and shared with no one.

And then his routine began to fall apart. Business dwindled to a standstill in Canada West. Britain's Free Trade policies had destroyed Canada's markets and there were now no ready buyers for the timber that grew so plentifully or the wheat that sprouted out of the ground. Mr. McFaul's affairs were not as complicated as they had once been. He had less business to conduct and less correspondence to see to. The businessman reluctantly informed Thaddeus that his services were no longer needed. He had hopes, McFaul said, that economic times might improve in the future, especially if trade continued to grow with the United States, but for the time being, financial prospects were dim.

"If some of these railways they're proposing actually materialize, that will help," McFaul said. "But in the meantime my business has contracted along with everyone else's. I'm sorry, Thaddeus, but there just isn't enough work to keep you on."

Things changed at the hotel as well. Custom fell off. There was still plenty of work to get through every day — especially since Sophie, the genius in the kitchen, was once again expecting, and after several disappointments hoped this time to complete the process of birthing a child. Her brother, Martin, though, was let go from the Wellington planing mill, and he was immediately, and quite rightly, offered a place at Temperance House. The hotel belonged, after all, to his mother.

Martin was young, and far more help than Thaddeus had ever been. Nothing was said, no hints were dropped, but it was clear that the hotel was trying to support far too many people, even with Thaddeus working for nothing more than room and board.

He was far more receptive to the notion of being a preacher again when Bishop Smith returned a second time and repeated his urgent request that Thaddeus ride Yonge Street in the name of the Methodist Episcopal Church.

The decision was made easier for him by the arrival of Luke's letter, with the news that he was considering a situation in Yorkville. Thaddeus hoped that the advice he gave his son was based on Luke's best interests and not his own, but it was extraordinarily convenient all the same. When he was tired of congregational hospitality, of lumpy mattresses and kitchen beds, when he had completed his circuit and needed dry socks and a clean shirt, he could go to Luke's. He wrote to Bishop Smith at once to accept the appointment.

Now, as his pony pulled him along Yonge Street, Thaddeus marvelled at how much the circuit had changed in the course of just a few years. He'd first come here in 1834, when he finally gave in to the siren call of the preaching life. He was received into the travelling connection at the Methodist Episcopal Church's annual conference at the chapel at Cummer's Settlement. Yonge Street was little more than a track at the time, muddy and perilous with holes and fallen brush. Now he found that whole sections had been macadamized, improvements paid for by the tollgates that halted travellers and demanded fees for passage.

Little villages clustered around mills and the inevitable taverns that lined the road on its long march toward Lake Simcoe. These inns had been the breeding ground for Mackenzie's doomed rebellion in 1837. Every grievance, every complaint was trotted out on the taproom floor and catalogued until the stolid farmers of North York rose up and formed a pitchfork army. They marched down Yonge Street only to be ambushed and overpowered. Too few of them had marched home again. But now all was forgiven, apparently. Even the rebel leader, Mackenzie, was beckoned home, and the villages themselves had settled into a pattern of slow, sleepy growth until the collapse of the wheat market threw them into crisis again.

These settlements were beads on the string of road as it led north. Yorkville with its breweries; Drummondville, famous for the Deer Park estate; Davisville and its potteries; Eglington and the infamous Montgomery's Tavern where the Rebellion had faltered so badly. And so on north to York Mills, Lansing, and Cummer's.

He had returned to Cummer's Settlement only once since he'd been appointed as a circuit rider. It had been a few years later — 1838 if he remembered correctly. He was a seasoned campaigner by then and was asked up onto the platform to preach at a camp meeting that had lasted three days. And when he finished exhorting the crowds to a frenzy of conversion and confession, he had been invited to share a meal with Jacob Cummer and his family.

Cummer was a German from Pennsylvania who had built a mill on the Don River and opened a tinsmith's on Yonge Street, but in those rough and ready days when the area was far from civilization, he had also trained himself to be the local doctor and veterinarian. Like Luke had done up in the Huron, Thaddeus reflected, except that Jacob had never bothered to acquire any formal credentials. The Cummers were Lutherans when they arrived in Canada, but when Jacob built his log meeting house he had invited all denominations to use both the church and the campground. Later the Cummer family formally joined the Methodist Episcopals. The old man died a few years after that shared meal, but the majority of his fourteen sons and daughters still lived either in the village or nearby and, in particular, the oldest son Daniel was proving to be a stalwart supporter of the church. Of all the villages on the Yonge Street Circuit, Cummer's Settlement was the place where Thaddeus would receive the surest welcome.

He looked forward to seeing Daniel Cummer again and was pleased that the man was waiting for him in front of the meeting house. He was far less pleased when he realized that nearly all the men present for the class meeting were Cummers, sons of Cummers, or married to Cummers. But then, he reflected, Yonge Street was never as rich a ground for the Methodist Episcopals as other parts of the province, and too many Methodist adherents had been drawn off by the Wesleyans, or by one of the other numerous versions of the doctrine.

When he completed the meeting, Daniel, as Thaddeus had hoped he would do, invited him to share a meal at his house. He confirmed that the Methodist Episcopals had lost ground on the Yonge Street Circuit.

"As you know, the Presbyterians and the Anglicans have always done well here," Daniel said as he dipped into the savoury stew his wife served up, "but there are a lot of New Connection and Primitive Methodists as well. And, of course, Wesleyans."

The British arm of John Wesley's church had attempted a union with the Methodist Episcopals some years previously. The partnership soon fell apart, but the Methodist Episcopals suffered greatly by the Wesleyans' claim on all of the property that had been brought to the merger at the time.

"It's an uphill battle to keep the old church alive," Thaddeus said. "Otherwise I doubt you'd be seeing me today. Bishop Smith must have been desperate to ask an old man like me to take a circuit again."

"I expect he is desperate, there are so few of you left. I dare say there are no more than a handful between here and Cobourg. And your work is made all the harder by the times. The fall in wheat prices has badly affected the farmers of York, although here and there you can see signs that things are stirring again. John Hogg has started to lay out lots at York Mills, I hear."

"If I remember correctly, most of the land there is swamp, isn't it? Swamp, and a murderous steep hill."

"Your memory is good," Daniel said. "No one can fathom what he's up to. People have started calling it Hogg's Hollow, which doesn't make it sound very appealing, but he must think he can sell the land. And now that David Gibson is home again, he's making plans to build a mansion."

Gibson had been one of the leading figures in the 1837 Rebellion. Like Mackenzie, he escaped to the United States before he could be arrested for treason. Unlike Mackenzie, he had fared well there. He was a surveyor, and found work building the Erie Canal. It must have been profitable, Thaddeus thought, if he could now afford to build a mansion.

"And farther up the line?" he asked. "What can I expect there?"

"More of the same, I'm afraid," Daniel replied. "You might do well in Langstaff, but I'm not sure it's even worth your while to stop at Thorne's Hill. Not with the cult that's sprung up around Holy Ann."

"Holy Ann? And who would that be? It sounds like something that belongs more rightly with the Catholic Church."

"No, no she's a Methodist. Wesleyan. But a very strange one. They say she has the second sight and can perform miracles in answer to prayers."

"Only God can do that." Thaddeus was immediately on the alert. He had experience with women who claimed miracles and turned out to be charlatans.

"I know, I know," Daniel said. "Just try and tell that to the ignorant folk who traipse up to Thorne's Hill to drink from her well, all of them expecting to be cured of their ailments."

"Who exactly is she?"

"Her name is Ann Preston. She's a poor, ignorant Irish girl, brought to this country by Dr. Reid as a servant. She seems to be particularly adept at locating lost articles, just by praying to God for guidance, but I don't think anyone took her seriously until the Reids' well went dry."

"What happened then?"

"She prayed to God, of course, and fetched up two buckets of the purest water," Daniel replied.

"Was it raining at the time?" Thaddeus wanted to know, and Daniel looked at him in astonishment, then started to laugh.

"I've wanted to ask that question myself," he said. "Good for you." And then he grew serious again. "There's a great deal of work for you to do here, Thaddeus. I'm afraid it's not the easy circuit you might have been led to believe it was."

"I've had harder," Thaddeus replied. "I took on a whole nest of Universalists near Rideau one time." But he was beginning to understand why Bishop Smith had been so anxious to have him return to the travelling connection. The Methodist Episcopal Church was fighting for survival.

He discovered how correct Daniel Cummer's assessment was as he trotted north. There were only three women waiting to meet him at the general store in Newtonbrook. And as his weary pony trotted into Thorne's Hill, he passed a knot of people clustered around a wellhead. Suppliants to Holy Ann, hoping she could cure them or reform them or make their chickens lay, he expected. And when he reached the wagoner's cottage where he was supposed to conduct a class, there was no one there but the apologetic owner. It was hard for an ordinary preacher to compete with miracles, he reflected, when all he had to offer was a sermon or two.

He was cheered somewhat by the number of people in attendance at the meetings in Langstaff. There were three Methodists at the men's class and five at the women's, and they all came again in the evening to hear him preach. Oddly, there were no taverns in Langstaff and Thaddeus hoped that the lack of liquor was as a result of the influence of the church, but he was afraid that it was more due to the lack of prosperity in the small settlement.

Langstaff was where his boundary ended, the villages farther north more properly part of the Markham or Vaughan Circuits, so he arranged times and places for his return, then turned the cart to work his way southwest through sparsely scattered settlements as far as the Humber River. From there he would circle around to Yorkville and take a day or so to visit with his son. It wouldn't be the same as going home to Betsy, but it would do.

Even though Yonge Street was by no means the largest circuit he had ever ridden, and in fact he hadn't had to cover it on horseback as he had in the old days, Thaddeus found that disappointment had exhausted him by the time he reached Luke's. He felt none of the exhilaration that came from preaching to overflowing halls or counting up new converts on this first round. He had accomplished nothing more than the humdrum exercise of reaffirming the faith of the already committed.

He was given a good dinner at the end of his last class meeting, however, so when he reached Dr. Christie's yellow brick house on Scollard Street he was content to go straight upstairs and sink into a deep sleep on the daybed in Luke's sitting room.

The next morning he found his way to the dining room, where a place had been set for him. Christie seemed pleased that he was there.

"More the merrier," he said, beaming. "When Luke asked if you would be welcome, my one question was whether or not you were capable of intelligent dinner conversation. He assured me that you were, and I suppose that applies to breakfast as well. I'm hoping it will compensate for the inelegant presentation of the meal. Never mind, here comes Mrs. Dunphy. Dig in."

Mrs. Dunphy turned out to be a rather large woman with a heavy gait and a dour expression. She stomped in from the kitchen and thumped down a gigantic bowl of porridge. Thaddeus filled his bowl, then looked in vain for a jug of milk and some sugar to go with it. Christie ladled out a huge serving for himself, sprinkled it liberally with salt, and then handed the saltcellar to Thaddeus. "Get yourself around a bowl of oatmeal every morning and you're content for the rest of the day, isn't that right, Luke, my boy?"

Apparently they were expected to eat their oatmeal Scottish-style: plain porridge with salt and nothing more.

"Wait," Luke said to his father, and a few moments later Mrs. Dunphy returned with a platter of scrambled eggs and side bacon. Thaddeus was relieved. There was a time when he would have been happy enough with a bowl of plain oatmeal, but he had since been spoiled by Sophie's cooking. Mrs. Dunphy's food didn't appear to be quite up to the standards of the Temperance House Hotel, but it was served hot and looked reasonably edible.

"Methodist Episcopal, eh?" Christie said between mouthfuls of porridge. "Not many of those around here."

"I'm finding that," Thaddeus replied. "I have my work cut out for me."

"Always found Methodist services a little hysterical for my taste — all that shouting and so forth. I'm a John Knox man myself, or at least I was raised that way. Some seem to like the excitement though. The Cummers up yonder, of course. And the Africans down along Richmond Street, but I expect, being in the city, they're not really part of your circuit."

"No, they're not. The African Methodist Episcopal Church is actually a separate body from us. It was organized by the coloureds themselves. They don't even fall under the jurisdiction of the Canadian Conference."

"Interesting that they've found their way here, isn't it?" Christie mused.

There had always been a small coloured population in Toronto, Thaddeus knew, but now their community had burgeoned, swelled by new laws in the United States. Local authorities, even in the anti-slavery northern states, were now required to assist in the recovery of runaway slaves. Since all that was required on the part of the slave owner was an affidavit confirming that a coloured person was his property, many free Africans in the northern cities were being scooped up and sent south to the plantations. Many of them deemed it wiser to exit the country entirely.

"Execrable business, this slavery stuff," Christie said, polishing off his porridge and reaching for the platter of bacon and eggs. "Slave owners should all be hanged. That would put an end to it, then, wouldn't it?" He suddenly glared in the direction of the kitchen door. "Mrs. Dunphy! Tea!" he shouted.

"You'll get it when it's ready!" Mrs. Dunphy shouted back. "You can't make it steep any faster by yelling at it!"

Christie looked at Luke and Thaddeus and smiled. "There you go. Tea's on the way. By the way, Luke, I wonder if you might attend the office this morning? I have some rather pressing business to see to."

"Of course," Luke said, although Thaddeus noted that his son didn't seem happy at the prospect.

Mrs. Dunphy trudged in and set a large teapot on the table. Then she settled herself in a chair at one end and glared at Christie, who, with an apologetic look, passed her the bowl of oatmeal.

"And what will you do with yourself today, Mr. Lewis?" Christie asked.

Thaddeus wasn't sure. He had a two-day rest period before he once again had to meet any appointments, but he hadn't given much consideration to what he might do when Luke was working. In the old days when his circuit was complete, he always returned home to discover that Betsy had numerous things that needed doing, and he seldom had time to complete all of the tasks before he had to leave again. Even his free days were full.

"You could go and visit Morgan Spicer," Luke said. "He wants to talk to you."

"Morgan Spicer?" Thaddeus was astonished. "Where on earth did you run across Morgan Spicer?" He had long since lost track of his one-time protégé.

"He hailed me as I was walking down the street the other day. He mistook me for you."

"But what is he doing in Yorkville?"

"Spicer?" Christie said, "Isn't he that weedy little character who looks after the Burying Ground? The one with the twins?"

"I don't know," Luke said. "But he wanted to speak with my father in connection with the Burying Ground, so I'm sure you're right. He said there had been a strange occurrence there. He said to say it was a *puzzle*."

"Ah yes, someone's been tampering with the graves, I hear," Christie said, reaching for the last rasher of bacon on the platter. "Resurrection men no doubt, looking for bodies for the medical students to cut up. Should do it the way they do in Scotland — just fetch them from the hangman." He stopped talking for a moment, wrinkled his brow, and chewed thoughtfully. "Mind you, there was rather a strange case in Edinburgh in '28. Not enough people hanged, you see, so cadavers were in short supply. Families soon found that they had to post guards at the graves of their newly buried love ones, so the bodies wouldn't be dug up and sold. And then two bright souls decided to expedite the process by dispatching a raft of old folks, drunks, and prostitutes, whom no one would miss, you see. Burke and ..." he hesitated for a moment and chewed thoughtfully on his bacon, "Hare. Yes, that was the other fellow. Rather a clever ploy, but they were careless with the victims' clothing and were soon caught. Hanged, of course, and dissected by the surgeons. Ironic, don't you think?"

"Where did the bodies come from at McGill?" Thaddeus asked Luke. It wasn't a subject that had previously ever occurred to him to inquire about, but he supposed that they had to come from somewhere.

"From the jails, mostly, I guess." Luke said. "There was some grave robbing, but not much within the city itself. It was more of a problem in the outlying districts. The Montreal graveyards are all within the city limits, with stores and houses around them. There was some talk of putting a new cemetery up on the mountain overlooking the city. That might make it easier for the resurrectionists, I suppose."

"If they'd just hang more criminals, it wouldn't be such a problem," Christie pointed out. "Enough of this nonsense of sending them off to penitentiary, where they sit around and eat their heads off. Hanging would save a great deal of money and ensure a steady supply of cadavers. They could start with resurrectionists and work their way up to slave-owners."

"I'm sure you're right," Thaddeus said. He didn't dare look at Luke. He was reasonably certain that if he did so, he would scarcely be able to stop from laughing out loud.

Chapter 4

Thaddeus had no difficulty recognizing Sally Spicer when she opened the door of the Keeper's Lodge at the Burying Ground. In spite of the years that had passed since he had last seen her, she was still the same raw-boned, red-haired girl he remembered. She, on the other hand, seemed to have trouble placing him, and her eyebrows lifted in a question.

"Sally!" he said, tipping his hat. "Or I should say Mrs. Spicer, I suppose. It's Thaddeus Lewis."

Her hand flew to her mouth. "Oh, I'm so sorry. I didn't know who it was at first. Come in, come in! Please sit down and I'll get Morgan. He's just out back."

The Spicers' parlour had only two hard chairs in it, both drawn up to a scarred wooden table. Thaddeus took the seat nearest the window. He heard Sally call Morgan's name, then she reappeared in the doorway. "He'll be along in just a moment," she said.

"So how did you come to be in Yorkville?" he asked. "I was surprised when my son said you were here."

Sally sighed. "Poor Morgan. He could never get the hang of writing. He can read well enough, or at least by my standards he can, but he has a terrible time whenever he goes to put the words down on paper. It's the one obstacle that's kept him from being a real preacher. Whenever he's applied for a trial, he's been turned down because of it. He knows his Bible inside and out, but I guess that's not enough."

"I'm so sorry," Thaddeus said. "I thought I'd done fairly well by him. I wish he'd let me know. I could have helped more."

"You had your own troubles at the time," Sally said, "and more since. Morgan tells me your good lady has passed on."

"Yes, although we had some fine years, even at the end."

"I'm glad for the good years and sorry for the loss," she said. "Any road, we fetched up here just after the girls were born and Morgan thought it was time to settle for a bit. The job here came up and he writes well enough to keep the burial records. Most don't like the work, you see, dealing with dead bodies all the time, so there wasn't much competition, and the job came with the house as well." She peered at Thaddeus anxiously. "He hasn't given up, you know, on the preaching. This is just until we're better situated, and then he'll try again."

"I know he will," Thaddeus said. "If there's one thing Morgan has, it's persistence."

"Here he is," Sally said, turning to look as Morgan appeared in the doorway, a gaggle of children crowding in behind him. Thaddeus had to look carefully to see that there were, in fact, only four of them, and even then he had to take a second look to assure himself that he wasn't seeing double. Judging by the way they were dressed, there were two girls and two boys, but they looked so much like each other that without the clue their clothing offered, any one of them might have been mistaken for any of the others. He judged them to be perhaps eight or nine years old — at the gangly stage — but the lankiness could well be another trait they had inherited from their mother along with carroty-red hair and an extraordinary number of freckles.

"Mr. Lewis! It's so good to see you again." Morgan entered the room, his hand out in greeting.

The years had in no way improved Morgan Spicer's appearance, Thaddeus thought. He was still scrawny and unkempt-looking, with lank hair and a straggly beard, his clothing cheap and ill-fitting. As Thaddeus looked more closely, though, he realized that Morgan stood a little straighter perhaps, and had developed a grave and deliberate way of moving. He could well have cultivated this mien because he felt it was appropriate for a minister, but it would certainly be fitting for his current occupation as well. Although, Thaddeus supposed, an effort at solemnity would be largely wasted on the customary clientele of a Potter's Field. At a Strangers' Burying Ground, there would be few mourning relatives on hand to usher the dead into the earth.

"Pardon me for not rising," Thaddeus said. "I've grown older since last I saw you."

Spicer sat in the opposite chair and beamed. "Those were good days, weren't they? When you and I rode together."

Thaddeus nodded, although he by no means agreed with this statement. They had been hard days, the whole colony stirred into an uproar by rebellion and invasion, and all the while a murderer was stalking young women. He and Spicer tracked the villain down, but Thaddeus had been shaken to the core by the experience.

The mob of children had filed into the room in Morgan's wake and now stood in a row against the wall, their collective gaze fixed on their father's unexpected visitor.

"These are our children," Sally said. "Ruth and Rebecca, Matthew and Mark. Children, this is Mr. Lewis, who is a very old friend of your father's. Or I guess that's a friend of long acquaintance, isn't it? Not an old friend."

"Either way is appropriate, I'm afraid," Thaddeus said. "Are these quadruplets?" He found their unwavering stares slightly disconcerting.

Sally shook her head. "No, two sets of twins. The boys are a year older than the girls, but they're at that age where the girls outgrow the boys. They all look the same right now, don't they?

Thaddeus had to agree. The duplication was astonishing.

"You go off now and leave your father to talk with Mr. Lewis," she said to them. "Go play outside."

The expressions on the twins' faces didn't change as they obediently filed out of the room.

"They've been a chore in some ways," Sally said, "coming as they did in batches. But now that they're older, all they want to do is follow their father around. Now, would you have tea, Mr. Lewis?" When Thaddeus nodded, she disappeared again, presumably to the kitchen.

"I was surprised when Luke mentioned that he'd seen you," Thaddeus said to Morgan.

"No more surprised than I was when I heard you were in the area as well. I mistook your son for you, when I saw him on the street, but he set me straight and promised to pass my message on. He's the new doctor then? The one that's taken over from Christie?"

"Not really taking over. *Assisting* would be a better word."

Morgan nodded. "Christie's a good doctor, but he's a bit odd. He always acts like he'll look after your ailment if you insist, but that he would really rather be somewhere else."

"I think that's why he took Luke on," Thaddeus pointed out. "So he can be somewhere else. Whatever his reasons, his decision certainly aided our plans. Luke needed a position and I needed a place to stay occasionally. But tell me about you and Sally."

"Sally's a grand woman, for sure. We seem to produce children only in pairs, but she's wonderful with them. It helps that we're settled now. It's better for all of us."

"She mentioned that you still hope to find a congregation somewhere."

Morgan glanced at the doorway before he replied in a low voice. "That's what I pretend — to Sally if not to myself — but I don't think that's what I'm meant to do. You know, I used to think that it would be such a fine thing to be on the road, to ride to a different town every day. See new sights. Meet new people. It wasn't so fine after I'd done it for awhile. To tell the truth, it got tiresome. And I like it here well enough. It seems almost as good, dealing with dead souls instead of the live ones. I take care of them. And after all, I already know all about gravestones, don't I?"

Thaddeus recalled then that Spicer was once apprenticed to old Mr. Kemp, the gravestone maker in Demorestville, before he had taken it in his head to go off preaching. It would not be so dissimilar an occupation, he supposed.

"I'm just sorry that the job won't last, that's all," Morgan said. "I may have to start looking for something else soon."

"Why? Surely dead bodies are a commodity that's in steady supply at a cemetery?"

"Some of the local businessmen want to petition the legislature to close the grounds so they can be given over to more shops and houses. They say the village will never amount to anything as long as it has a cemetery in the middle of it."

"But what about the people already buried here?"

"They'd move them all over to the new Necropolis. There's been talk of it for years, but the Board of Trustees seems to be taking the notion seriously this time." Spicer shrugged. "The grounds are getting full anyway, so even if nothing happens, I probably wouldn't be needed that much longer."

"I'm sorry to hear it."

Just then Sally reappeared with a pot of tea and two mugs on a tray. She set it down on the table. "I'll leave you two to talk," she said. "I know Morgan has something to ask you."

"Yes, your puzzle," Thaddeus said. "Luke delivered your entire message, you know. He said you needed my advice on something."

"Something very odd happened, and I'd like your opinion of it." Morgan briefly filled him in on the strange desecration, and the constable's reaction to it. "I don't see how it could have been grave robbers," he said. "And I don't believe it was hooligans, either. They seldom do more than topple the grave markers."

"I agree, although I must admit that my first thought would have been of resurrectionists."

"They weren't interested in the body. They threw it aside. He wasn't very fresh anyway. He had been in the grave a long time. He died in 1848."

"Then there must have been something of value in the coffin."

"I don't understand how that could be. The man had no relatives and was buried by the county," Morgan said. "But if there *was* anything there, it was taken."

"Who, exactly, was it who was dug up?" Thaddeus asked.

"A man by the name of Abraham Jenkins."

"And who was he?"

"I don't know. Just another poor soul who died alone, as far as I can tell. I don't even know how old he was. There wasn't a birthdate to put on the stone. He died of a pain in the stomach, but other than that, there was no other information in the record."

It certainly wasn't much to go on, Thaddeus thought, but in the interest of being thorough, he supposed he should have a look at the disturbed grave itself.

Morgan led him out of the cottage to the laneway that led through the burying ground. The twins materialized, seemingly out of nowhere, and followed them, a little parade that straggled past a small building in the centre of the cemetery. A chapel, perhaps? Or a deadhouse? Probably useful for either function, Thaddeus figured.

Morgan turned into one of the right-hand rows and stopped in front of a grave with loose soil heaped over it. As soon as their father stopped, the twins hunkered down on their haunches to watch, two of them with thumbs in their mouths. They were like little imprinted chicks, Thaddeus thought, programmed by nature to follow. Morgan appeared not to notice that they were there.

"This is it," he said.

The raw soil looked out of place next to its undisturbed neighbours, but that was the only extraordinary thing about it as far as Thaddeus could see. Abraham Jenkins's headstone revealed little. It was a plain square piece of granite, as befitted one buried by charity, with a simple statement of name and date of death. Other than the fact that the grass on the nearby graves had been trampled and suffered a spade mark or two, there was nothing nearby that offered any other clue.

Thaddeus made a slow survey of the grounds. It was an old-style cemetery, more thought given to the efficient use of space than to the comfort of dead souls, the graves laid out in regimented rows with a minimum of space left between them. It would be a sorry place to spend eternity, Thaddeus reflected, but then, he supposed, it provided a last resting place for the sorriest of people.

Nearly the entire ground appeared to be filled, except for small empty sections at the back, and there was no direction in which it could be expanded. Yonge Street and the concession line along Tollgate Road hemmed it in on two sides. Buildings crowded up against it on the other two.

"Show me where they went over the fence."

Morgan led him to the back of the cemetery, the twins flapping in a line behind them.

"I think it must have been here," he said. "At least this is where they ran to when I surprised them." And then he stood back and waited while Thaddeus examined the fence and stared at the buildings beyond it. There was nothing at all remarkable about any of it: an ordinary paling fence and a huddle of wooden houses. He turned and walked back to the gravesite, but the backside view of it was no more informative than the front side had been.

"Can you think of any reason at all why they would have chosen this particular body to dig up?" he asked.

Morgan shook his head. "No. The grave has been here for several years. There's nothing special about the headstone that marks it. Nothing special about the person in it. I have no idea why this happened."

Thaddeus knew that Morgan was expecting him to discover some piece of information or small item that would set them on a path to resolution of the mystery, but there seemed to be nothing that suggested so much as a line of inquiry. He would make a circuit of the grounds, he decided, just to be thorough, but he had little expectation that anything useful would come of it.

As soon as he moved, Morgan made to follow.

"Just stay here for a minute," Thaddeus said. "I'll shout if I have any questions."

To his relief, the children stayed with their father. He was finding their presence hugely distracting.

The burial ground wasn't large, only five or six acres in all, he judged. Back in the 1820s, when the field was established, no one could have foreseen that there would be so many strangers to bury, although it had obviously found favour with some affluent families, as well, for here and there more elaborate stone and marble memorials towered over the plain blocks that were planted for the indigents. He went up and down the rows, idly scanning the information recorded on the markers. Most of the names meant nothing to him, but one small slab with two familiar names caught his attention. Samuel Lount and Peter Matthews were buried here, a fact that he had not known, but he supposed he should have guessed it. When Mackenzie fled the colony after his failed rebellion, it was Lount and Matthews who were fingered as ringleaders. In spite of pleas from across the colony, they were both hanged and their bodies buried with strangers. Ironic that Mackenzie himself had now been welcomed back, all forgiven. Thaddeus wondered whether or not the little rebel had ever visited the graves of the men he had led to their deaths.

He continued his survey, but no clues presented themselves. The key to the riddle must lie elsewhere. He returned to where Morgan was waiting, his brood of identical children hunkered at his feet.

"I'm sorry," Thaddeus said. "I can't see anything that would explain what happened, unless someone was after the body itself. And without knowing who he was, it's unlikely that we'll ever think of any reason for him to have been dug up."

Morgan's face fell. "At least you tried, which is more than the constable was willing to do. Ah, well, come back inside and we'll finish our tea."

Thaddeus's first inclination was to protest that he needed to be getting back, but then he realized that both Luke and Dr. Christie were no doubt occupied, and that there would be little for him to do and no one for him to talk to at the doctor's house. Better to chew over old times with Morgan and Sally, he decided, even if it meant being subjected to the unwavering stares of the twins. Maybe he'd get used to them.

Chapter 5

Luke sat in the armchair behind the big desk in the office, glumly trying to ignore Mul-Sack's toothy grin. After breakfast Dr. Christie disappeared into the kitchen with Mrs. Dunphy. Thaddeus went off in search of Morgan Spicer, not even stopping to ask the way to the Burying Ground. No doubt, Luke figured, he already knew where it was.

His father and Dr. Christie seemed to hit it off. That was a relief. Although Luke's rooms were ostensibly his home now, they didn't feel like it, and he was too aware that he was living in someone else's house. Christie was more than gracious in welcoming Thaddeus, but the dynamic of the household could have been difficult had the two men detested each other on sight.

It seemed very odd to Luke to be doing nothing after the frantic years at medical school, when every day was filled to more than capacity with knowledge that must be learned, tasks that must be done. No one had told him that real doctoring would entail long periods of waiting for something to happen, yet he knew that no one would call for a doctor unless there was an accident, or some illness that swept through the village. He would need to find something to keep himself occupied while he waited for calamity to strike the residents of Yorkville.

Books: Dr. Christie had whole shelves of them. It was books that had led him to the shop in the little lane off Notre Dame Street in Montreal. As soon as he'd arrived in the city he had gravitated to the cluster of booksellers on St. Vincent Street, drawn both by the knowledge their books contained and the warmth of the shops. Most of the texts he needed for school were sold, usually at exorbitant prices, at the university, but all of the Montreal book dealers had small sections of medical books. Some of the titles were on the local curriculum, but many of them were obscure, out-of-step with current medical theory, or English and French translations of foreign texts. Even so, he browsed through these as long as he dared, in particular lingering over the illustrations of anatomy, trying to absorb as much as he could in preparation for the lectures he would hear during his classes. Most of the proprietors of the shops chased him away after half an hour or so, cautioning him to either buy or be gone.

Ferguson's was different. To begin with, it wasn't in the heart of the bookselling district, but just at the periphery of it. The tall, thin proprietor seemed not to mind how long Luke dawdled in front of the heaped tables and shelves of books, or how long he stood in the aisle reading them. It was a tiny shop, crowded with bookcases and bins and racks, but there was a stove in the corner that filled the space with a fragrant heat that seeped into his frozen limbs. He stood for hours, comfortably lost in the mysteries of the human body.

Eventually Luke hadn't bothered with any of the other shops. As the season turned to a hard winter, he tramped along the snowy streets to Ferguson's, where he consulted the texts on matters that had puzzled him during the day's classes. He seldom bothered to stop at his room first. The temperature in the attic was only a few degrees warmer than outside and he knew that he would not be able to study there. He would fall into a fitful sleep, huddled under a thin blanket with his coat still on. At least at Ferguson's he could accomplish something useful.

And when he tired of tracing the veins and arteries and muscles shown by the illustrated plates in the medical books, and when he grew weary of reading about the symptoms of the many complaints that could plague a human body, he turned to some of the bookstore's other offerings. He found a wealth of literature — accounts of daring explorations and doomed expeditions, memoirs and biographies, bins full of maps, shelves full of novels and stories. He delved into these and stood with his nose in them until hunger or closing time chased him out of the shop.

He wasn't sure how long the owner would have been content to let him haunt the store without saying anything. Possibly forever, he reflected, had he not walked in one day just as the man had finished tying a bundle of books together with twine.

"Would you like to earn a few coins?" he asked in a soft Scottish accent. "A customer needs these books delivered right away, and if I take them myself I'll have to close the store while I'm gone."

Luke was happy to run the errand, and although he was quite desperate for money, refused the coins the man offered in payment.

"It's the least I can do," Luke said. "I've read my way through most of your stock."

"Fair enough," the man agreed with a smile that transformed his long, thin face. "I'm Ben, by the way, Ben Ferguson."

Luke often ran errands for Ben after that, in exchange for reading privileges. He began taking his class notes with him to the store. He could sit at a small table by the stove and study them. Ben supplied him with regular servings of tea and coffee while he worked. Gradually Luke stopped being so jittery and started sleeping again. Lectures were no longer the torment they had been, and when he didn't understand something that had been said, he had no hesitation in raising his hand and asking for clarification. He was no longer afraid that this would make him appear inadequate. He was there, after all, to learn.

As he struggled to absorb the information he needed to get through the examinations that were looming, he began to turn to Ben for help. The older man knew nothing of medicine, of course, but seemed happy enough to use the notes Luke had taken to grill him on the indications for the use of cupping and plasters, the pros and cons of administering ergot in cases of prolonged labour, and the pharmacological properties of recipes, compounds, and formulae from the endless list of preparations commonly encountered in a modern medical practice.

It was clear that Ferguson was an educated man, but when Luke asked about this, he merely shrugged, and said that he had had "a few years of schooling, but not in anything useful." He had a grounding in classical studies, "like all good Scots," but beyond that he had little to say about his life before he had come to Canada and opened his store.

Luke asked no further questions, although he was curious about Ferguson's background. The man appeared to love anything that was printed on paper. He constantly tidied the bins of maps that became disarranged when a customer shuffled through them, straightened shelves, and dusted books with a reverent care.

"Knowledge is everything," he said one time as he rearranged a section of reference books, "and this is where it's kept."

Dr. Christie seemed to share Ben's respect for the printed word, if not his liking for tidiness. The small parlour at the front of the house was filled with encyclopedias and dictionaries, compendiums of English literature and periodicals of every nature. Newspapers spilled from a table under the window and the office itself was home to a stack of leather-bound medical texts jammed, in no particular order, into a bookcase behind the desk.

Luke ran his finger along the titles. There were the usual tomes on medical chemistry, surgical techniques, and midwifery, but Christie had collected numerous other related publications as well. Randomly, he pulled out a book with handsomely marbled boards. It was *The Complete Herbal and English Physician Enlarged* by Nicholas Culpeper, apparently an addendum to a book called *The English Physician* by the same author. It was no more than a curiosity, its medical theory based on the movement of the planets, but it did have a number of handsome coloured plates that illustrated the herbs and other botanical sources that Culpeper had found useful, and which Luke recognized as the basis for the current knowledge on pharmaceuticals. He was soon absorbed in the work, fascinated by the careful drawings and acute observations — so absorbed that he jumped when the door behind him slammed open.

Dr. Christie stood in the doorway glaring at him. "For God's sake boy, there's been someone pounding on the door for the last five minutes. Are you deaf?"

Luke rushed to the front door and opened it. A young girl stood there, her face streaked with tears.

"Please, could you come, sir? It's my gran. We think she's going."

"Of course," Luke said. "I'll just get my bag."

As he returned to the office to grab his leather instrument bag, he realized that Dr. Christie was still standing at the interior doorway, and that he looked most peculiar. He had removed his jacket and rolled up the sleeves of his shirt, over which he had tied a white apron of the sort that a butcher might use. Or at least the apron had once been white.

The entire front of it was covered in ugly brown smears and rust-coloured stains. Again Luke was aware of a most peculiar smell emanating from the kitchen behind him.

"You'd better get in here." Mrs. Dunphy's voice floated out into the room.

Christie glared at Luke again, then returned to the kitchen, slamming the door behind him.

Luke followed the girl down the street. She led him across Yonge Street and past the Red Lion Tavern, where, even at this early hour of the day, three openly intoxicated men loitered in front.

She turned into one of the short streets that led toward the edge of the escarpment that marked Yorkville's boundary. Beyond this lay the complex of ravines that scarred the lands around the Rosedale estate.

The girl turned in at a modest wooden cottage, its front dooryard neatly fenced to protect the riot of flowers that bloomed in the beds beside the plank walk. The front door led directly into a small parlour, where Luke's patient had been installed on a daybed. Not only to facilitate her care, he figured, but also to afford her a degree of privacy in her final days. Judging from the girl's tear-streaked face, the old woman was a beloved grandmother whose passing would be mourned.

Luke knelt beside the cot and took the woman's hand. It was covered with dry, parchment-like skin tinged with the blue of the veins underneath. He stroked it lightly and was rewarded when the woman's eyelids fluttered a little, although the eyes did not open.

"What's her name?" he asked.

"Bessie." The name startled him for a moment. Almost the same name as his mother's, and this woman, he judged, was close to the same final circumstance — death was not far off.

A middle-aged, careworn-looking woman and a young man who appeared to be in his late teens crowded into the room.

"I'm Dr. Lewis, Dr. Christie's partner," Luke said in response to the question on her face.

"Thank you for coming. I'm Margaret Johnson. I hadn't heard that there was a new doctor, but then I've been so busy with Ma."

"How old is she?"

"Seventy-eight her last birthday."

"And has she been ill for a long time?"

"Oh yes," Mrs. Johnson said. "She has a growth in her stomach. Dr. Christie told us it was cancer."

Luke peeled back the light blanket that covered the old woman, but he didn't have to search long to find the problem. Her abdomen was huge, the outline of the tumour clearly visible.

"Has she been in a lot of pain?"

"She was before today. Now she seems to have sunk too low to feel anything."

There was no mercy in doing anything to prolong this battle, Luke knew. The best he could do was to make sure she went peacefully. He turned to the family members.

"I don't think she can last much longer," he said. "But I don't want to see her go in pain, even if she can't let you know she's feeling it. I'll give her something, just to make sure she's comfortable."

"How long?" Mrs. Johnson asked.

"It's impossible to predict," Luke replied, "but I would be surprised if she lasts the day."

The young girl burst into tears at this, but the daughter just nodded. "I thought as much."

Luke pulled a bottle of commercial laudanum preparation from his bag, then hesitated a moment before he also retrieved the tiny bottle that was beside it. Pure opium extract. He would strengthen the dose to speed her along. There was no point in letting her linger.

"Could I use your kitchen for a moment?" he asked. "I need to mix this."

The young man led Luke through the doorway and hovered nearby while he carefully added a few extra drops of opium to the laudanum bottle, pouring it over the kitchen basin in case he spilled it.

"Be a good lad and rinse the basin for me?" Luke directed, before returning to the parlour. Mrs. Johnson lifted the old woman to a sitting position and Luke spooned a little of the medicine into her mouth.

"Let me know if anything changes," he said. "I'll come back as soon as it does."

Luke left them clustered around the dying woman, certain that it wouldn't be long before he returned.

It happened even faster than he expected. Dinner was ready when he returned to the Christie house, but he had scarcely finished his custardy dessert when there was a rap on the door. It was the young man who had watched him mix the medicine he had given to the old woman.

"We think she's gone," he said. "She took a big deep breath and then nothing."

Luke collected his bag and accompanied the young man down the street toward the cottage.

"It's for the best, you know," Luke said.

"I know."

They walked in silence for a minute or so and then the young man suddenly said, "Can I ask you something?"

"Of course." Luke hoped he wasn't about to be questioned about the dose of opium he had given. He was sure that the daughter knew what he had been doing, but younger people sometimes had little perspective on dying.

"Are you married?"

It was such an unexpected question that Luke stopped

walking and stared at the boy for a moment before he said "No. Why do you ask?"

The boy blushed. "It's just that …well … do you know anything that will stop urges? You know … at night."

"Urges to … oh, I see what you mean."

Luke could feel himself blushing in turn. At medical school there had been entire lectures devoted to the dangers of onanism. Self-abuse could lead to lethargy, sapping of physical strength, blindness, madness even, they had been told. All manner of disease was ascribed to the shameful solitary act, and Luke sometimes wondered if it was responsible for his own difficulties. The professors had certainly claimed that this was so.

"Well … I'm sorry, what's your name?"

"Caleb."

"Well, Caleb," he said, "sometimes cold baths help. And lots of exercise, so that you're tired at night and fall asleep right away." It was the standard advice given on the subject. There were some schools of thought that advocated complicated devices that would interrupt the urge with pain — rings with spikes to deter the swelling, heavy gloves designed to control the hands, electro-magnetic apparatuses that delivered a disruptive shock, but Luke thought these excessive. He couldn't imagine applying them to himself, and was reluctant to prescribe them for anyone else. "Sometimes I'm not sure it's so big a problem as they make it out to be," he ventured. "It's so common that I expect it's probably pretty normal."

Quackery. Blasphemy. Heretical advice of the worst sort. But he couldn't bring himself to censure this boy so obsessed with his own failings that they concerned him even as his grandmother lay dying.

"Really?" The boy looked a little relieved. "But the church says it's a sin."

"Well, you know, sometimes I wonder why God gave you those urges if he didn't intend you to do something about them."

"I suppose." He looked doubtful.

"How old are you?"

"Seventeen."

"Then you'll soon find someone. Once you're married, your troubles will go away. Until then, I wouldn't worry about it too much."

This seemed to be enough to set the boy's fears to rest. His face brightened. "Thanks. I didn't feel right asking Dr. Christie about it."

Luke could well understand the reluctance. The crusty doctor's response would most likely be a call to have all self-abusers trotted off to the hangman.

They had reached the small house, and when Luke went in to the parlour it was immediately clear to him that the old woman had finally breathed her last. He went through the motions of listening for a heartbeat and looking for a pulse. Then he confirmed her death and left the family to mourn.

The whole encounter left him in an unsettled mind. There had been nothing he could do for the old woman, and she was probably happy enough to leave life behind, but it had reawakened the sense of impotence that had dogged him in Kingston, where nothing he did seemed able to slow the march of bodies to the burial pits. It also reminded him of his own mother's death, and his heart went out to the grieving family he had just left. Worst of all, his conversation with the boy had reminded him of his own frailties. Caleb would be all right eventually, Luke was sure of it, but without Ben, what was he himself going to do?

Chapter 6

The next morning, Dr. Christie asked Luke if he would mind going into the city, to Lyman and Kneeshaw's, the apothecary shop on King Street. They had run low on antimonial powder, he said, and gauze for bandages.

"Oh, and while you're there," he said, as if it were an afterthought, "could you also get five packets of magnesium carbonate?"

Luke found the last request puzzling. Although the compound was useful as an antacid and laxative, it was seldom required in any quantity. Most patients took care of their own digestive problems rather than bother a doctor with them. But as he was happy enough to get away from Christie's skeleton for a morning, and curious to see Toronto's commercial core, he cheerfully boarded the omnibus that trundled down Yonge Street from Yorkville to the new St. Lawrence Market.

King Street still showed the effects of the devastating fire that had engulfed nearly half the city in 1849, although many of the buildings that replaced the old market square were now completed. Their dignified facades were in stark contrast to the warehouses and mills farther south that crowded the waterfront and belched their fumes of sulphur and coal smoke over the entire city whenever there was an onshore breeze.

As he walked along, Luke was able to pick out the familiar lilt of Irish voices. Irish emigrants had settled mostly on the edges of the city, he knew, their temporary shelters becoming more permanent and gradually spreading out until they formed neighbourhoods of a sort. Some of the emigrants found work in the nearby manufactories; some of them migrated into the west in search of farm work, only to wander back to the city when the harvest was over. Luke wondered if he would meet any of the people who might remember him from Kingston, but no one spoke as he walked along. He didn't know how many Irish had found a home in Toronto. Too many, if some of the outraged citizens of Toronto were to be believed. Every issue of the newspapers featured an irate letter or two about the "drunken Irish" and their outlandish behaviour, including their practice of bathing in the Don River, their thin, pale bodies exposed for all to see. With no water available to the majority of the tenements and shacks that housed them, Luke wasn't sure what other option they had if they wanted to stay clean.

It was not only Irish accents he heard. The street scene was a veritable Babel of voices. Irish cadence warred with the guttural tones of German immigrants, the burr of Scottish brogues, and the starchy inflections of England, all of them sounding peculiarly foreign against the flattened accent of the Canadian-born.

He soon found Lyman and Kneeshaw's, guided by the brightly coloured glass globe in the front window, a beacon to the illiterate in search of relief. As soon as he entered the front door, he inhaled deeply, soaking up the spicy astringent smell that permeated the apothecary. Shelves on both sides of the shop were heaped with toiletries, infant feeding bottles and aids, razors and miscellaneous devices to aid the self-medicator, from enema boxes to comfort containers that could be filled with hot water or coals and placed in a bed to warm an invalid.

The items of particular interest to Luke were found at the rear of the shop, stacked on painted shelves that stretched from one side of the room to the other. At the top, large green carboys held bulk quantities of the most popular oils and tinctures. The shelves below them were filled with shop rounds, their distinctive shapes signalling their contents: narrow-necked bottles of liquid preparations, spouted stoppers for the pouring of oils, wide-necked jars for powdered substances. Along one shelf he saw the familiar labels for opium-based products, OPII, OPHO, RHOEA.

He approached the massive walnut counter with its brass scales and mortar and pestles and handed his list to one of the apothecary assistants. While he waited for his order to be filled, he idly scanned the labels of the multitude of pharmaceuticals available. Extract of belladonna, tincture of calumbra, arsenate of potassium.

When his order was completed, he directed the assistant to bill Dr. Christie's account, and after one last look around the jumble of proprietary formulations and medical paraphernalia that filled the store, he stepped back out onto King Street.

Luke found he was enjoying the crush of street vendors, newsboys, and housewives on their way to shop at the market. Yorkville had seemed very sleepy and small after his years in a city as big as Montreal. He would walk along King Street and take in the sights, he decided, before heading north. If he grew tired, he could simply board an omnibus that would take him home.

He had turned north when he saw the smoke, a thick, black spume spiralling up from a cluster of frame buildings three blocks away. At first he wasn't sure if it was a cause for concern or just a greasy emission from someone's chimney. Then he heard shouting and several men raced past him. He broke into a run and followed. He was a doctor, after all, and might be able to render some assistance should anyone have been caught by fire. Even if there were no casualties, he was willing to man a water pump or pass a bucket if needed. Indeed, he was probably obliged to. He assumed that Toronto, like every other city, had an ordinance that required passersby to assist firefighters when asked.

As he drew closer he could see that flames had engulfed a one-storey wooden building sandwiched between two brick houses. The water wagons arrived at nearly the same time he did — and not one cart, but two. Neither of the parties was happy to see the other.

"I've got this," one of them growled to the other carter. "You go on."

"I'm staying put. I'm not giving up the bonus for being here first."

As Luke watched the carters argue, two pumper wagons arrived. He was surprised to see them respond so promptly. Both sets of firemen began to unload their hoses and axes, jostling each other and getting in the way of any effective response. Occasionally, one of them would shout at another. The fire and the altercation between the fire companies were drawing a crowd of curious onlookers, who only added to the tumult by shouting out insults. It was no way to fight a fire, and Luke could see that the flames were beginning to lick at the roofs of nearby buildings. Then, as the crowd of people pushed him closer to the burning building, he saw one of the carters throw a punch.

Pandemonium erupted as men from the fire companies joined in the fray, the raging fire forgotten.

Whether there were any injuries or not, Luke needed to get away from the riot. He turned and began to push himself through the mass of people, although they were little inclined to give way. A judiciously applied elbow to a short, stout man in a butcher's apron finally parted a path in front of him.

Just then the police arrived. Luke heard shouting behind him, and pressed himself against the wall of a shop before he'd even ascertained who was arriving on the scene. The police waded into the skirmish, swinging clubs as they went. Slowly, Luke inched his way along the storefront, using the structure as a balance to keep himself from falling as people rushed past him, anxious to get closer to such an entertaining diversion.

He reached a winding alleyway, and debated whether or not he should go down it. It would get him off the street and away from trouble, but if he couldn't get out again at the other end he risked being trapped by the spreading flames. He thought he could just see daylight at the end of the narrow passage, so he took a chance and slipped into the shadowy space. It was full of garbage, rotting produce, and discarded articles, and, here and there, puddles of filth where slop jars had been emptied.

It was hard to see inside the alleyway until his eyes made the adjustment from the bright sun outside, and Luke had to pick his way carefully around the piles of muck. He was only ten paces down the length of the passage when he heard a muffled yell, and a mutter or two. He wasn't at all sure that the noises had come from inside the alleyway — they could just as easily be from the street — but then there was a scream, and he heard, quite clearly, a cry of "Leave me alone," followed by a jeering laugh. "Shut up, nigger bitch," someone said.

Luke rushed forward, no longer concerned about stains to his shoes and trouser cuffs, and close to where the passageway emptied into the street beyond, he could see a group of three people. One of them was a woman, who was huddled on the ground, hands over her head to protect it from the blackjacks wielded by the two burly men who stood over her. One of the men kicked at the fallen figure, while the other watched, the sound of his laughter drowning out any noise of Luke's approach.

Luke chose to barrel into the laughing man at full speed. The man fell, the club in his hand making a graceful arc as it flew out of his hand. One kick to the body, and he rolled into a defensive ball, his head tucked and his legs pulled up. Luke turned in the direction of the other assailant, arm raised to ward off the anticipated blow of the blackjack, but to his surprise the woman on the ground leapt up and took advantage of the second man's surprise to land a hard kick between his legs. The man doubled over, and Luke was able to step forward and rip the club out of his grasp. Then he scurried back a few paces, out of reach of either of the attackers. He stood, club at the ready.

The man who had been kicked was in no condition to offer any resistance. He was moaning, his hands cupped over his injured genitals. The man Luke had tackled, however, uncurled himself, reached down into his boot, and pulled out a long, lethal-looking knife. Luke's club would be no match for it.

"Run," he said to the woman, and when she hesitated, he was more insistent. "Go on, run and get help." She turned then and ran toward the end of the alley, but before she could reach the street the yells from the crowd watching the fire grew suddenly louder and echoed down the low-roofed alley. It was enough to distract the man with the knife for just a moment, and in that time Luke let loose a swinging blow at his hand. The woman ran back, and between them she and Luke pulled the knife out of the man's grasp.

They backed out of the alleyway, wary of another attack, but the man made no move to follow them. When they reached the street, Luke shoved the knife under his jacket and slid the club into his pocket, but there was no one to see them anyway. The street was deserted. Everyone had gone to watch the fire over on the next block.

Now that he could see her in the light, Luke realized that the woman he had rescued was younger than he thought, a girl really, no more than eighteen or twenty, he judged. She was tall — almost as tall as he was — and slim, and her coffee-coloured skin stretched over high cheekbones below enormous brown eyes. She was, he thought, extraordinarily striking. She was also far more finely dressed than Luke, her dress beautifully cut and her boots made of fine leather.

"Oh," she said, her hand patting her head," I've lost my hat." She took a step back toward the alley, but Luke stopped her.

"Wait a few minutes to make sure the alley is clear," he said, "then I'll go back and get it. I've left something behind, as well." He had dropped Dr. Christie's package of powders and bandages when he leapt to the rescue. "Who were those men anyway?"

"Catchers," she said, "from the States. They were trying to grab me so they could take me over the border and claim a bounty."

"What do you mean?"

"Because of the new law there. They claimed I was a runaway slave, and men like that are paid to track down runaways and take them back to their owners."

"But this is Canada," Luke protested. "They have no call to be here."

"Nevertheless, they are," she said, "and they aren't fussy about who they grab up. Any old African will do, whether they're freeborn or not. Thank you for your assistance. I'm Cherub, by the way." She held out her hand.

It was an odd name, Luke thought, but strangely appropriate for so beautiful a woman. He took the hand and shook it. "Lewis. Luke Lewis."

She nodded, but said nothing more as they waited until Luke judged it was safe to return to the alleyway. There was no sign of Cherub's attackers. Her hat was on the ground close to the entrance, the brim lying in a puddle of muck. He found the package from Lyman and Kneeshaw's a little farther down the alley, none the worse for wear.

He emerged into the street, Cherub's hat held at arm's length. "I'm afraid it might be ruined," he said, handing it to her.

She sighed. "I'm afraid you might be right. I don't know if this will clean up or not."

She began walking north. Luke fell into step beside her. After they had walked two blocks, she stopped at a handsome, gaily-painted buggy. "This is my carriage. Thank you again, Mr. Lewis."

"My goodness, aren't you going to introduce me to your friend, Cherub?" said a voice from under the vehicle's leather canopy. It was a deep, velvety voice that made Luke immediately want to see the person it belonged to. He ducked his head into the confines of the covered buggy.

"How do you do, ma'am," he said.

"A pleasure." A gloved hand was held out for him to take, but he still couldn't see the woman clearly. She sat back in the padded seat, her face shadowed by the deep brim of her straw hat.

"Mrs. Van Hansel, this is apparently Mr. Lewis," Cherub said. "He saved me from a very unpleasant situation."

"Unpleasant in what way?"

"Yankees looking for runaways."

"Are you all right?"

"Yes," Cherub said. "But they very nearly had me."

"Then we owe Mr. Lewis a very great debt," Mrs. Van Hansel said. "And at the very least a ride home. Do you live near here, Mr. Lewis?"

"I'm much obliged, ma'am," Luke replied. "But that's not necessary. I'm a long way from home."

"And where exactly is home?"

"Yorkville."

Mrs. Van Hansel laughed. "Why, Mr. Lewis, that's not a long way at all, unless you came down Yonge Street on foot. It will take us no time at all to get there. Cherub can ride in the jump seat. You climb up here beside me." She patted the seat beside her.

"But …" Luke's protest was only a mild one. He was still shaken by his encounter with the thugs who had attacked Cherub, not to mention the riot that had erupted at the fire. The prospect of being jammed onto an omnibus was unappealing after so much excitement.

Mrs. Van Hansel patted the seat again.

"Much obliged." Luke climbed up beside her.

She flicked the reins and the buggy started forward, but when they reached the next intersection, Luke realized that the mob had grown in size and had spilled farther along the street. Mrs. Van Hansel urged the horse through the crowd, but just as they reached the thickest part of the throng, a cheer went up and the horse shied a little. The woman beside Luke expertly tightened the reins and the animal steadied.

"They're throwing fire grenades," she commented. "Much good that will do."

Luke had to agree with her. The glass bottles filled with carbon tetrachloride had little effect on the flames that were consuming the building and did little more than fill the air with a noxious odour.

Just then a hook and ladder truck appeared at the head of the street. The driver of the wagon made little effort to avoid pedestrians as he barrelled through the crowd. Here and there people were knocked aside and Luke thought it fortunate that none of them ended up beneath the wheels of the wagon. Three policemen rushed forward, ordering the driver to halt. The driver ignored them, and one of constables leapt up onto the wagon to try to wrest the reins away. The driver launched a haymaker at the policeman, which missed the intended target of his face but landed squarely against his shoulder. The officer toppled backward onto the ground.

The rest of the police force abandoned their efforts to break up the original altercation and rushed to the aid of their colleague. Two of them ministered to the fallen policeman while the others scrambled onto the wagon, pushing the driver out of the way and grabbing at the reins. When the firefighters saw the driver being attacked, they dropped their axes and grenades and waded into the fray. Onlookers immediately joined in willy-nilly, seemingly unconcerned about whether their fists connected with constable or fireman. The scene was turning to riot, and Luke felt panic welling up in his chest. This was too much like what had happened in Montreal.

Mrs. Van Hansel managed to turn the buggy in spite of the numbers of people crowding against it, but now they were moving against the flow of traffic, as everyone not actively involved in fighting desperately tried to crowd closer so they could watch the unexpected entertainment. Either that, Luke thought, or to judge whether or not they should join in.

After several anxious minutes, the vehicle cleared the last of the crowd and the horse settled down to a steady pace. As they rode along, Luke searched for something to say to the finely dressed woman beside him.

"Cherub is an unusual name," he ventured.

"Yes it is," Mrs. Van Hansel agreed, "but it suits her perfectly. That's what she looked like when she was a child — like a little cherub fallen down out of the sky. She's become even more angelic-looking as she's grown older."

"You've known her for a long time, then?"

"Oh yes. And her mother before her. She was a genius with a needle. Cherub grew up in my household. I'm very fond of her and she helps me in many ways."

Luke assumed from this that Cherub occupied a servant's position. Or was an assistant of some description. Something in the nature of hired help, at any rate.

"And what do you do, Mr. Lewis?" Mrs. Van Hansel asked. She turned to him as she said it, and he was able for the first time to get a clear view of her face. To his surprise, she looked not at all like he had expected from the timbre of her voice. She was not nearly as old as she sounded, although there were a few fine lines beginning to gather at the edges of her full-lipped mouth and at the corners of her eyes. She could be no more than a few years older than Cherub, he judged. Her very round, very blue eyes dominated her heart-shaped face, and together with her porcelain-like skin gave her the look of one of the imported china dolls that he had often seen in shop windows.

"I'm a physician," he responded in answer to her question.

Her eyebrows arched in something that was more like calculation than surprise, but the gesture still made her face seem more doll-like than before. "Oh really? You seem so young for such a responsible profession."

"I'm just a junior partner, really," he admitted. "I've been taken on to assist an older doctor in Yorkville."

"How wonderful!"

"Yes, I was very lucky to find a position."

"And why is that?" she asked.

"I didn't have the money to set up on my own, or the connections that would help establish me."

"I see," she said, but she made no further comment, turning her full attention once again to the horse.

Luke could think of nothing more to say and they trotted along in silence. He wondered who this woman was. She had to be the wife or daughter of someone important, he figured, judging by the quality of the horse and buggy she drove. And if the clothing she wore was anything to go by, she was well-acquainted with seamstresses — her skirts were made of a fine cloth, her hat fashioned in some new mode that featured lacquered straw and yards of ribbon. The wife of someone important, he decided. And quite probably rich. He wondered if this was the sort of "connection" that might do him some good in the future, but he had no idea what he should do or say in order to nurture it.

"It's just up here," he said as they trotted past the Red Lion. He directed her to Christie's house and clambered down from the buggy as soon as they reached it.

"Thank you so much." He held out his hand for her to shake, and shifted from foot to foot as he desperately tried to think of some way to turn the chance encounter into something more.

"But aren't you going to invite us in for a cup of tea, Dr. Lewis? It's a long, dusty drive back to the city."

Tea. Of course. Luke mentally kicked himself for overlooking the obvious. The rules of hospitality eased all difficulties. In all the years he was growing up, anyone who had ever shown up at the door had been invited in. And even when his mother's stores had been depleted, she would find something to offer, even if it was only chicory coffee or nettle tea. Guests must not be allowed to go thirsty.

"Yes, of course, please," he stammered. "Won't you come in?"

He hoped that Dr. Christie would not mind, and that Mrs. Dunphy was up to the task of producing tea on such short notice. He helped both women down from the buggy, then ushered Mrs. Van Hansel to the front door while Cherub tethered the horse to the gate. He saw Mrs. Van Hansel into the hall, then turned to Cherub, who stood waiting, one hand stroking the horse's head.

Luke smiled and held the door open, gesturing her inside with one hand. She blinked a couple of times, then stepped along the short walk and into the front hall. He showed both women into the small, musty parlour at the front of the house.

"Please, sit down. I'll just be a moment."

He knew there was no point in ringing the bell that connected the parlour with the kitchen. Mrs. Dunphy ignored bells and when reproached by Dr. Christie for her negligence retorted that she wasn't a trained circus animal and had no intention of jumping at bells or whistles.

Just as he reached the kitchen door, it flew open and there stood Dr. Christie in his blood-spattered apron.

"Oh! Luke! It's you!" he boomed. "I didn't expect you back quite so soon."

"I got a ride," Luke said. "And I've brought people home for tea. Do you think Mrs. Dunphy could provide a pot?"

Christie turned and bellowed over his shoulder. "Mrs. Dunphy! Tea! And cakes if you have 'em."

"What? Tea at this hour? And cakes? Of course, I'll just conjure 'em out of thin air. It's the easiest thing in the world to come up with cakes when you're least expected to. I'll just wave my hand and —"

Christie slammed the door shut against the muttering and strode down the hall toward the parlour.

"Visitors, eh?" he said. "I must say, Luke, I hadn't thought that you'd be such a social creature. It might take me some time to get used to the notion of having company."

Luke scrambled after him. "Don't you think you should take your apron off first?" he said. But Christie had already reached the parlour doorway.

"Hello! Hello! Welcome!" he boomed into the room, in spite of the remarks he had just made about sociability. "I'm Stewart Christie. How do you do." And he strode forward, his hand out.

Luke had no idea what either of his guests made of the loud man with the filthy apron, for he could discern no astonishment on their faces. Christie, however, made no attempt to contain his surprise at the presence of Cherub.

"An Ethiopian! How do ye do, miss, how do ye do? Now there's something you'd never see in Edinburgh. An Ethiopian in the parlour. And a very pretty one at that! You would be an addition to any Scottish sitting room, I can tell you that!"

Luke thought he would die of embarrassment, but Cherub seemed to take Christie's remarks with good grace, and Mrs. Van Hansel positively beamed.

"It's true," she said, "Cherub is an ornament wherever she finds herself. I'm Lavinia Van Hansel."

Christie bent to take her hand, but at that moment must have realized what an impression he must be making. He stopped and peered down at his stained apron.

"Oh my goodness, you must excuse me," he said. "I was working and I didn't realize that I was quite such a sight." He ripped the apron off, balled it up, and then seemed at a loss as to what to do with it, opting finally to throw it behind the settee.

Luke was having severe second thoughts about his decision to invite guests home with him, but the women seemed to be taking the doctor's odd behaviour in stride.

"Now then, tell me, how did you make the acquaintance of my young assistant?" Christie said as he settled himself down on the settee beside Mrs. Van Hansel.

"He saved me," Cherub said.

"Saved you? My goodness, from what? Cholera? A palsy? Relapsing fever? Details! You must give me details!"

It was Mrs. Van Hansel who answered. "Poor Cherub was set upon by a pair of Yankee catchers. Dr. Lewis manfully fought them off and delivered my friend safely back to my carriage."

Luke felt himself blushing. "I didn't do much," he said. "I really only surprised them. Miss Cherub seems quite able to look after herself if she's not woefully outnumbered."

"Yankee catchers?" Christie said. "You mean they're snatching Africans off the streets in broad daylight?"

"I'm afraid so," Cherub answered. "It's the second time I've been set upon in the last few weeks."

"They were carrying knives, as well," Luke said.

Christie shook his head. "It can't be countenanced. Did you find a constable and report the incident?"

"No," Luke said. "There was a fire and the police were too busy fighting with the fire brigade."

Christie snorted. "Sometimes I wonder whether this country will ever be civilized." He turned to Cherub. "You are, I hope, recovered from your ordeal?"

"As well as can be expected, I suppose," she replied. "I must say I appreciate the opportunity to sit and collect myself for a moment." She turned and smiled at Luke. "I don't think I thanked you properly — not only for coming to my aid, but for the invitation to tea."

The statement seemed to spur Christie to action. He leapt up and went to the doorway. "Mrs. Dunphy! Tea!"

There was a muttered reply, which, mercifully, Luke couldn't quite make out, and a few moments later Mrs. Dunphy trudged in with a tea tray containing not only a pot, cups, milk, and sugar, but also a plate of gingersnaps. She plunked it on the parlour table and promptly trudged out of the room again, leaving Christie to pour the tea and pass the cookies.

"You live in Toronto, do you, Mrs. Van Hansel?" he said, handing her a cup.

"Yes. On Shuter Street."

Christie seemed impressed with this information and Luke guessed that it must be one of the city's better neighbourhoods.

"And you, sir, hail from Scotland, I take it?"

"Been here thirty years now. I've seen a lot of changes in the place in that time." And with that he launched into a long description of what the colony had been like when he first arrived, and the progress that had taken place since, although, he pointed out, "there's plenty of room for improvement yet," at which point he outlined the specific areas he judged still lacking and finally ended his discourse with a prediction that most of the politicians currently in office would end their days on a gibbet.

"Well," Mrs. Van Hansel said when it appeared that Christie had finally subsided, "you must come and visit me in turn. By and large I find social occasions rather dreary. One sees the same old people time and time again. It would be pleasant to have an educated man like yourself to liven things up."

"Oh no, oh no," Christie protested, although Luke could see that he was flattered by the invitation. "I've long since forgotten how to behave in a drawing room. Dr. Lewis, on the other hand, would no doubt be a brilliant addition to any occasion."

Mrs. Van Hansel turned her gaze to Luke. "Why yes, I do believe you're correct. An eligible young bachelor never comes amiss at any function. The unmarried ladies will be all aflutter. You are a bachelor, aren't you, Dr. Lewis?"

"But … I couldn't possibly," Luke said. "I have so little free time. I'm needed here."

"Nonsense, my lad," Christie said. "After all, you're entitled to the occasional day off. I am still quite capable of seeing to patients, you know. I did for years before you arrived."

"Then it's settled," Mrs. Van Hansel said, setting her tea cup down on the table. "I'll send you an invitation." She fished around in the bag she carried until she located a calling card, which she handed to Luke. "And now, Cherub," she said, rising, "we've dallied long enough. We must be on our way."

Dr. Christie saw them out the front door and handed them into the buggy while Luke trailed behind, his manners forgotten. Once he saw them off, Christie beckoned Luke back into the parlour.

"Well, well, well," he said, "since there's tea at such an unexpected time of day, we might just as well finish it off. It will save Mrs. Dunphy some trouble later if we make a meal of this." He scooped a gingersnap off the plate and crunched it loudly.

Luke was too dumbfounded to eat anything. He had hoped to nurture his chance encounter, of course, but he hadn't expected it to turn into anything more than a nodding acquaintanceship. He didn't know what would be expected of him at a social occasion. And he certainly didn't like the sound of "unmarried girls all aflutter." He hoped he wouldn't be invited to anything that involved dancing, or drinking, or any of the other temptations that his father had always warned him against. He didn't know how to dance, and had never touched anything stronger than beer.

"Well, my boy, I must send you off to the city more often," Christie said, snatching another gingersnap. "That's just the sort of person who could do us some good in terms of raising the tenor of the practice."

"How?" Luke asked. He had only the vaguest notion of how connections worked, since he had never had any.

"Well," Christie said, "she might introduce us to a better class of patient."

"In Yorkville?"

"There are not many, I admit. But there are a few. Although I'm not sure they pay their bills any more promptly than anybody else. Still, they were a decorative pair of women, weren't they? Nothing wrong with having a couple of fine-looking ladies in your parlour."

"I suppose not."

"Of course not! Now," he said, pouring himself another cup of tea and settling himself back comfortably, "tell me everything that happened."

Chapter 7

The pounding of feet on pavement. The shattering of glass. Shouts in the street.

Luke woke up trembling and drenched in sweat. He sat up in bed and tried to calm his panicked breathing and still his wildly pounding heart. Slowly he calmed down and oriented himself. He was in bed. He was in Stewart Christie's house. He was in Yorkville. He had had a nightmare. He must have been asleep for some time if the positioning of the sliver of moon in the sky was any indication. The day's events had conjured frightening memories, he decided. Being trapped between a burning building and an excited crowd had taken his mind back to Montreal.

Ben had been standing by the front window of Ferguson's book shop. "There's a mob out there," he said. "I could hear something before — voices and a few cheers — but it sounded as though it was quite a long way away. I couldn't tell where it was coming from at first, but now it seems to be moving this way."

"Who are they?" Luke asked.

"The same crowd you saw this afternoon, I expect."

Luke had been returning to the shop after the delivery of a parcel of books to a customer at the edge of the city limits when he noticed a stream of people headed south toward the river. Just like today, or rather yesterday, he supposed it was now, he feared a fire or some other catastrophe, and wondered if he could be of some assistance. He followed the crowd along the street to St. Anne's Market, recently conscripted to house the Parliament of the United Province of Canada. A mob was assembled in front of the massive porch at the front of the building — a restless, surly bunch that muttered and shouted in English.

"No money for traitors!"

"Go back to England!"

"You'll be the last governor we'll ever have, Elgin!"

As Luke watched, a distinguished-looking gentleman flanked by policemen emerged from the porch. He realized that it must be Lord Elgin, the aristocratic governor general of Canada, whose sympathies were said to be aligned with the current reform government of Baldwin and LaFontaine. Elgin ignored the crowd and made his way to a waiting carriage.

Luke could see that some of the people at the front of the crowd had arms raised to launch turnips and potatoes obtained from the nearby market stalls. As they threw them, the vegetables came perilously close to hitting the governor general. He appeared oblivious to the assault, but as soon as he reached his carriage the crowd surged forward, shoving against Elgin's servants and a handful of police. The noise was deafening. Luke turned and fled back along the street toward the bookshop. It was an ugly scene and he wanted no part of it.

"Ah," Ben said, when Luke related what he had seen, "Lord Elgin must have signed the Rebellion Losses Bill into law. It's an unpopular move, but I didn't think his opponents would go so far as to attack him physically."

The Rebellion Losses Bill was a piece of legislation designed to compensate those in Lower Canada who had lost property in the Rebellion of 1837. A similar bill had already been applied to Upper Canada, where a nearly simultaneous rebellion had been led by William Lyon Mackenzie. In Quebec, however, there was violent opposition to the bill from the old political elite who were pining for the power they had lost when the colony was granted its own government and from the merchants whose commercial empires were in danger of dissolving in the sudden economic depression. They were cheered on, aided and abetted by the anti-Catholic Orange Societies. All three groups saw the bill as an opportunity to wrest power away from the Reform government that had been elected.

"Treason!" they cried. "The government is paying out compensation to those who caused the rebellion in the first place." It was an issue tailor-made to discredit the coalition led by French Canadian Louis-Hippolyte LaFontaine and English Canadian Robert Baldwin and to call into question the loyalty of everyone who supported them, from Reform proponents to Roman Catholics to French Canadians, the last by virtue of their language and origins alone.

Luke was familiar with the old "loyalty to Britain" mantra that had been used so effectively in the past to shore up the position of privilege. He had heard his father rail on about the ruling Tory elite in Upper Canada, and how they had used the Methodist Episcopal Church's American roots to claim that Methodists were, by definition, a threat to the Crown. It was an old, tired ploy, but the Rebellion Losses Bill could well be the spark that would fan it into flames once more.

"What do you think will happen?" Luke asked.

"I don't know," Ben said. "But if they've gone so far as to pelt a British lord with old neeps and tatties, they may be prepared to go further. There will be trouble tonight, I'm afraid. One of us should stay up, to protect the store if there's a riot."

"We'll both stay up," Luke said, although he wasn't entirely sure what he could do if a mob descended on the bookshop. But then again, why should they? Ben had made no public show of support for anyone, Tory or Reformer, and Luke had been so busy with his exams that he had only barely been aware of the crisis that had been brewing.

That evening, Ben locked the shop door and put the CLOSED sign in the window. Luke went upstairs and heated up two bowls of soup and took them, along with some bread and cheese, downstairs to where Ben was waiting. He had no sooner placed the food on the little table by the stove at the back of the store when they heard the clang of the fire brigade coming down the street. Ben ran to the door and flung it open.

"Loyal Britons, join us!" a man called from the wagon. "On the Champ-de-Mars! Come to the Château Ramezay!"

A newsboy running behind the hook and ladder wagon threw a thin paper at Ben's feet. It was a special issue of the *Montreal Gazette* rushed into print as an extra evening edition. "The Disgrace of Great Britain Accomplished" the headline screamed, and below it "Canada Sold and Given Away — Rebellion Is the Law of the Land."

"They must have had it already printed, to get it out on the streets so fast," Luke said. "It's only been a couple of hours since Elgin was at Parliament."

"I don't know what kind of crowd they'll get over at the Château," Ben said. Château Ramezay was the current Government House, the residence that Elgin used when he stayed in Montreal. "Maybe no one, now that the bill is law. Maybe a lot of people. But there will be speeches, I suspect. A lot of ranting. It will take some time to get a mob mobilized, if there is to be one. It could be a long night."

"Let's eat," Luke said. "And then we'll watch together."

It was nine o'clock when the distant roar of the crowd swelled and drew nearer. The mob was streaming down Notre Dame Street with lighted torches, shouting and smashing as they went. Ben shaded his lamp and stood to the side of the window so he wouldn't be seen. Luke grabbed the poker from beside the stove and stood at the ready, a few feet from the front door. If anyone broke in, he would defend the shop, and Ben, from anything they might do.

The crowd seemed to be focusing on the establishments of known Reform supporters, Ben reported, rather than indulging in full-scale destruction. They watched as the mass of people marched west, fuelled by indignation and alcohol and led by the hook, ladder, and hose brigade.

"There are thousands of them," Ben said. "I'm guessing they're headed for the Parliament Building."

They stood and watched for an hour or more, until the crowd began to thin, the stragglers too cold or too drunk to keep pace. They relaxed then, and Ben turned to Luke.

"You should get some rest. I think the worst has passed us over, for tonight anyway."

He had no sooner spoken the words than they heard a renewed disturbance, one voice strong above the others.

"Let's get the Sodomite," it said.

"No, it's Reformers were after," came a slurred reply.

"Reformers, Catholics, nancies — they're all scum. We should clean 'em right out of the city." And then there was a crash as the front window of the shop smashed, a flying shard of glass hitting Ben in the face.

Luke rushed forward as two men began pounding at the door in an attempt to force it. He slipped the lock and flung it wide, his poker held high. And then he let it fall, cracking it against a head, then a shoulder, then a shin.

Fortunately, the men had been drinking heavily. They stood, befuddled by the sudden attack.

"Go on," Luke hissed from the dark shadow of the shop. "You have no business here. Join the others. Go get the Reformers."

"He hit me," one of them whined. "We should burn him out."

"We have no torch. We'll have to come back later."

And then they staggered back out to Notre Dame Street in pursuit of the more focused protesters.

Ben grabbed a cloth and held it against his bleeding face. Luke gently pulled it away to find that the flying glass had carved a two-inch gash in Ben's cheek.

"This needs to be sewn up," he said.

Ben shook his head. "I'm not leaving the shop. No one should be on the streets tonight."

"At least let me bandage it."

Luke found a freshly laundered towel and ripped it into strips, then tied them, as best he could, over the cut. "You'll have a scar."

"I'll just look all the more rakish," Ben replied, but Luke could see that he was shaken by the assault.

"How did they know?" Luke asked.

"Everyone knows everything about everybody in this place. It's too small a city for secrets. I've always been careful. If you're careful, no one seems to make an issue of it."

"They did tonight."

"Those men were drunk. They won't even remember what they did. In the meantime, we'd better see what we can find to board over the window."

There were packing crates at the back of the store. Luke hammered them apart and used the wood to fashion a barrier against further attack, and Ben tacked up a curtain that would provide some protection against the cold night air.

And then they waited, listening, but it appeared that Ben was right. Their assailants had been too drunk to remember that they were hunting nancies as well as Reformers.

* * *

The next morning they locked the shop door behind them and ventured out into the streets to hear that the unimaginable had occurred. The unruly crowd, aided by the fire brigade's long ladder, had rammed open the front doors of the Parliament building, where the legislature had been sitting in a late session. Rioters stormed up the stairs and into the chamber. They were met by fierce resistance from the members of parliament themselves. Then the crowd outside pried up paving stones and began hurling them through the windows. One of the chunks of pavement struck a gaslight. The shade ignited. The fire spread. And by the early hours of the next morning the Parliament Building was a smoking ruin.

Luke and Ben stood in the street in front of what had once been the seat of the government of Canada. Lost along with the building were the library and archives, twenty-three thousand books in all, a chronicle that stretched back to the very first European settlement of the country.

"The building was just stone and mortar," Ben said, "but the books can never be replaced. Canada's history is gone." The man who loved anything printed on paper had tears in his eyes. For him, the loss of so much knowledge overshadowed anything that had happened to him personally.

The madness continued for days. Rioters took over the downtown area and surrounded the Government House. Prime Minister LaFontaine's house was sacked, his stables burned, his furniture and library destroyed. All across the city, Reformers' houses and businesses were attacked.

LaFontaine and his ally Baldwin calmly reassembled the government and recalled the legislative assembly, using Château Ramezay as a meeting house. Police, even assisted by a makeshift militia of Irish Catholics and French Canadians, were unable to control the frenzy. Finally the military was called in to restore order, but was given extraordinary instructions — as little force as possible was to be used to contain the rioters. Restraint was to be the order of the day.

In hindsight, Luke could see how effective this policy had been. There were further incidents, to be sure, but eventually the excitement died down. Reformers from other places rushed in to provide support. There were a small number of arrests. But there were no martyrs.

From Luke's perspective, the main casualty in the disturbance had been Ben. Some inner vitality had burned away as surely as the books had. And then the malady that made him so thin gained a greater hold. It had been a downhill course from there.

Chapter 8

The next morning, Luke, Thaddeus, and Dr. Christie were at the breakfast table when a knock came at the door. Christie heaved himself to his feet and plodded off to answer. He returned with a buff-coloured card, which he placed in front of Luke.

"What's that?" Thaddeus wanted to know.

"It's an invitation, apparently," Luke said. He read it out: "Mr. and Mrs. Phillip Van Hansel request the pleasure of your company on the evening of Friday, July 11, commencing at 8:00 p.m., for an evening of musical entertainment featuring Miss Sadie Gleeson."

"July 11?" Christie said. "The Van Hansels must be holding an Eleventh Night Party."

"What's an Eleventh Night Party?" Luke asked.

"It's a party on the evening before the twelfth."

Luke sighed. "What's the twelfth?" He was hopeless with these social references that everyone else seemed to navigate so easily.

"Why, the Glorious Twelfth of July," Christie said. "When all the good Orangemen march down the street waving banners and singing. There'll be a crowd gathered to see them, that's for sure, what with the marching band and everything."

"Load of nonsense," Thaddeus said. He'd had run-ins with the Orange Lodge before and didn't think much of them.

Neither did Luke. He had spent weeks tending to typhus-stricken Irish and he had nothing but good wishes for those who had survived. But he knew the arrival of so many Irish Catholics had upset the already uneasy balance between the mostly French-speaking Catholics of Canada East and the mostly English-speaking Protestants of Canada West. With the priests of the eastern province openly preaching that government must bow to the authority of the Pope, the western Protestants assumed that the Irish would agree, and that without action, Canada would soon be ruled directly from Rome. It was this terrifying prospect that, in part, had helped fuel the rioting in Montreal.

The Orange Lodge positioned itself to provide a rallying point for that fear. An organization transplanted directly from the arguments of the Old World, the Lodge found favour not only with Irish Protestants, but with Scots and Loyalist families as well, and now Lodge members controlled nearly everything in the corporation that was Toronto. And they trumpeted that fact, loudly and forcefully, at the annual Orange Day Parade.

"It's a shame the government couldn't outlaw the marches when they wanted to," Thaddeus observed. The very first legislatures of the Province of Canada, back in the early 1840s, attempted to suppress the lodge, along with other secret societies, and had been successful in passing legislation to that effect. Unfortunately, the bill also needed to be approved by England, and the English governor of Canada simply chose not to pass it along to them.

To Luke's surprise, Dr. Christie agreed with Thaddeus.

"Orangemen should all be hanged," he said. "They'd be nice fat, overfed bodies for dissection, wouldn't they?"

"I would have thought that as a good Scotch Presbyterian you'd be all in favour of the Orange Lodge," Thaddeus said.

"I don't hold with the Pope," Christie said, "but I don't hold with a bunch of self-satisfied bigots running things either. If you ask me, the Orange Lodge in Toronto has less to do with anti-Catholicism and more to do with another group setting themselves up to control everything. Might just as well have left the old Tory class in charge."

"Now you're starting to sound like an American. Every man equal to the next."

Christie snorted. "Oh that's a high ideal, all right, but the Yanks are just as bad as anybody else when it comes to dealing with immigrants. Worse, probably. And just as anti-Catholic. 'Life, liberty and the pursuit of happiness,' my foot. Only if you're one of those on top to begin with."

"About this party," Luke said, desperately hoping he could steer the conversation back to the issue at hand. Mealtime conversations had been spiralling off into political and philosophical discussions ever since Thaddeus first arrived. It was as well that his father had a circuit to ride; otherwise Luke felt he would never get a word in.

"Ah, yes, the soiree," Christie said.

"There won't be dancing, will there?" Thaddeus asked. "Methodists don't dance."

This was one of the questions that Luke had wanted to ask. If there was to be dancing, it was a good excuse to stay home.

"I doubt it," Christie said. "The invitation says 'musical entertainment.' More like a recital, I should think."

"I can't possibly go," Luke said. "I have nothing suitable to wear."

"Oh, just brush off your frock coat and shine your shoes," Christie said.

"I'll starch a collar for you," Mrs. Dunphy offered. Luke was startled. She so seldom said anything during meals that he hadn't been sure she was listening at all.

"You see," Christie said. "You'll be fine. And of course you're going. You need to make the most of this chance encounter. It could do you no end of good to hobnob with moneyed people."

"I thought you didn't approve of a privileged class," Thaddeus said.

"I don't," Christie replied. "That doesn't mean I have to spend my days grovelling in the dust with the poor and the ignorant."

And they were off again, one comment igniting another, while Luke sat and worried about what might be expected of him at something as exotic as a soiree.

* * *

The day that Luke had been dreading for two weeks finally arrived, and he was still unsettled in his mind about attending the Van Hansel party. He kept hoping that some medical emergency might intervene — an outbreak of measles, perhaps, or an accident with a runaway wagon. Anything that would keep him in Yorkville without offending either Christie or Mrs. Van Hansel.

However, it turned out to be a singularly uneventful day. Old Mrs. Cory had an attack of heart palpitations, for which Luke prescribed a glass of brandy at bedtime; a four-year-old girl broke her arm when she took up her older brother's challenge of jumping off the shed roof; Mr. Frederick needed a bottle of laudanum mixture for his rheumatism. Except for those three cases, Luke had nothing to do but stare glumly at Mul-Sack and wonder if he should practice making polite conversation with the skeleton.

At four o'clock he left the office and went up the stairs to his rooms. He removed his coat and brushed it down as well as he could and selected the newer of his neckties. Mrs. Dunphy consented to iron his best shirt, and while she was doing this, Luke wiped the mud from his boots and gave them a polish. When he was as presentable as he felt he could make himself, he went looking for Dr. Christie, to remind him that he would be out for the evening.

Christie was sitting in the dining room, having become immersed in reading the newspapers. He looked up, dumbfounded, when Luke announced that he was on his way.

"On your way? To where?"

"This is the day that Mrs. Van Hansel is having her party."

Comprehension dawned on the doctor's face. "Oh yes, of course. My goodness me, it's Friday already, is it? Well, off you go then. Do give my regards to the fine lady and, of course, the lovely Cherub."

Luke boarded an omnibus in front of the Red Lion Tavern with a handful of other passengers. He was relieved that the bus was not crowded, and that he did not have to share a seat, which helped to keep his coat from getting creased. Nor did he have to engage in conversation with anyone. The traffic would be going the other way, he realized, as workers and shoppers left the city after their day's activities.

Lavinia Van Hansel's house was located in a respectable-seeming neighbourhood of similar-looking three-storey brick houses, although a little farther along the street Luke could see newly built row houses, it having become fashionable to forego a front garden in favour of a good address.

The front door of the Van Hansel house had a huge brass knocker and was opened by a maid as soon as he let it fall. He was ushered into a drawing room, which appeared to be full of flounced dresses and paisley shawls, the young women and their fussing mothers reflected and multiplied by the large mirrors that hung around the room. Here and there knots of men stood huddled in discussion. Luke was relieved that none of them was wearing anything but a simple frock coat. He would not stand out too much after all.

Mrs. Van Hansel rose from her chair when he entered and came over to greet him, signalling that he was a guest of some importance. The young women certainly thought so, for they rushed over to him, jockeying for an introduction. Luke was soon lost in a sea of Isabels and Harriets and Georginas, all of whom ventured polite remarks about the weather. He looked around the room for Cherub, as someone he already knew, and if they could find no other topic of conversation, he could at least inquire as to whether she had recovered from the attempted abduction. But she was nowhere to be seen.

Finally, after an excruciating half-hour of agreeing that the weather was indeed fine, Mrs. Van Hansel signalled that the entertainment portion of the evening was about to begin. A clean-shaven young man languidly made his way to the piano that stood in one corner of the room. He was soon joined by a plain and somewhat overweight young woman, who positioned herself with one hand resting on the tasselled throw that covered the piano top. When all conversation ceased and everyone's attention was focused, she took a deep breath and nodded at the pianist.

"Oh the sky was clear, the morn was fair
No breath came o'er the sea

When Mary left her Highland home
And wandered forth with me ..."

Luke was no connoisseur of music, having grown up with only the thump of Methodist hymns, but even he could tell that the young woman had a sweet voice and that it had been trained to sustain a repertoire. He was equally impressed with the young man at the piano, who augmented the accompaniment with well-placed flourishes.

"Sweet rose of Allendale
Sweet rose of Allendale
By far the sweetest flower there
Was the rose of Allendale."

At the end of the song, there was nothing more than polite applause, and Luke felt mildly offended on behalf of the musicians. He thought the rendition had been remarkable. Perhaps the assembled guests would warm as the concert continued. The next piece had a long introduction and showcased the pianist, whose fingers flew across the keys in complicated arpeggios. Finally, the melody settled in and the singer began.

"Sleeping, I dream'd love — dream'd love of thee
O'er the bright waves, love, floating were we ..."

On through a song about a willow tree, several waltzes that had everyone swaying with the tempo, some more sentimental ballads, and then the singer finished with "Oh, Susannah," a popular song whose lyrics seemed to be known by everyone except Luke, and to which everyone else joined in. The chorus was repeated three times, to the delight of the audience, and at the end of the song there was enthusiastic applause.

Afterward, Mrs. Van Hansel led the way to the dining room, the gentlemen waiting politely until the ladies were through the door. Then they followed, one man standing aside to usher them through: their host, Mr. Van Hansel, presumably. He was rather an ordinary-looking man. Medium height. Medium brown hair. A medium build. Altogether rather nondescript except for one arm that hung at an odd angle. As Luke watched him, he realized that the arm did not move from its dangling position. It just hung, useless. And suddenly Luke knew exactly who this man was — and he knew exactly what had happened to his arm. Luke remembered back to the night that a furious Irish emigrant girl had fired a small brown pepperbox pistol across a local cabinetmaker's yard. The bullet had struck this man in the shoulder. There had been three people killed that night, but Luke and Thaddeus hadn't waited around to find out if there would be a fourth. They had rushed out of the yard with a burly thug in pursuit.

They had known this man only as "Hands." Hands because "he has his hands in everything," the Irish girl had told them. Now Luke realized that the nickname was a far cleverer play on words than that — it was obviously short for Van Hansel, as well.

"Hands" Van Hansel, whose flunkies had lurked around Toronto's waterfront in 1847, ready to pick off stray girls for the brothels. Who stuffed extra bodies into coffins in order to defraud the city. Who siphoned profits from the brandy provided for fevered immigrants, and who didn't like it when there were mistakes. Luke had been invited to the one house in Toronto where he was sure to find an enemy.

The ladies had all crowded through the door and now the gentlemen were moving forward. Luke didn't know if Hands would recognize him or not. It had been nearly dark in the yard that night, and so much had happened so quickly. Luke had been covered in blood and dishevelled from hard travel. Still, it would be foolish to take a chance that the man wouldn't remember.

He slipped to the side of a portly gentleman with bushy side whiskers and did his best to keep the man between himself and Hands as they entered the dining room. When he was safely through the door he made for a set of heavy tapestry curtains that were swagged over French doors at one side of the room and made a great pretence of stepping behind them to peer through into the garden. As soon as he possibly could, he decided, he would work his way back to the drawing room and out the front door.

"We should stick together, you and I, or we'll be married off before we know it," said a voice in his ear.

He turned to find the pianist at his side. "You're much safer here," he said. "The girls will be occupied for a time with trying to stuff down as much cream cake as they can eat while protesting that they have the appetites of birds, but sooner or later they'll zero in on you."

The figure that stood in front of him seemed every elegant when sitting at a piano, but now that Luke had a closer look, he found the man rather odd-looking. He had a very pale complexion and brown, almost black eyes above a very pointed nose. His eyebrows slanted upward in an attitude of perpetual surprise. He reminded Luke of some small animal, a chipmunk maybe, or a deer mouse, but his thin body exhibited none of the frenetic busyness of either. Instead, he lounged against the frame of the French door and waved one hand in lazy emphasis to his words.

"They're like crows circling carrion, aren't they?" the young man said. "And their mothers are worse. I don't like the feeling of being dead meat. I'm Perry Biddulph, by the way. Peregrine, actually. My misguided parents named me after Peregrine Maitland, the governor of Canada at the time of my birth, and now, mercifully, gone off somewhere else to rule in an arrogant and high-handed way."

"Luke. Luke Lewis."

"What a wonderfully simple name. I wish I had it. My brother is named Theophilus, after an ancient and only remotely connected ancestor. He goes by Theo, of course."

"I've always just been plain Luke," Luke said.

"Well, just plain Luke, what is it you do to keep yourself occupied?"

"I'm a physician. In Yorkville."

Perry looked at him with a puzzled expression on his face. "Really? Way out in the woods? How odd. Although I suppose a physician would be useful."

"Yorkville isn't that far away," Luke pointed out. "And why should it be odd?" He was finding that Perry had a very disconcerting way of expressing himself.

"Only that our dear Mrs. Van Hansel must want something from you, if she's gone to all the trouble of luring you in from the wilds."

"What could she want from me?"

Perry shrugged. "I don't know. Something she'll find useful. She wants things from me as well. Lavinia rather collects useful people."

Luke had no idea how to respond to this.

Perry noticed his puzzlement. "Everyone is here for a reason," he went on. "They all have something they want from someone else. None of them are quite top-notch, if you know what I mean. The men are all merchants and traders who hope to make deals. Their daughters and wives are hoping to meet people who are on a little higher rung up the social ladder. It's all about making connections. And if the connections are made, Lavinia is the gracious hostess who has facilitated them. Beyond that, her parties provide an opportunity for the married women to socialize with each other. It smoothes the way, apparently, for the husbands to do their bits of business with one another."

"But I have no interest in deals," Luke said. "I'm not in business. And I'm certainly not very high on any social ladder."

"Oh, I don't know about that," Perry said with a crooked grin. "A handsome young doctor would be a decent enough catch for any of these girls, even if you do live out in the woods."

"Oh." Luke suddenly understood why he had been swarmed by so many young women when he entered the Van Hansel's drawing room.

"Of course, you would be even more appealing if you were a lawyer. More money in law than in medicine. Unless, of course, your family has money?"

"No. None."

"Really? Well, if you're not here to do business, I suppose you're useful as a prize to dangle in front of the mothers until Lavinia figures out what she wants from you."

Perry seemed to know the Van Hansels well. Well enough, at any rate, to be slightly contemptuous of them. Luke wondered what he knew about Hands.

"Can you tell me what it is that Mr. Van Hansel does? I met Mrs. Van Hansel quite by accident, and I'm afraid I don't know the family." Luke was curious to hear how Hands presented himself to the regular world. His party guests might not be "top notch," as Perry put it, but they certainly looked respectable enough. The people in this room did not come from the world of thugs and whores that Hands ruled.

Perry shrugged. "Some sort of businessman. Business, business, business. It keeps them all busy. And their wives and daughters in dresses and cake, of course."

And as if Perry had magically called to them, two of the young women detached themselves from the food table and started walking toward them. At the same moment, Hands glanced around the room. Luke quickly looked out the window again.

"Are you terribly interested in more chit-chat about the fairness of the weather?" Perry asked.

"No. In fact, I've been standing here desperately trying to figure out how to get back to the door without being seen. I'd like to leave."

"Ask and ye shall receive." Perry reached out and turned the handle on one of the French doors. "Ah. Not locked. That makes sense. There are to be fireworks after the meal." He slipped through to the garden.

Luke took one last look around the room. The two girls had been waylaid by an elderly woman who was determined to get closer to the pastries, but was having difficulty balancing both a plate and her cane. Hands was nowhere to be seen. Luke slid through the door after Perry.

Although the evening was fine, as Luke himself had remarked in conversation several times during the evening, the temperature had dropped, but he found the night air refreshing after the stuffiness of the drawing room. His eyes took a moment to adjust to the darkness, and then, by the light of the half moon, he spotted Perry waiting by the garden gate.

"There's an alleyway beyond, but the gate's locked," he said. "We'll have to climb over."

"I can do that." Luke made a stirrup with his hands and more or less heaved Perry over the fence. Then, with a leap, he grabbed the top of the ironwork gate and hauled himself up and over. He landed with a thump on the other side to find Perry brushing the dust from his trousers.

"So what would you like to do now, Dr. Lewis? Fancy a drink?"

"I … I don't drink," Luke stammered. "And I promised that I'd return to Yorkville as soon as I was finished here. Perhaps some other time," he added hastily, even though Perry seemed not at all upset by his refusal.

"Any time," he said. "Just send me a note and we'll make a date." He handed over his card. "I'm nearly always available."

Luke hesitated. He was finding Perry very odd, but as he had made no other friends since he'd arrived in Yorkville, he didn't want to close the door on the first person he had met who was willing to be one. Besides, maybe Perry would turn out to be one of those elusive connections that everyone kept going on about. If so, he hoped it would a less dangerous association than the Van Hansels.

"Well," he said, "perhaps I could spare a half-hour or so."

"Excellent!" Perry beamed and then led him down Shuter Street to Yonge. "Tell me, Dr. Lewis," he said as they walked along, "where did you study?"

"Please, call me Luke. My formal training was at McGill University in Montreal. But my real education was quite practical."

"Oh really? Is your father a doctor as well?"

"No, he's a saddlebag preacher," Luke replied.

"Which explains why you don't drink?"

"Well, yes."

"So how does the son of a saddlebag preacher end up with practical experience in doctoring?"

"I went with my brothers to the Huron Tract to farm," Luke said. "I soon discovered that I wasn't cut out for it, but I liked looking after the animals. I spent a lot of time with my hand up cows' backsides."

Perry startled several passing pedestrians by hooting with laughter. "That would fit you not only for a career in medicine, but as a prime candidate for capture by the flouncy girls in Lavinia's drawing room," he said. "They're all rather bovine, don't you think?"

"It wasn't all just cows, of course. I went from doctoring livestock in Huron to disposing of dead Irish bodies in Kingston. They put them all in a pit, you know." Luke hadn't ever said much about his experiences in the fever sheds, other than to Ben. But for some reason, he was finding it easy to talk to this newfound acquaintance.

"A rather large number of Irish seem to have survived in spite of everything, haven't they?" Perry said. "All you hear on Toronto's streets these days are Irish accents. My father thinks the government should pack them all up and ship them back to Ireland now that the potatoes are growing again. He firmly believes they'll never be good for anything."

"They'd do just as well as anyone else if they were as well fed. It's too bad they can't get themselves invited to a soiree sometime. I'm sure they'd love a cream cake or two."

"I agree. I admire their resilience, if not their habits. It's this way."

Perry led them from the main street into a warren of side laneways that twisted and turned and, Luke was quite sure, doubled back on themselves. He was lost after the second turn. Then Perry stopped in front of an unassuming one-storey building with an oddly scratched wooden doorframe. There was nothing that Luke could see that would mark it as a tavern, yet when Perry swung open the door, Luke's nose was assailed by the sour smells of whisky, beer, and tobacco.

There were only a handful of men standing at a counter that stretched along one wall, but they all seemed to know Perry.

"Peregrine, my good man," said one of them. "Haven't seen you for a time."

"I was reined in," Perry replied. "Father said I needed to stay at home and peruse the absolutely tedious course of study he's laid down. He still seems to think that some university somewhere will allow me to grace its doors someday. George, may I present Luke. Luke, this is George."

"Welcome, Luke. I haven't seen you here before."

"Luke is new to town. Actually, he's not even in town, but not far away either. This is his first visit."

There was a warning in Perry's voice that the other man seemed to comprehend, but Luke wasn't sure what was being warned against. He also didn't know why no last names were offered in the introduction, but he decided to merely follow Perry's lead and see what happened next.

Perry ordered a whisky, but Luke declined anything but a mug of ale. They took their drinks to a table in the corner.

"What do you think of my little hidey-hole, Dr. Luke?"

Luke didn't think much of it. He had only ever been in a tavern or two in his life, but there didn't seem to be anything special about this one. The same scarred tabletops, the same sawdust on the floor and spittoons in the corners. He had never understood the lure of such places, or why hard liquor had such a hold on some men.

"It seems all right," he replied. "It's more congenial than Mrs. Van Hansel's drawing room at any rate."

"Yes, all those eager girls. And their dreadful mothers."

"I enjoyed the musical part of the evening," Luke said. "Where did you learn to play the piano like that?"

"Oh," Perry said with a wave of his hand. "My education has been extensive and, generally speaking, a complete waste of time, save for piano lessons. I just dabble, really, but I play well enough for an evening at the Van Hansels."

"Do you know Mrs. Van Hansel's … assistant? Cherub?" Luke wasn't sure what position Cherub held exactly, except that she seemed very much in favour with Lavinia.

"Ah yes, the fascinating Cherub. So you've met her?"

"Yes. I was hoping she would be there this evening, but I didn't see her."

"Of course not. Some of the merchant wives would not allow their daughters to attend if she'd been there. Silly, isn't it? She's far more presentable than any of them. So, tell me, how did you fall into Lavinia's clutches?"

"Two men were attacking Cherub in an alley. I just happened to be going by and intervened. When I escorted her back to her carriage, she introduced me to Mrs. Van Hansel. It seemed like a propitious meeting at the time."

Perry looked puzzled. "Only at the time?"

"I've met Mr. Van Hansel before, although I didn't realize it until this evening. There are … reasons why it would be better if he didn't meet me again."

"You crossed him?"

"In a manner of speaking." Although Luke felt that he needn't guard his tongue overly with Perry, a voice in the back of his mind cautioned him not to be too free with details either. He'd only just met this man, after all, and he had no idea how close Perry really was to the Van Hansel family.

After a few moments, during which it became clear that Luke would be no more forthcoming, Perry shrugged a little and smiled. "A man with a past. You get more and more interesting all the time, Luke Lewis. Never mind, someday you'll tell me, I'm sure."

"And you? How do you know the Van Hansels?" Safer to steer the conversation away from matters that were best left undisclosed.

"Mister is a friend of father's. Well, acquaintance really. They know each other through the lodge."

"The Orange Lodge?" That would explain the remarks about the Irish.

"Is there any other lodge in Toronto? Anyway, the Van Hansels, as I said, aren't really top drawer, but father is convinced that I might someday find a wife if exposed to enough female companionship, and he's willing to lower his standards to make it happen, especially if her family has a little money. And of course Lavinia is delighted that I'm available as an extra unattached man for her functions. There aren't so many of us, you know. The eligible ones tend to get snapped up in a hurry. There's a surfeit of women in this city."

"So why haven't you been snapped up yet?"

"I'm a black sheep, of course. Welcome enough in most drawing rooms, but not considered good marriageable material."

"And why is that?"

Perry rolled his eyes at the ceiling. "Oh let me see ... there are so many reasons. I've been asked to leave numerous educational institutions due to an apparently incurable lack of application on my part. I drink. I spend far too much money that isn't mine." He stopped and looked at Luke directly. "And Father may not realize it, but I'm sure you know the fourth reason."

Luke felt the blush creep up to his hairline. He took another sip of beer and noticed that his hands were shaking.

"I'm right, aren't I?" Perry was looking at him closely. "I haven't made a mistake, have I?"

"I ... I don't know what you mean."

"I'm reasonably sure you do."

Luke didn't know how to deflect this overture. He had known Ben for many weeks, had lived in the same rooms with him for some time before the subject was even alluded to. It was so patient, so slow, that it seemed like a natural extension of what had already become a warm friendship. And then, after Ben died, Luke vowed to wall off that part of his life. But here it was again, this time offered openly by someone he had only just met. He looked around the taproom, trying to find words to say, and noticed that there were two men in the corner by one of the stinking spittoons who were leaned over very close to each other. A man at the bar slapped his hand on his companion's shoulder, but as Luke watched, he realized that the hand lingered just a little too long. It suddenly became very clear to him that the tavern was full of men just like him. He didn't want to be one of them.

"Look," Perry said, "I don't mean to press you. You have my card. You can drop me a note anytime. Even if you just want someone to show you around the city, that's fine. It doesn't have to be anything else." He dropped his eyes to the drink in front of him for a moment, then looked up at Luke. "I'd like it to be, though."

Luke finished his ale in one gulp, then rose from the table. "I have to get back."

"Of course. But I'd better walk you out of here. You'll never find your way otherwise."

When they reached Yonge Street, Perry hailed a passing horse cab. "Do you want to take this?" he asked. "I can get another one."

"No. You go on. I'm fine," Luke said. He would catch an omnibus, if any of them ran so late at night.

"I hope we meet again, Dr. Lewis," Perry said as he climbed into the cab. "Thanks for the drink."

No buses passed Luke as he walked north, so he just kept walking toward Yorkville. He had covered greater distances delivering books in Montreal. Besides, there wasn't a great deal he needed to get back to, other than Christie's questions about the evening. And, he realized, the accusing skeletal finger of Mul-Sack.

Chapter 9

Thaddeus was roused from a very deep sleep by the sound of a knock at the front door. He supposed it was not an unusual noise to hear at a doctor's house. Knocks on the door in the middle of the night must occur occasionally when there were sudden emergencies or turns for the worse. Whoever was knocking must be desperate indeed, however, for there was no let up in the pounding until Thaddeus heard Christie stumble down the stairs and unlatch the door.

To his surprise, he then heard Christie shout "It's for you, Lewis!" Thaddeus assumed this must mean Luke, but when he rose and looked in the other room the bed was empty, the bedclothes undisturbed. Apparently Luke had not yet returned from the Van Hansels' party. Puzzled, he grabbed his jacket and, shrugging it on over his nightshirt, started down the stairs. In his hurry he slipped on the bottom step and his left foot hit the floor hard. He felt something in his knee shift and when he stepped again, a sharp pain shot through it.

Morgan Spicer stood just inside the door. "It's happened again," he said when Thaddeus reached him.

"What, another desecration?"

Morgan face was red with exertion and anger. "Whoever it was ran this way, but I couldn't catch up with them. Did you see anyone go by?"

"I'm sorry, I was fast asleep," Thaddeus said.

"My room is at the back of the house," Christie said. "I can't see the street from there. Nor hear much either."

"I was afraid of that," Morgan said. "I wouldn't have seen them myself, except that one of the twins has a fever and I was up with her. I caught a glimpse of them just as they were slipping out the front gate. I ran after them, but they had too much of a head start."

"Let me put some clothes on and we'll go look at what they did," Thaddeus said.

"Better you than me," Christie grumbled. "People who disturb other people in the middle of the night should be hanged." He scowled at Morgan.

"Sorry," Morgan said, "I just thought …"

"Never mind, laddie, never mind. Not the first time, won't be the last." And he plodded back up the stairs.

Thaddeus climbed the stairs behind him, but much more slowly, using the banister to help haul himself up. Once upstairs, he didn't bother with putting on a proper shirt, just pulled on his trousers and found his socks and boots. Morgan waited impatiently by the door as Thaddeus limped back down the stairs.

Just as they were about to set off for the Burying Ground, Thaddeus spied Luke walking up the street toward them. "What's happened?" Luke asked when they reached him. "Why are you outside at this time of night?"

"There's been another incident at the Burying Ground," Thaddeus said. "We're just going along to have a look at the damage."

Luke fell into step beside his father. "What have you done to yourself? You're limping."

"Stepped the wrong way. How was your party?"

"Disconcerting." Morgan was leading the way, several steps ahead of them. Luke spoke in a soft voice, so that only Thaddeus could hear. "It turns out that Mrs. Van Hansel is the wife of Mr. Van Hansel."

"That would stand to reason," Thaddeus said.

"And Mr. Van Hansel is none other than Hands."

"Oh." Thaddeus had also been in the cabinetmaker's yard when Van Hansel was shot. He helped the Irish girl get away afterward. He had also written a letter to the emigration agent, Anthony Hawke, to inform him of the fraud they'd uncovered. If there was anyone in Toronto he didn't want to meet, it was Hands.

"Did he know it was you?" he asked.

"No. Fortunately I saw him first and kept out of the way, so I don't think he noticed me at all."

If Hands was able to recognize either of the Lewises from that night, it would most likely be Thaddeus. Luke had been crouched over a dead body. It was Thaddeus who urged Hands to call a constable, and Thaddeus who rushed them out of the yard after Hands was shot down. And it had not been Hands, but one of his burly henchmen, who had chased them through the streets of Toronto. With any luck, Thaddeus thought, Hands wouldn't remember Luke at all from that night. But it would be foolish to take a chance on it.

"I hid behind the curtains and left as soon as I could slip away, so I don't think there's any harm done," Luke said.

"Really? You're awfully late for having left the party early."

Luke reddened. "I went off with a friend. We talked for a while."

Thaddeus noticed his son's embarrassment, and wondered if Luke had met a girl. Now that he was finished with school and was more or less settled, there was no reason he shouldn't start looking around for a wife. But now was not the time to ask questions about it. Luke would tell him when he was ready.

Instead, he said, "You didn't mention anything about Hands to your friend, did you?"

"No."

"Good. The fewer people who know about that night the better. Hands has far too many friends in odd places. If Mrs. Van Hansel ever invites you to her house again, you'll have to make some excuse not to go."

"I don't intend to go again regardless. I didn't enjoy it much."

"It's as well we're in Yorkville. He's unlikely to run across either of us as long as we don't venture into the city too often." Thaddeus couldn't help but be curious, though, about the consequences of that strange night. "So he survived the gunshot wound? I thought he must have."

"Yes, but his left arm was damaged. He doesn't seem to have much use of it at all."

"Serves him right."

As they reached the gates of the Burying Ground, Luke and Thaddeus followed Morgan past the Keeper's Lodge and into the cemetery. This time Spicer led them to a grave near the fence that ran along Tollgate Road.

"It's the same as before," Morgan said, the dismay evident on his face. The marker was knocked roughly aside, the grave opened, the corpse thrust up onto the bank of dirt. "It's another old grave. This part of the cemetery has been filled up for some time."

Thaddeus once again looked at the grave, and then in all directions around it, hoping the orientation of the site would give him some clue as to why this coffin in particular had been ripped out of the ground. But there was nothing in the location that offered up any clue, or anything he could see that would connect it with the first violation.

"Where were the men when you saw them?" he asked.

"They slipped out the front gate just as bold as anything. I expect they got in the same way."

"But the last time they went over the fence."

"Only because I surprised them."

Thaddeus peered at the fence that separated the cemetery from the road. There was nothing about it that was out of the ordinary. Nothing to see except the dusty street and the buildings on the other side. "Luke and I will help you set things to rights. Then I want to look at your records."

"Here, let me," Luke said, when Thaddeus stooped to grasp one end of the shrouded corpse.

"You don't have to do that," Morgan said. "I can take care of it later."

"It's all right. I've handled dead bodies before. This one is less disturbing than most I've seen. At least he was given a proper burial."

"Is it a he or a she?" Thaddeus asked.

Morgan pointed to the dislodged stone. "Isaiah Marshall."

"Poor soul. Let's get him back to his resting place then."

As Morgan and Luke manoeuvred the body back into the coffin, the folds of Isaiah Marshall's shroud ripped open and fell away to reveal an arm and part of his chest. A pungent smell wafted up at them, making Thaddeus's eyes water. The exposed upper arm had a cheesy, whitish appearance, but a section of brown skin was intact over the bony part of the shoulder.

"Was Mr. Marshall a coloured man, or has the skin darkened after death?" he asked.

Luke knelt and pulled the folds of cloth away from the man's head. Here the skin had shriveled, the lips pulled away from the teeth in a grimace, the eyes absent, consumed by insects or maggots. But the man's hair was grey and kinked, the cartilaginous remains of the nose wide and flat.

"I'd say he was. The skin darkens after death, but always on the underside of the body, not on top of the shoulder like that, and the hair looks right." He opened the grave clothes a little further, recoiling from the smell that was released.

"What are you looking for?" Morgan asked. Thaddeus wished he would stop looking. With every shift of cloth the stench grew worse.

"This body has been dissected," Luke said.

"How can you tell?" Thaddeus asked.

"The body has decomposed a great deal, but I can still recognize the incisions. He's been more or less put back together again for burial, but rather sloppily, I'd say."

"He may have come from the Anatomical School," Morgan said. "A lot of their bodies are sent here. If they're unclaimed to begin with, no one knows where else to send them."

Luke rewrapped the man as well as he could, then he and Morgan laid him back in his coffin.

"I'll get some tools," Morgan said and walked over to the lodge to fetch shovels and a hammer and nails.

While he was waiting, Thaddeus picked away some of the moss that had grown over the gravestone and found a date underneath the name: October 15, 1847.

"It's sad, isn't it?" he said. "This is the date he died, but there's no corresponding date of birth."

"A stranger in the Strangers' Burying Ground," Luke said. "No one would have known what it should be, I suppose."

Thaddeus picked away at a little more moss, but there were no other markings. Then he moved the stone to one side, so that they wouldn't trip over it while restoring the grave.

When Morgan returned, he and Thaddeus nailed the coffin shut again, but when they both reached for shovels,

Luke stopped his father. "We'll do the heavy work," he said. Thaddeus was about to protest, when he realized that he was just as happy to let them go ahead. His knee hurt. *I'm such old bones,* he thought. *The younger men take the heavy load now. It won't be long before I join poor old Mr. Marshall. When that happens, I'll see Betsy again. I wonder if there was anyone waiting for this man?*

Luke and Morgan mounded the soil over the coffin and tamped it down as best they could, but it looked raw and wrong in such a settled part of the cemetery.

"Shall I say a word or two?" Thaddeus asked.

Morgan looked grateful. "I wanted to before, with the first one, but I didn't think it was right for me to do it."

Thaddeus nodded, then the three men positioned themselves around the grave, Morgan at the foot, Luke at the head, Thaddeus between them.

"Oh Lord," Thaddeus began, and then he hesitated. He knew prayers for the newly interred and prayers for those who had experienced a delayed burial. He even knew prayers for those who had never been properly laid to rest. He wasn't sure what he should say for someone who had been committed once and then dug up again.

Finally, he decided that a few simple words were all that was needed. "Dear Lord, we are again giving you the earthly remains of Isaiah Marshall and trust that you remain guardian of his immortal soul." And then he began the familiar prayer "Our father, who art in heaven ..."

Morgan joined him. Luke did not, although he stood with his head bowed respectfully. Thaddeus was aware that Luke professed no great faith, and this saddened him, but even as he intoned the familiar words, he reflected that his son must find his own way. He could only hope that the way led down a righteous path.

At "amen" they all three stood for a moment, then turned and walked slowly back to the lodge. Sally met them at the door.

"I've put the kettle on," she said. "I thought you might like something after such a horrible chore." Then she disappeared down the hall and Thaddeus could hear her climbing the stairs.

"She's a good girl," he said as he slumped into a chair at the kitchen table.

Morgan nodded. "She is. I'd wish a wife like her for every man if I could."

Luke sat down on one of the wooden stools that had been pulled up to the table, while Morgan fussed with the teapot. When he had served each of them a mug, he reached down a brown ledger from the kitchen shelf and began leafing through it.

"Here it is. Isaiah Marshall. Died October 15, 1847. Birth-date unknown. Cause of death: Congestion. Interred: October 28, 1847."

"Nothing there to tell us much," Thaddeus said. "Other than the fact that he was a long time being buried."

"That would fit with the evidence of dissection," Luke said. "He may have been taken to hospital, where he died from his illness and was sent on to the Toronto School of Medicine when no one claimed the body. Either that or he died in his bed and no one knew what else to do with him."

"May I see the entry from the time before?"

Morgan flipped forward a page and handed over the book.

"Abraham Jenkins," Thaddeus read. "Died: May 4, 1848. Birth date: unknown. Cause of death: Pain in the stomach. Interred: May 15, 1848." His burial was delayed, as well. Does that suggest that both of the bodies came here via the dissecting rooms?"

"I should think so," Luke said. "Nobody else would leave a body lying around for ten days. Not in May."

"So neither of them had family. Or at least no family who cared to go to the expense of burying them. You reburied the first corpse yourself, didn't you, Morgan?"

When Morgan nodded, Thaddeus asked, "Was he a coloured man too?"

"I don't know. I didn't look that closely. Only his arm slid out of the grave clothes and it was mostly bone. I just tucked it in before I put him back."

"It would be interesting to discover if he was. In any event, we might be able to track down more information for Mr. Marshall if he was a member of one of the African congregations. We could talk to the medical school as well. Do they keep records of where they obtain their corpses?" Thaddeus looked at Luke in expectation of an answer.

"I doubt it," Luke said. "They didn't in Montreal — there would have been far too much explaining to do if they had. There were never enough cadavers to go around. I know some of them must have come from resurrectionists. I expect it's the same situation here. But Dr. Christie might know better than I about the records."

"Let's consult Christie and we'll see where we go from there," Thaddeus said. He flipped idly through the rest of the book, taking note of the kind of information the cemetery recorded. Dates of death. Names, although in one or two instances even these were missing. Occupations, when known. Occasionally a date or place of birth. He suspected that these more complete entries were made in cases where a church maintained no cemetery of its own and used the Burying Ground instead.

The very first entry in the book was for Mary Carfrae, the infant daughter of Thomas Carfrae, alderman, customs collector, harbourmaster, and one of the early proponents of a non-denominational cemetery. The Carfraes had lent dignity to the potter's field they supported by burying their own in it. The name appeared a number of times in the record, the last entry being for Thomas himself, who died in 1841.

"Well," he said, handing the ledger back across the table. "I think we should visit the African churches and the medical school, but I have to leave in the morning so it will have to wait until I get back. And now I'd like to visit my bed again, unless Morgan can think of anything else I should see."

"Nothing that I know of," Morgan said. "Thank you for doing this. I know it must not seem that important to anyone else, but it is to me."

"There's no guarantee we'll ever be able to make any sense of it," Thaddeus said. "But at least now we have a place to start."

* * *

The reinterment of a dead body at the Strangers' Burying Ground seemed to Luke to be only the final episode in what had been an altogether bizarre evening. How many people lived in Toronto? Thirty thousand perhaps? Maybe more. Streets and streets of shops and factories and houses that stretched as far as the eye could see. And yet he had inadvertently wandered into the home of the one man in the city who might wish him harm.

As he tossed and turned in an effort to find sleep, he went around and around the events that had led him to the Van Hansels' drawing room. It had seemed a chance encounter. Any stranger might have stopped to assist a young woman in distress. What were the odds that it would be Luke Lewis? He wondered if Van Hansel had known he was in the area, and engineered the circumstances in order to snare him. But he couldn't see how this could have been done. If Hands knew of

Luke's whereabouts, he had a whole cadre of thugs who would be perfectly happy to waylay him at a street corner and deliver him up for punishment. Besides, it hadn't been Luke who had fired the shot that night. He was merely present. And it was his father who had written to Anthony Hawke. He was told that Van Hansel was a vindictive man, but would he go that far to exact his revenge?

No. It had to be coincidence that had brought them face to face. "Coincidences as strange happen every day without anyone taking the slightest notice" his father was fond of saying, and Luke supposed he was right. Still, he found it all rather alarming.

Less dangerous, but more disturbing, was his encounter with Perry Biddulph. Luke really couldn't ascribe any sinister construction to their meeting. The drawing room had been full of people, and Perry had obviously been invited along to accompany the singer. And it was only natural, in a roomful of women, that two young men should seek each other's company. What Luke did find surprising was Perry's willingness to lead him to the tavern, and his directness about his designs. Was it so obvious? Was it something in the way Luke walked or talked or presented himself that signalled what he was? Ben had known. And so had Perry. Could everyone see it, or just those who were looking for it?

In any event, he had no intention of seeing Perry again. He had closed the door on his history with Ben. That was in the past, and he resolved to keep knowledge of it firmly locked away.

So much for his foray into Toronto's social life. The two connections he managed to make were both impossible. Perhaps, he thought, it would be best if he stayed in Yorkville only long enough to replenish his coffers and gain a little experience. Then he could return to Huron, where his life had been far simpler. He would look after cows and pigs and horses and farmers and spend his days discussing the price of potash and the year's yield of wheat with his brothers, and give no one reason to speculate about why the local doctor remained so firmly a bachelor.

And with that decided, he finally fell into a deep sleep.

*　*　*

The second incident at the Burying Ground dominated the breakfast-table talk the next morning. Luke was grateful that Christie's attention was diverted from asking about the Van Hansels' party, but he did think that Christie's questions about the disturbed grave took an odd turn.

"Did you see the corpse?" he asked. "Were there just bones, or was there still flesh on it?"

"I didn't look at it any more than I had to," Thaddeus said as he took advantage of the doctor's momentary distraction to make a dive for the bacon. "We left that to Luke."

"A great deal of the flesh was still intact," Luke said. "Enough, at any rate, to tell that he was coloured."

"An African? Really?"

"He'd also been dissected. The incisions were unmistakable."

"Which brings me to a question you might be able to answer for us," Thaddeus said. "Do you know if the medical schools keep records of their cadavers?"

"Do you mean in terms of where they were obtained?" Christie snatched the last two pieces of toast from the plate. "I'm not sure. There would be records of any felons who were sent on, of course, but those may well be kept at the jail. The same would hold for unclaimed bodies delivered from the hospitals, but if the corpse arrived by any other means it would be madness for them to write anything down. There would be a vested interest in making sure that there was no written account of any body that was illegally obtained."

"Would it be worth asking? There was very little information about either body in the ledger that's kept at the Burying Ground."

Christie shrugged. "You can always ask, but don't be surprised if you get no answer."

He turned to Luke. "Tell me more about the state of the body," he said. "I've never seen coloured bones. Are they different from ours?"

"Not that I could see," Luke replied. "Same composition. Same colour. Except for a scrap of intact skin and what was left of his hair, there was little to distinguish him from anyone else."

"Did you look at the whole body?"

"Well, no," Luke said. "The grave clothes had become disarranged and we had to put them back together, that's all. I wasn't there to make a full examination."

"Unfortunate," Christie said. "I'd have been very interested in the condition of a body that had been buried for that period of time. Perhaps, should it happen again, you might come and fetch me so I could have a look?"

"I don't think so," Thaddeus said firmly. "It would just be a further violation of the poor soul."

Christie seemed not at all put out by this. "I suppose you're right," he said. "Pity. So there was nothing in common between the two corpses except that someone had tampered with their graves?"

"None that I can find, other than the fact that they both died several years ago and there was a longish stretch of time between their deaths and their burials. I'm heading up Yonge Street this morning, but when I get back I'll ask about them at the Medical School. And at the coloured churches.

I've been wanting to visit the African Methodist Episcopal Chapel anyway."

"Excellent idea. They may well be able to tell you something."

"Only if someone there remembers an Isaiah Marshall."

"They might," Christie said. "There's been an influx recently because of the troubles in the States, of course, but there has always been quite a close-knit coloured population here. When I arrived in the 30s they were already well-established in St. John's Ward. Industrious bunch. Blacksmiths and carpenters and shoemakers. Far less trouble than the Irish — the coloureds never seem to ask for anything." Christie chewed a mouthful of toast thoughtfully. "Except once, that I can recall. They petitioned the mayor of Toronto to prevent a circus performance."

"Why was that?" Luke was intrigued that such a harmless diversion could be a point of contention.

"The circus included a minstrelsy act and the coloureds took offence at the way these shows always portray them as dim-witted and lazy."

"Then I can't say I blame them for objecting," Thaddeus said. "What did the mayor do?"

"Why, he shut the circus down, of course. Silly entertainment anyway, if you ask me, with their plantation songs and fast-talking Yankees. Actors should all be hanged. I hope nothing of the sort comprised the repertoire of last evening."

Luke was startled at the sudden shift of focus to his own activities. "No … it wasn't like that at all," he stammered. "It was a singer and a pianist. They performed a number of songs — popular ones, I'm guessing, although I had no familiarity with them." He hesitated for a moment while he tried to recall the music he had heard. "There was one about a sweet rose of somewhere."

Christie's face lit up. "Sweet Rose of Allendale?"

"Yes, that's it," Luke said.

"Excellent choice of material!"

Christie suddenly burst into song.

"Sweet rose of Allendale
Sweet rose of Allendale
By far the sweetest flower there
Was the rose of Allendale.

"Reminds me of home, don't you know!" he said jovially before continuing.

"Oh the sky was clear, the morn was fair
No breath came o'er the sea
When Mary left her Highland home
And wandered forth with me ..."

And he continued to hum happily around mouthfuls of buttered toast all the way through breakfast.

Chapter 10

Thaddeus turned the events that had occurred at the Burying Ground over and over in his mind as his pony plodded up Yonge Street against the steady stream of traffic headed in the opposite direction. All on their way to the city, he assumed, to watch the parade march by. He doubted that many of them knew anything about the Orange Lodge or the significance of July 12, but the lure of a marching band was enough to draw them down from the outlying regions to the north. They would line the street and cheer for whoever was walking by.

He himself was not in a cheering frame of mind. The hot, suffocating heat of an Upper Canadian summer had settled over Toronto in the middle of June and now extended its hold into July. The muddy ruts on unimproved sections of road crumbled into dust with every step the pony took and swirled a cloud of fine particles into Thaddeus's face. He pulled his hat lower as a shield, but then he could feel the hot sun burning the back of his neck. His discomfort made it hard to think.

He could see little connection between the two corpses, other than the fact that they had both been men buried by charity. There was no clue to be found in their relative positions in the graveyard. One was on one side, one on the other. There were roughly two weeks between occurrences. The moon had been waning the night before, which meant that it had been a half moon, or close to it, on the first occasion. Thaddeus supposed that partial illumination was a better camouflage than a dark night. Any light that spilled from a shuttered lantern would be less noticeable under the veil of the shifting graveyard shadows. No help in determining the cause of the desecrations, but it might well be an indication of when the next might occur. Utilizing the phase of the moon would be dependent on the weather, of course, but he resolved to discuss this possibility with Morgan upon his return to Yorkville. Perhaps they could circumvent a third incident.

Poor Morgan, he thought, his ambition to join the ministerial ranks thwarted by his inability to wrestle the English language to the ground. This lack was difficult for Thaddeus to comprehend. Language and its efficacious use had always been one of his strengths as a preacher and his best tool as a teacher. He had been sure that he could bring Morgan along, and was distressed that he had apparently failed in this. On the other hand, he reflected, Morgan seemed resigned to his current position. No, not resigned, happy almost — and who wouldn't be happy with a girl like Sally and four fine children to spend his days with? Thaddeus was suddenly hit with a wave of grief at the loss of his wife. Hurriedly, he shoved the pain away, before it could take hold of him, but no sooner had he put this thought away than he realized with a start how much he missed his granddaughter Martha. She had always been good company for him and Betsy. She had a lively curiosity about everything and at times her observations were so shrewd that she took Thaddeus aback. When he had completed his duties on Yonge Street, he must speak to her father about her future. She should be educated beyond the basic rudiments offered at a village school.

When, dirty, thirsty, and bemused, Thaddeus finally reached his host's house in Davisville, he was only momentarily encouraged to discover that the women's class had attracted two new faces, both wives of men who worked at the potteries.

"I was brought up in the old Methodist Episcopal Church," one of them said. "I remember hearing you preach at a camp meeting near Napanee. When I heard it was you taking the class, I was curious to come along. I thought you'd retired ages ago."

"So had I," Thaddeus allowed, making light of the comment. "But when the Lord calls, I have to answer."

The exchange cast him down again and made him feel old, and he suddenly realized why he was taking so much delight in helping Morgan Spicer discover who was responsible for the raids on the Toronto Burying Ground — it made him feel like he was in the thick of things again, and that made him feel young, in spite of the fact that his arthritic knee still hurt from his misstep of the night before. Vanity, he knew, and the words from Ecclesiastes came to him: *Remove vexation from your heart and put away pain from your body, for youth and the dawn of life are vanity.* He could cast away the vexation, he knew, but putting away the pain of his body was proving far more troublesome.

When he reached York Mills a number of people were lining up along the street. There was to be a small march, one of them said when he asked, to celebrate the glorious victory of King William at the Battle of the Boyne. Local Orangemen would parade through the street carrying banners. No band, of course, but an entertaining diversion nonetheless.

Even here, so far out of the city, they subscribe to this nonsense, Thaddeus thought, although he did not share this thought out loud. The Methodist Episcopal Church apparently had few adherents in this place as it was, and he would not attract any more by criticizing out of turn. He couldn't resist a small piece of mischief, however, and asked a red-faced man which King William had been victorious, and where exactly was Boyne.

The man looked at him with suspicious confusion.

"Well, you know, good King William. And he put down the Catholics."

When Thaddeus persisted in his questioning, the man had no answer but to say that he, for one, had no intention of being ruled by the Pope, and if that august personage should ever happen to wander into York Mills, he'd be given the pummelling he deserved.

Shaking his head at the ignorance of men, Thaddeus made his way to the cottage where he was to lead a women's class, only to discover that no one was there. Lined up along the street to watch the Orangemen, he supposed.

There was no one to meet him in Lansing either.

He was to preach the next day's sermon at Cummer's Chapel, so with relief he continued on to the Settlement. Again a number of Cummers were waiting at the meeting house for the men's class, among them Daniel, who as usual extended a dinner invitation and the offer of a bed for the night. The meal was excellent, and Thaddeus was cheered up a little by the unwavering support shown by the Cummer family.

After dinner he and Daniel sat out on the spacious farmhouse veranda to watch the setting sun, unmolested by the swarms of mosquitoes that would have pestered them earlier in the year.

"It's too dry for them," Daniel said. "The bugs all seem to wither away as soon as the streams do. We desperately need some rain, but if it comes the skeeters will, too, no doubt."

"How are the crops holding up?" Thaddeus knew that many of the Cummers had farms in the area.

"The wheat is definitely looking peaked. I'm not sure it matters. There's no market for it anyway. At least here we can keep the livestock and the kitchen garden watered — we have a spring-fed well and it has yet to run dry in the summer. 'Look for willow trees, that's where you find the water' my father always said. Of course if wells go dry, people can draw from the mill pond, but even it's getting low."

"Your father was a wise man."

"He was. Sometimes I think it's as well he didn't live to see all this Orange Society nonsense that seems to have gripped the province. He was no supporter of the Pope, but he was always willing to accept the fact that there could be many ways to approach God."

"There was a march in York Mills, of all places," Thaddeus said.

"Ironic, given Prime Minister LaFontaine's close connection with York County."

It was a Quaker sect, the Children of Peace at Sharon, who had led the way in 1841, Thaddeus recalled, when Robert Baldwin formed a coalition of reformers with Louis-Hippolyte LaFontaine. The two men shared a vision of a Canada where French and English could flourish together under a government that was guided by the will of the people. When LaFontaine ran into difficulties in his Quebec riding, Baldwin asked the farmers and villagers of the fourth riding of York to elect him to a seat in the legislature. The local reform-minded voters, urged on by the leader of the Sharon Temple, had obliged. Later, LaFontaine returned the favour and found Baldwin a safe seat in Rimouski, a French riding east of Quebec City.

"Are the Reformers going to be able to hold the union together, or do you think it will fall apart after all?" Thaddeus asked.

Daniel took a few moments to answer. "I mislike the amount of influence Orangemen have in Toronto, but if the province was going to fall apart it would have happened when the Parliament buildings were torched."

"My young lad was in Montreal when it happened," Thaddeus said. "He doesn't talk about it much. Apparently it was an ugly scene."

"And could have been much uglier if LaFontaine had been heavy-handed. I, for one, will put my faith in him and Mr. Baldwin. And God, of course, who surely must approve of their tolerant approach."

Thaddeus wasn't sure he agreed with Daniel Cummer's assessment. It seemed to him that there were too many divisions in Canada. Protestant against Catholic; English against French. Everybody, it seemed, against the Irish. Even the Methodist Church, never united in the first place, continued to splinter into fragments. Methodist Episcopals, Wesleyan Methodists, Protestant Methodists, New Connection Methodists, Primitive Methodists, Bible Christians, African Methodists....

Perhaps it would be better if they were all one, he reflected — if they could all put our differences aside and concentrate on the work at hand. Methodist schisms were odd things, in many cases ruptures occurring not due to different interpretations of the scripture, but along the fault lines that opened over political and organizational considerations. Maybe it would make more sense to take a page from the Baldwin-LaFontaine book and work toward a common goal.

It was an ironic conclusion to reach, given the fact that he had toiled so steadfastly for the Methodist Episcopals in the past and was now working so hard to lure people into their fold. If the Methodists ever became one church, he would no longer need to trot his pony along Yonge Street preaching to an ever-diminishing handful of people. He found that he was not in the least distressed by this notion.

In light of these ruminations and the events of the previous day, he chose to base his Sunday sermon on the subject of tolerance. It wouldn't be a popular choice, he knew, but he had followed his conscience before and, no doubt, he would do so again. He noted that there were several new faces in the congregation. Perhaps he could do some good work on this circuit after all.

He drew from Matthew for his text: "Judge not, that ye be not judged. For with what judgment ye judge, ye shall be judged and with what measure ye mete, it shall be measured to you again.

"And why beholdest thou the mote that is in thy brother's eye but considerest not the beam that is in thine own eye?"

Here and there he saw a downcast face, which told him his words had hit the mark, but if he had to sum up the general response to his sermon, he would say it was one of puzzlement and disinterest. Maybe it was a mistake after all.

His mood darkened even further when he reached Newtonbrook to discover only three people waiting to hear his service, delivered in the yard of a local farmer. It was as though the clock was cranked back fifty years, to when the Methodist Episcopal circuit riders travelled from farm to farm, cabin to cabin, buffeted by intemperate weather, indifference, and hostility.

He hoped for a breeze as he travelled northward. Yonge Street climbed steadily uphill from the city, taking him away from the steamy heat near Lake Ontario; but even though he reached a greater elevation, the wind died away to nothing. He was soon boiling from the sun and thirsty from the dust. Daniel Cummer had provided him with a jug of water to speed his travels, but when Thaddeus reached for it, he realized that it was already empty.

He looked in vain for a stream where he could stop and fill it. Here and there brooks and rills had dried away to stagnant puddles and he could find no fresh-running creek that invited him to scoop up a palmful of water. Best to wait, then, until he reached Thorne's Hill.

His knee was paining him badly, as well, from the effort of bracing his legs against the footboard of the buggy as it rumbled over the more poorly graded sections of the road. It was with relief that he finally reached the wagoner's house at Thorne's Hill, where he hoped to hold a men's class.

When he stepped down from the buggy he felt a sharp pain in his knee, as if there was a shard of glass embedded in the joint, and at the same time his leg gave way. He was saved from a tumble in the dust only by reaching out at the last moment and steadying himself on the buggy's dashboard. He waited for a few moments and then took a tentative step on his bad leg. The pain was still there. He limped over to the front door of the house and knocked, but no one answered. He knocked a second time and waited, but with the same result. There appeared to be no one at home. He peeked in through the windows, but it was clear that the man had forgotten that he was to host a meeting. Either that or he had changed his mind, Thaddeus thought, and was too embarrassed to say so directly. The class promised to be sparsely attended anyway, as there was no one else waiting to gain entry.

His throat felt scratchy and parched and he knew that he had to find a drink before he could continue on his way to Langstaff. He returned to the main street, but the only public well he could find appeared to be the one that attracted a line of supplicants — Holy Ann's Well — the well that was said to be the site of a miracle. He didn't believe in miracles of that nature, but surely the water itself would be good enough, he thought. He would get his drink there and be on his way.

The woman waiting in front of him was inclined to be friendly and struck up a conversation with Thaddeus as soon as he joined the line.

"I'm hoping Holy Ann water will cure my goiter," she said. She had a huge lump at the front of her throat that bulged past the scarf she had wrapped around her neck to hide it. "It just keeps getting bigger and bigger and nothing seems to work. I've been taking Syrup of Naptha and Oriental Balsam for years, but it just keeps growing. My sister-in-law said that maybe Holy Ann could help."

"Did you travel far?" Thaddeus asked.

"Yes. All the way from Brockville. It was a tiresome journey, but I'm at my wit's end with this thing."

By the time they reached the wellhead, Thaddeus had learned nearly everything there was to know about this woman. The most interesting development in her life, however, was the growth of the ugly tumour at her throat. He heard about the opinions of the various doctors she had seen and the pieces of advice given by various members of her family, both of which were numerous, and a history of the affliction as it pertained to the aforesaid family, several of whom were similarly stricken. It was with a sigh of relief that he watched her dip an old mug into the bucket of water and drink. Then he stepped forward for his own turn.

The water was cool, clear, and sweet, and he drank his fill. He replenished his jug and poured several mugfuls into his hat for his pony to drink. Then he boarded the buggy and trotted out of town with a farewell wave from the chatty woman.

For the first half mile or so he mentally grumbled about the folly of believing in miracles from anyone but God, the growing stridency of the Orange Lodge, and his own lack of success on the circuit thus far, but as he headed farther north, he found that his mood lifted. Even though the sun was now high overhead, the relief of his thirst and the cooling effect of the damp hat on his head improved his outlook immeasurably. Even the pain in his knee started to ease off.

As he trotted into Lansing, he felt better than he had at any point during the previous two days.

Chapter 11

Over the course of the next few days three elegantly written notes were delivered to Dr. Christie's house, two of them addressed to Luke directly. In the first, Lavinia Van Hansel thanked Luke for attending her soiree and expressed regret that she had not had time to say goodbye to him at the end of the evening. Luke knew that it had been ungracious of him not to send a letter of thanks the day after the party, but he was determined not to have anything more to do with the Van Hansels and he was reluctant to provide any opportunity for further communication. He burned the note in the office grate and hoped that his lack of response would mark an end to the matter.

Two days later another letter arrived, in the same elegant handwriting that had graced the first. Luke carried it upstairs to his rooms and laid it, unopened, on his bureau, where it stayed until it was time for him to retire for the night. Then curiosity got the better of his caution and he ripped it open.

Dear Dr. Lewis, the letter read. *We enjoyed your company the other evening and look forward to furthering our acquaintance.*

I know you are under an obligation to attend to the needs of your practice, but is it possible that you might be free for tea next Tuesday? I know our attractions are poor to an up and coming young man as yourself, but as an enticement to your attendance, I have also invited Peregrine Biddulph, the young man with whom you seemed to hit it off so nicely at our party. Please let me know if Tuesday is convenient — if not, I would be happy to select another time.

Lavinia Van Hansel

Luke felt a rush of nausea. Lavinia had noticed him leaving with Perry, in spite of the fact that they had slipped so stealthily into the garden. What had she construed from this action? Did she know about Perry, and by extension, Luke? For a moment he had a vision of his world crumbling, of vilification and ostracism, of his innermost secrets exposed for the scorn of all who cared to look. He began to shake as he imagined what could happen to him — he would be dismissed from Dr. Christie's practice, that much was sure, and quite probably hounded from Yorkville. He might even lose his licence. He had no idea where he would go if that happened. The taint would follow him everywhere, even if he returned to Huron resigned to a farmer's life. And worst of all, his father would find out, the sympathetic fellowship between them smashed beyond repair.

He threw the letter on his bed and went to the window, where he hoped the evening's breeze might calm him. He drank the air with deep gasps and eventually his breathing slowed and became more regular, the cascade of unwelcome thoughts evened out and resolved into a question. *What exactly did Lavinia mean?*

He walked over to where the letter lay accusingly on the bed. Gingerly, as though the paper might be infused with a hidden poison, he picked it up by the corner and reread it. It didn't seem so sinister on the second reading. *We enjoyed your company.* A standard statement for the hostess of a party. *We look forward to furthering our acquaintance.* In his panic at the mention of Perry, Luke had overlooked this part of the sentence. As far as he was aware he had contributed absolutely nothing to the evening beyond his mere presence. He neglected to speak to Lavinia after the first greeting. He did his best to ignore the young women present. And then he bolted over the garden fence without saying goodbye. He had, in fact, been extremely rude. Why would Lavinia want to see him again after such a poor showing? On reflection, he found it very puzzling.

As for the rest of it — the mention of Perry as someone he seemed to hit it off with — he decided that he might well have read too much into the observation. It was only natural that they would have sought each other's company, wasn't it? Especially at a function that was so over-represented by young women. No, there was no reason to think that anyone suspected anything untoward. His nerves had got the better of him again, that was all.

He would not, however, respond to the invitation. With any luck, Lavinia Van Hansel would conclude that he was abominably boorish and not worthy of any further consideration.

"Lavinia wants something from you," Perry had said. Well, she wasn't going to get it. Not if it took Luke anywhere near Hands.

* * *

Two days later another letter arrived. It was apparently addressed to Dr. Christie directly, for he appeared at the office door and waved it at Luke.

"Another invitation!" he said. "Well done, Luke. You've obviously made a great impression."

From where he sat behind the desk, Luke could see that the thin sheet of paper Christie held was covered in the same handwriting as the previous two letters.

"I didn't think I'd made any impression at all," Luke said. "I can't imagine why I'm getting another invitation."

"It's for Tuesday. For tea," Christie said, "and we're both invited."

"Oh, that's too bad. We can't both go."

"No, we can't," Christie agreed, and just for a moment Luke hoped that the matter was resolved, but Christie went on. "I'm relatively certain that I'm not the one the lady would like to take tea with. It's you she wants to see. You must take advantage of these opportunities, Luke. By all accounts, Phillip Van Hansel is turning heads in the business world. A mover and a shaker. If you're in his wife's good graces, he could well be in a position to help you get ahead."

"I don't want to get ahead," Luke said. "I'm perfectly happy here."

"Nonsense. You won't feel that way when you have to start collecting your own accounts, trust me. Every practice needs a few patients who are well-heeled enough to pay their bills on time, and this one currently doesn't have nearly enough of them. You're a very personable young man, Luke. I think you should take advantage of this unexpected connection. Plan to take Tuesday off so you can attend. I'll hold the fort." And with a nod of the head, Christie disappeared into the rear of the house again.

Luke wondered if he should confide his misgivings to his employer. After all, the old doctor could hardly be pleased at an association with someone who Luke knew for a fact controlled at least one brothel in the city and had been involved in several cases of fraud. But when he thought about it, Luke realized that he had no way to prove that Hands was connected with Toronto's criminal underground. He and Thaddeus had been present when Van Hansel ordered his henchmen to place two dead bodies in one coffin, but anything else they discovered about him was assumption, based on a few overheard conversations and a great deal of guesswork. And any witnesses willing to back their story were either dead or long since disappeared. After all, the matter of fraud had been investigated by the authorities, but no conclusions were reached and no charges were ever laid.

During the confrontation in the cabinetmaker's yard, Hands claimed to have the local constabulary in his pocket, which, if true, would have afforded him protection during the investigation. Now Christie described him as "a mover and a shaker in the business world." His empire must have grown in the intervening years, his power consolidated. The investigating officials themselves could well be under his control.

Even if he were sure that Christie could be sworn to secrecy, any accusation against Hands would be a dangerous thing to make. If it ever became known, Luke could well find himself in court for defamation, and he would have no way to defend himself. And if the case were to hinge on the moral rectitude of the complainants, one hint of Luke's relationship with Ben would sink him.

He would have to go to tea on Tuesday, he decided. There was no way around it. He could only hope that a tea party wasn't the sort of thing that husbands normally attended. And, he promised himself, if he managed to get through the occasion unscathed, he would save every penny he could and return to the Huron as fast as was humanly possible.

As he was deciding this, he happened to glance over at the skeleton in the corner. He could have sworn that Mul-Sack was laughing at him.

* * *

To Luke's great relief, Lavinia Van Hansel's tea party proved to be a small and intimate affair.

He once again brushed down his jacket and removed the street dust from his shoes before he boarded an omnibus that took him down into the city. Once again a maid answered the front door as soon as he let the brass knocker fall, but this time he was not ushered into the drawing room, but into a small parlour to the left of the hall. Here a round table with a paisley cloth and six chairs stood in the centre of a cozy room filled with shelves of bric-a-brac. Lavinia was there already, as were Cherub and another young woman whom Luke didn't know, although she could well have been in attendance at the soiree and he just didn't remember her. Lavinia rose when he entered the room and ushered him to a seat beside Cherub.

"You two already know each other, so there will be no difficulty in making conversation," she said. Luke nodded to Cherub, who rolled her eyes at Lavinia's remark.

"How are you?" he asked politely. "I trust that you have recovered from your attack?"

"An attack?" the other girl squeaked, "How thrilling!"

"It was nothing," Cherub said. "And I am quite fine, thank you. By the way, this is Grace Thomas. Grace, this is Dr. Luke Lewis."

"A doctor! How thrilling!" Grace said. "And where do you practise, Dr. Lewis?"

"In Yorkville. And it's not very thrilling at all actually."

Grace looked puzzled, but his remark was rewarded by a small twitch of Cherub's lips.

Just then someone let the knocker fall against the front door and everyone's attention was diverted in expectation of the arrival of more guests. Luke tensed, prepared to duck under the tablecloth and make a pretense of tying his shoe should the newcomer turn out to be Phillip Van Hansel. He had no idea what he would do after that, but the subterfuge might at least buy him a little time. This desperate measure proved unnecessary. Two people were shown into the parlour, Perry Biddulph and a young, remarkably good-looking man with a scowl on his face. In spite of the scowl, his appearance made Luke gasp. The man had a shock of wavy chestnut hair that swept back from a wide brow and a physical presence that dominated the room. He was like a ghost risen from Luke's past, for he was like the twin of the priest who had laboured in the fever sheds at Kingston. Luke had been quite enamoured of Father Higgins, although he was disturbed by his feelings at the time; as far as he knew, the priest had been unaware of anything untoward. And Higgins had died. Surely he couldn't have come back to life.

Then as the man walked farther into the room, Luke realized his mistake. This man was taller and more heavily built. His eyes were blue, not brown. His hair wasn't quite the right shade of chestnut. And Luke began to breathe again.

He wondered if the man had been invited along with Perry, or if the two merely arrived at the same time. Then he became aware that Grace Thomas was making hasty, fluttery adjustments to the voluminous sleeves of her dress, straightening them and brushing away imaginary crumbs.

Lavinia beckoned the young man to the chair beside Grace, which only deepened his scowl. This was a matchmaking exercise, apparently, but only one of the sides seemed at all interested.

Perry remained standing, his eye assessing the china figurines that were lined up on the shelves. He walked over and picked one of them up to examine the potter's mark on the bottom.

"You seem to have quite a taste for shepherdesses," he remarked. "This one is quite good, but most of the rest of it is dreadful. You might think about getting rid of a lot of it and giving this one a shelf by itself."

It was an incredibly rude thing to say, but Lavinia laughed. "Oh, those aren't mine. Mr. Van Hansel collects them. He has terrible taste, doesn't he?" Then she turned to the guests at the table. "I don't think everyone has met our special guest yet," she said. "Everyone, this is Dr. Luke Lewis. Dr. Lewis, this is Grace Thomas and Arthur Ryan to her left. You, of course, know Miss Ebenezer, and you met Mr. Biddulph the other evening."

Luke was grateful for the introduction. He hadn't been told Cherub's last name before, and it seemed disrespectful to continually address her by her first name.

Perry took the seat to Luke's right. "Yes, Dr. Lewis and I had quite a charming conversation the other night. It's lovely to see you again, sir." He smirked a little as he said it.

Luke nodded in acknowledgement and told himself to act normally.

Lavinia rang the bell that connected the parlour to the kitchens and soon two maids bustled in with a large silver tea service and plates of cakes.

As soon as the cups were filled and the plates passed, Lavinia turned to Luke. "I'm so sorry that Dr. Christie couldn't join us as well," she said. "He seems such an interesting gentleman. A Scot, I take it from his accent, but in Canada for quite some time?"

Luke understood that Lavinia was making conversation for the benefit of her other guests. "Yes, I believe he's originally from Edinburgh, but came to Canada in the thirties. I was very fortunate to be taken into the practice, as I had just graduated."

"And do you enjoy it?"

"Some of it is interesting. A great deal of it is pretty humdrum. Like any practice, I expect, although I originally intended to return to the Clinton area where my brothers farm. I expect medicine would be more challenging there. Machinery accidents, trees falling on people, farmers gored by bulls, that sort of thing."

Grace Thomas gave a little squeaky gasp and Luke was suddenly aware that his statement was probably inappropriate as teatime conversation. He tried frantically to change the subject, seizing on the first thing that came to mind.

"And what do you do, Mr. Ryan?"

Ryan fixed Luke with an intent gaze. "Oh, father has a mind to put me to work in the family business. He seems to think I should develop a head for figures so he can concentrate on opening the new warehouse."

"Mr. Ryan's father owns an ironworks," Lavinia interjected. "It's very successful and he has hopes of expanding. And Miss Thomas's father owns a cooperage."

A marriage not only of children, but of business concerns, Luke thought. He didn't give the merger much of a chance, if Arthur Ryan's scowl was anything to go by.

"What do you hear of the proposal for a Toronto industrial exhibition, Arthur?" Perry asked.

Arthur shrugged. "Oh, I don't really know," he said.

"Exhibition?" Luke asked. Both his father and Dr. Christie had been fascinated by newspaper accounts of the Great Exhibition of the Works of Industry of All Nations and had spent an entire mealtime regaling each other with snippets of information about the wonders that were on display. The London palace of iron and glass that housed the exhibition was itself a marvel, the perfect setting for thousands of displays of mechanical and industrial ingenuity, from the latest in agricultural implements to a demonstration of Mr. Colt's repeat action revolver. Thaddeus was intrigued by the newest contraptions; Dr. Christie, on the other hand, read out descriptions of the more novel exhibits like the Koh-i-Noor diamond, the largest in the world; a four-sided piano; huge Russian vases twice the height of a man fashioned from porcelain and malachite; and an elaborate howdah draped across the back of a stuffed elephant. They were both fascinated by the descriptions of the retiring rooms, where a system was set up to flush away human waste using water.

"Everyone wants an exhibition now that the one in London has proved so successful," Perry said. "The good burghers of Toronto are rubbing their hands in glee at the notion of charging people for the privilege of inspecting their wares. There's talk of using the Caer Howell Pleasure Grounds, especially if Mrs. Boulton can be persuaded to loan out the horse park next door. No doubt someone will want to build a replica of the Crystal Palace — in which case I would think that Mr. Ryan's father might do quite well out of it if he moves smartly."

"What are the Caer Howell Pleasure Grounds?" Luke had a mental vision of harems and Turkish baths, but he found it difficult to believe that anything so exotic could flourish in a city as staid as Toronto.

"Oh, it's just a place to play cricket and rackets," Perry said. "Full of sweaty athletic types. It's quite boring really, but I'll take you there sometime if you like. There's an archery range — I could shoot an arrow through you."

Luke wasn't sure how to respond to this. Perry's innuendo made him uncomfortable, although the only other person at the table who appeared to notice was Lavinia, who shot a sharp glance at Perry.

"It would be quite wonderful to see the London Exhibition first hand, wouldn't it?" Cherub said. There was a dreamy note to her voice. "I'd love to travel to different places, see different things."

"Oh, I don't know," Grace said. "It seems such a bother when everything you could want is right here. All the fuss of packing, just for starters. And then there's the journey itself. I'm sure I'd get quite queasy on a ship. And there's no guarantee that I'd like anything once I got there. Different food, different customs. No, I'd rather stay put, thank you."

"And so you shall," Arthur said. "Much the best plan."

Cherub indulged herself with a small grimace. Perry laughed. Luke wanted to, but his good manners stopped him just in time.

* * *

As it turned out, Arthur Ryan had not travelled with Perry. The party began to break up after they all consumed several cups of tea, exchanged a few bits of gossip, and participated in three or four long conversations about a number of determinedly non-controversial topics. It was a far cry from the spirited debates that took place at Christie's table. Luke wondered what would happen if he suddenly, *à la* the good doctor, announced that someone or other should be sent to the hangman. He suspected that Perry would laugh. So might Lavinia. And Cherub. He stifled the impulse. He didn't want to be considered an amusing guest. He didn't want to be a guest at all.

Perry left first, then Luke said his goodbyes and found himself standing in front of the house with Arthur.

"It was nice to meet you," he said.

Arthur merely nodded at him and set off down the street, signally quite clearly that he was uninterested in a companionable walk. As he was travelling in the same direction, Luke let him get a good head start, then trudged after him. He had walked as far as the corner when someone hailed him. It was Perry.

"Climb up," he said. "I've got the carriage for the rest of the day. I'll give you a ride home."

Luke hesitated. He didn't really want to associate with Perry any more than he did with the Van Hansels, but unlike Arthur Ryan, he felt it was churlish to decline and walk off when they were going the same way.

"Oh, come on, I don't bite."

Luke climbed up into the vehicle.

"Well, that was a tedious afternoon," Perry announced. "What would you like to do now?"

"I really need to be getting back to Yorkville," Luke said, although this wasn't strictly true. Dr. Christie had urged him to take his time and make the most of the occasion.

"Surely you have time for a small drink of something besides tea?" Perry said. "Especially since I'm saving you all sorts of time. I need a reward for being so bored."

"No, Perry, I can't. I have to go back," Luke said with what he hoped was a firm tone.

"I promise not to make eyes at you. We had quite enough of that from the young lady — what was her name again? Walter Thomas has a raft of girls and they're all called something like Patience or Prudence or Charity. I can never keep them straight."

"Grace," Luke said. "Her name was Grace."

"Grace? Was it really? In any event, there's quite a passel to get safely married off. Lavinia must be rubbing her hands with glee at the prospect of how much the good Mr. Thomas will owe the Van Hansels if she engineers suitable matches for them all. Poor Arthur. He's as good as hogtied and delivered at this point and he knows it. So what do you say?" Perry was about to pull the carriage into an alleyway.

"No. Drive."

Perry frowned, but did as he was directed.

More to break the silence than anything, Luke said, "So has Lavinia found a match for you yet?" He meant it as a joke, but it seemed to have the opposite effect.

"No, but I'm sure she's looking." Perry sounded glum. "One of these days she'll find one. And I may have to agree to it."

"Does she know? That you're …"

"Basically not interested?" Perry was silent for a moment before he confided, "Of course she knows. She's no fool. Father, on the other hand, hasn't a clue. He thinks my lack of eligibility is a result of my lamentable lack of initiative. My brother Theo, now, there's a catch. Everything a father could hope for. Lavinia would love to get her hooks into Theo, but there's little chance of that. He'll be found a suitable wife within our own circle here. Here or in England. No chance for anyone the Van Hansels might know. I, on the other hand, can be fobbed off on anyone as long as her father has enough money."

"I don't understand how you got tangled up with the Van Hansels in the first place," Luke said.

"I knew Arthur and he invited me along to a party one night." Perry cast a sidelong look at Luke. "No, it wasn't that. I just knew him. I can't even remember where I met him. Toronto's not that big a place, you know. Everybody meets everybody sooner or later. Anyway, when father found out where I'd been, he suggested that I cultivate the connection. Lavinia was delighted, of course, to be able to present a Biddulph to her bevy of prospective brides, and I was just as happy to do it, since it meant that father stopped ranting at me, at least for a while." He pursed his lips while he chose his next words. "At first I thought it was just my name she was after — as an ornament if you like — and then it became something else."

He flicked the reins and turned the horse into a side street off Yonge. "You see this stretch of trees?"

To Luke it looked like every other section of undeveloped land in the northern regions of the city. Undivided park lots, most of them, not yet carved up into a patchwork of shops and houses.

"This belonged to Alexander Wood," Perry said.

The name meant nothing to Luke.

"Most people call it Molly Wood's Bush."

"Was Molly his wife or something?"

No, Alexander Wood had no wife. The story goes a long way back. Back to when Toronto was still Muddy York. Wood was a magistrate. There was supposedly a rape, and the victim went to Wood to lodge a complaint. The young woman claimed that she didn't know the identity of the man who attacked her, but that she scratched his privates while fending him off. Wood decided to personally inspect the genitals of the suspects — of which there seemed to be rather a large number. He also inspected very closely. Someone complained and soon rumours were flying that Wood had made the whole thing up as an excuse to fondle young men. He became the object of ridicule and scorn. Someone dubbed him 'The Inspector General of Private Accounts' and the nickname stuck like a piece of horse dung."

"What happened to him?"

"He was persuaded to leave Upper Canada for a time to escape the scandal. He returned a few years later, but the old stories kept following him around. He owned this lot but he didn't ever get around to building a house on it. It's been known as 'Molly Wood's Bush' ever since. Now have you figured out what a molly is?"

Luke felt slightly sick. He didn't like the way this conversation was playing out.

"Anyway," Perry went on, "he died a few years ago. He had no heirs, of course. So while the courts try to decide what's to become of his property, his woods have become a favourite meeting place."

"Why are you telling me this?" Luke had no intention of going anywhere near Molly Wood's Bush. He didn't want to meet anyone. He just wanted to go back to Dr. Christie's house, sit in the office, and do his best to ignore Mul-Sack.

"I'm telling you because there's something Lavinia wants me to find there. But I don't know what it is."

"What sort of something?"

"I don't know. And neither does she. But she's starting to get frantic about it. I'd tell her to go away and leave me alone, but I'm afraid she'll carry tales to my father. She's quite capable of doing something like that if she's crossed."

Luke felt so tense he thought some of his bones must soon crack. "What would your father do if she did?"

"Throw me out. Cut me off. Have me charged. I don't know."

"What do you mean charged? With what?"

Perry turned to look at him, astonished. "With sodomy, of course. It's a hanging offence in this province. Hardly anyone is ever arrested, mind you, and even then no one has ever actually been executed for it. But there are a few who have been sent to jail. I can't go to jail, Luke."

"Would your father really do that?"

Perry flicked the reins and the carriage began to move again. "I wouldn't put it past him. I'm not in very good favour as it is, and that would probably be the last straw."

Luke couldn't imagine his own father turning on him to such an extent. Thaddeus would show extreme displeasure, yes. Would refuse to ever speak with him again, quite probably. But have him arrested? But then Luke realized that he really had no idea how his father would react if he were ever to find out. He was nauseated just thinking about it.

"So," Perry continued, "now you know why I need to keep Lavinia happy. I wish I could find what she wants, but I can't."

"What exactly did she ask you to do?"

"Have a look around Molly Wood's Bush."

"For what?"

Perry shrugged. "That's the problem — she doesn't know. She seems to think there's something hidden there, but I've been all over that lot and there's nothing but trees and bushes. Well, and men, of course, but I don't think she's interested in that."

Luke was puzzled. Lavinia had an imperious manner that had set him on his guard from the beginning, but otherwise she seemed like any other well brought up lady, perfectly at ease with teas and dances and recitals. Was she even aware of her husband's illegal activities? Most wives wouldn't be. They were kept in the dark about their husbands' financial dealings and business affairs, even in some cases the expense entailed in running their own households. But the more he thought about it, the more he was inclined to think that Perry was right, and that Lavinia Van Hansel was every bit as ruthless as her husband and would use whatever means she could to get what she wanted. She was obviously not above blackmail.

"Why is your father so eager to cultivate the Van Hansels?" he asked. "It can't be that important to get you married off, can it?"

"No, although that would be a bonus," Perry replied. "It's because Phillip Van Hansel is becoming an important man. The old families don't run Toronto anymore, you know. Things have changed. Men like Van Hansel are building empires. He controls a lot in the city, mainly through his connections with the Orange Lodge. Father's smart enough to know that and he's using me to curry a little favour."

"But Van Hansel is a crook." The words came out of Luke's mouth before he even stopped to think about it.

Perry seemed unsurprised by his outburst. "Of course he is. I know that. Father knows it, too. So does everyone at the lodge. Is that why you went running out the garden door that night? Because Van Hansel is a crook?"

"It's a long story," Luke said. And he had no intention of telling it to Perry. Or to anyone else for that matter. If Phillip Van Hansel was as powerful as Perry claimed, Luke and Thaddeus would be wise to stay well out of sight. Luke would have to find some way to deal with Lavinia's persistence. After the first rebuffs, anyone else would have given him up as a lost cause, but she had gone to the extraordinary measure of appealing to Dr. Christie. Perry was right. There was something she wanted from Luke. He was determined not to give it to her.

Perry slowed the carriage as they approached the intersection of Tollgate Road and Yonge Street. There was a disturbance ahead, with vehicles stopped and people milling in the street.

"It looks like there's been an accident of some sort," Perry said.

"I wonder if I should see if anyone needs help."

"Oh … I'd quite forgotten that you're a doctor. By all means, gallop to the rescue. I'll wait here."

Luke hopped out of the carriage and made his way through the crowd. He had not brought his medical bag with him, so he knew that whatever help he could render would be rudimentary, but an unequipped doctor was still better than no doctor at all. But when he arrived at the scene of the commotion, he discovered that the cause of the holdup was a dead horse. It was a poor, skeletal beast hitched to a cart that carried a load of hay. It had apparently given up on life and fallen over just as the wagon reached the middle of the busy intersection. Two men were trying to remove the harness that still tethered the horse to the wagon.

There was nothing he could do for the horse and nothing that anyone could do about the bottleneck but wait until the obstruction was cleared. He turned and walked back to where Perry was waiting, intending to send him on his way. It was an easy walk from there to Christie's, but a number of carts and buggies and wagons were jammed together in a line down Yonge Street, causing as much obstruction to traffic as the mishap ahead of them. Perry would be unable to turn the carriage until it cleared. Luke could scarcely walk off and leave him sitting there by himself. He would have to wait, too.

Just as he climbed up into the carriage, he happened to notice a rather handsome buggy a hundred feet or so down the street. He couldn't be sure, but he thought it might be the same vehicle that Lavinia had been driving the day he rescued Cherub.

He was about to point it out to Perry, but suddenly decided against it. Even if it was the same buggy, he had no way of knowing if it was just happenstance that it was on the same road. It could be anyone from the Van Hansel household driving it. And even if it was no coincidence, and Lavinia had arranged to have he and Perry followed, he decided it didn't really make any difference. He wasn't going to have anything to do with any of them ever again.

They had to wait only a few minutes until traffic started to move again. As they went through the intersection, Luke saw that the horse had been carted away and the hay wagon pushed to the side of the road, awaiting another horse to complete its journey. He pretended he was studying it, so he could take a look behind him again, but the handsome buggy he had spotted was nowhere in sight. Maybe he was mistaken after all.

He directed Perry to Dr. Christie's house and quickly climbed down when they reached it. "Thank you for the ride," he said. He knew that Perry was expecting to be invited in. Good manners can go to the devil, Luke thought, and he tried not to notice the look of disappointment on Perry's face when he was left sitting in his carriage.

Chapter 12

Thaddeus had worked his way through most of his circuit and was hoping to make it back to Christie's for dinner, but the men's class in Davisville ran far later than he anticipated and he arrived in Yorkville long after the household had retired for the night. He went straight up the stairs to Luke's sitting room, intending to fall into bed immediately, but once he got his boots off he realized that he wasn't in the least sleepy. He could light a lamp, he supposed, and read for a while, but he had neglected to grab a paper from the pile on the hall table and he was reluctant to risk waking someone by thumping down the stairs again. He could always read his Bible, but as he had long since memorized most of it there seemed little to be gained by reading it again. Eventually he pulled an armchair over to the open window and sat looking out at the deserted Yorkville street, a faint breeze blowing in to chase away the stuffiness of the room. As he watched a bank of low stratus cloud scud across the face of the moon, he wondered if Morgan Spicer was awake, as well, vigilant lest yet another grave be disturbed.

Thaddeus knew that there was a clue somewhere, a tiny piece of thread that he would have only to pull and the story would begin to unravel, but it was elusive, hiding out of sight. Maybe he could find it the next day in the city, but he would need to look carefully and consider everything.

* * *

Thaddeus was startled awake when a stray beam of sunlight flashed into his eyes. He had fallen asleep in the chair. Tentatively, he stretched his legs out. It wasn't the first time he had slept upright in a chair, and certainly over the years he had nodded off in far more uncomfortable circumstances, but that was when he was young and limber, before accident and injury and age stiffened his muscles and ate at the strength of his bones. To his surprise, however, there was no twinge of pain as he moved. He felt marvellous. And he was ravenous.

Luke and Dr. Christie were already at the breakfast table.

"Mr. Lewis! Home again! Wonderful!" Christie said as he passed him the customary bowl of oatmeal.

"Successful circuit, I hope," Luke said.

Thaddeus thought his son looked a little low, and wondered if there was a particular reason. "Fair to middling," he replied. "Nobody at all in some places, picking up in others. What's been happening here?"

"Oh, Luke has turned into quite the social butterfly," Christie said. "In great demand at all the parties in the city."

Thaddeus shot a glance at Luke, who signalled with a frown that they would have a private discussion later.

"Came home in a carriage, he did," Christie went on. "Hobnobbing with the local gentry. A Biddulph, no less."

Biddulph was a name that carried a fair degree of weight in Upper Canada. None of the Biddulphs had been members of the old Family Compact that once controlled nearly everything in the colony, but they had certainly been welcome in their drawing rooms. Lawyers and land speculators, Thaddeus seemed to recall. Advantageous marriages. Lucrative investments.

He was curious as to how his son had connected with someone like a Biddulph, but Luke's frown seemed to indicate that there was more to the story, and that he didn't particularly want Christie in his audience while he told it.

"Well, it's nice to see that you're making some friends," he ventured.

"And helping the practice at the same time," Christie crowed. "Good stuff, my lad, good stuff."

"Any plans for today?" Luke asked his father.

"I thought I'd collect Morgan Spicer and take him with me into the city. I'm not optimistic that I'll find any of the answers that I'm looking for, but I think it's at least worth nosing around." He turned to Christie. "Do you happen to know specifically where dissections are done?"

"In a rather squat two-storey building on Richmond Street," Christie replied. "It's part of the School of Anatomy. Go, by all means, but I somehow doubt anyone there will be inclined to talk to you."

"What about the hospitals?"

"I think you can exclude the lying-in hospitals, as both of your corpses are male. That leaves the General Hospital and the Asylum. And the House of Industry, of course." Christie stared thoughtfully at his bowl of oatmeal for a moment. "Any of those might be willing to confirm that the gentlemen in question were patrons at some point, but I doubt they'd be willing to tell you much more than that. Might I offer my assistance in this? I have a contact or two who might be able to help. I could drop a note and ask for details. Better the request comes from a doctor, you see."

"Or you could just come with us," Thaddeus said.

"Oh no," Christie protested. "Far too much to do here. Happy to help if it means writing a letter. Not keen on traipsing all over the city."

Only then did Thaddeus recall the old doctor's reluctance to travel any distance. It was why Luke was hired in the first place. However, it would be most helpful to have Christie make the inquiries, even if it was only by mail. "I'd be most obliged for any assistance you can offer."

Christie beamed. "Consider it done."

"I'd like to talk to the people at the African Methodist Chapel as well," Thaddeus said. "That's on Richmond Street too, isn't it?"

"Do you think they'll know anything about it?"

"Probably not," Thaddeus admitted. "But I'm curious to see the church and I'll be in the neighbourhood anyway. Would you like to come with us, Luke?"

"No, I'd better stay put," Luke said. "Dr. Christie has been good enough to stand in for me on several occasions already."

"I do have one request," Christie said. "Should you happen to gain entry to the dissecting rooms, I'd appreciate it if you could keep an eye open for any interesting bones."

Thaddeus nodded. "Yes, of course." And then he dove into his oatmeal. He was starving.

* * *

Luke waylaid his father just as he was leaving to collect Morgan. Dr. Christie had once again disappeared into the back rooms of the house. Even so, Luke spoke in a low voice.

"Christie thinks it's a wonderful thing that I've been taken up by the Van Hansels," he said. "And he's quite over the moon that I've met a Biddulph. I was quite prepared to ignore them all, but Mrs. Van Hansel sent an invitation for us both. I couldn't get out of it gracefully. Fortunately, Hands wasn't present."

"If you keep going there you'll run into him sooner or later," Thaddeus said. "You're going to have to think of some way to disentangle yourself. Would it help if I put my foot down about you going to fancy parties or something of that nature? Claim our Methodist scruples? I have half a mind to do so anyway, truth be told."

"Maybe. If I can't think of any other way. Thanks."

"Let me know."

Thaddeus walked the short distance to the Burying Ground. He and Morgan could take an omnibus into the city, he decided. The horse and cart he used to cover his circuit was for church-related business, and he intended to be scrupulous about not using them for anything else.

Sally opened the door at his knock.

"Mr. Lewis. How nice to see you again. Are you looking for Morgan?"

Thaddeus explained his plan for the day.

"Oh dear, Morgan's still abed. He had a late night."

And before he could offer to come back later, she sent the children clattering up the stairs to wake him.

When Morgan appeared a few moments later, Thaddeus was shocked at his appearance. He had never been a prepossessing figure, but now there were black circles under his eyes and he seemed to have lost weight.

"I thought we'd go into the city to ask some questions, but we can do it another day if that would be more convenient," Thaddeus said.

"No," Morgan said. "The sooner we go the better."

He bade Sally and the row of look-alike children goodbye and followed Thaddeus to the road.

"They tried again last night," Morgan said as soon as they boarded the bus and found their seats. "There was someone by the back fence, but I had a lantern ready. That was enough to chase them away."

"Have you been staying up every night to watch?" Thaddeus asked.

"Yes."

"Then the sooner we sort this out, the better. Do you have any idea which grave they were trying to get to?"

"No," Morgan said. "They didn't get that far."

"Well at least it's certain that the first two incidents weren't isolated," Thaddeus said. "I suppose that's something."

"I suppose," Morgan replied, but he looked gloomy for the rest of their journey.

They disembarked in front of Osgoode Hall at the corner of College Avenue. The city had grown enormously in the four years since Thaddeus had last been there. Back then, Queen Street was the northern limit of the city and Osgoode Hall was situated on six acres of country parkland. Now it was being encroached upon by the untidy bustle of Macaulaytown, with its liveries, blacksmiths, shoemakers, and barbershops. The modest one- and two-storey buildings that crowded the streetscape looked insubstantial next to the towering grandeur of Osgoode, with its dome that poked past the massive wings added to each side of the original building. It was in this hall that law students pored over the statutes and regulations of the province, and where the august body of the Superior Court handed down its decisions. Osgoode Hall's expansive lawns were fenced, access granted through an ornate cast-iron kissing gate, designed, Thaddeus guessed, more to keep the cows off the grass than to provide the opportunity for a romantic encounter. To the west the grounds terminated at the broad chestnut-lined street that led to King's College, guarded at either end by a gatekeeper. The approaches to these public institutions had been intended, Thaddeus knew, to blend into the park lots laid out along the north side of Queen Street, but the owners of this land had been unable to resist the temptation to subdivide their properties to accommodate spillover from the labourers' district to the south. It was from this working-class neighbourhood that two enterprising coloured gentlemen, Mr. Carey and Mr. Richards, established the very first ice delivery service in Toronto. Their wagons often rumbled up and down Yonge Street with cargoes of precious ice carved from mill ponds north of the city. Horse cabs sprung from this community, as well; a novelty at first, but now a convenience that most Torontonians took for granted.

"According to *Rowsell's Directory*, the African Baptist Church is just east of Yonge Street," Thaddeus said. "Let's try there first."

"I don't know where I'm going at all," Morgan said, "so I'll just follow you."

As they walked along Queen Street, they saw placards posted on walls and in windows. Thaddeus stopped to read one of them.

> CAUTION!
> *Coloured People of Toronto, one and all*
> *You are respectfully* CAUTIONED *and advised to keep a* SHARP LOOKOUT *for* KIDNAPPERS AND SLAVE CATCHERS *who by illegal means are harassing the Coloured People of our city, freeborn or no, with intent to claim a bounty for them in the United States of America.*
> Be VIGILANT and have TOP EYE OPEN

The incident that Luke had been involved in was not unique, apparently. The kidnappers must be growing bold, indeed, if they were so common on Toronto's streets.

There were even signs nailed to each side of the front door at the church. These were similar to the handbills and notices posted all along the street, urging the coloured citizens of Toronto to be wary of slave catchers.

When Thaddeus knocked at the front door of the church, no one answered. He tried the handle, but the door was locked.

"So much for finding anything here," he said. "It doesn't look as though there's anyone around."

They were about to leave when three men appeared, seemingly out of nowhere.

"Was there something you wanted?" one of them asked.

"Just a little conversation, that's all. My name is Thaddeus Lewis. And this is Morgan Spicer. We have some questions about a man who may once have been a member of your congregation."

"And why would you need this information, if you don't mind my asking?" The man's face was wary and mistrustful.

"Mr. Spicer is the Keeper at the Strangers' Burying Ground. There have been two graves tampered with recently. One of them was that of Isaiah Marshall, whom we discovered was a coloured man." Thaddeus shrugged. "It's a very small detail to base an enquiry on, but we have no other information to start with and we would like to prevent any further desecrations."

The man shook his head. "I don't know anybody named Marshall." He continued to regard them with suspicion, but Thaddeus noted that the other two men appeared to relax a little.

"Me either," one of them said. "I only came here three years ago. I don't know the old-timers."

The third man nodded. He, too, was a newcomer. "For a minute there, we thought you were kidnappers," he said.

"I understand your caution. We saw the posters. I don't understand it, though. Why are slave catchers coming here? They have no legal claim in Canada, and I would think that coming so far north would cost them more than any bounty they could collect." The question seemed to loosen the reserve of the trio even more.

It was the man who had spoken first who answered. "It wouldn't be worth it for one fugitive. But some of the plantation owners don't bother chasing their runaways — they just sell the right of ownership to someone in the north who sweeps up whatever coloureds he can snatch. They don't have to be taken all the way back to the plantations, you see. They're just sold in blocks on the open market."

Thaddeus was appalled. "What are the authorities doing to stop this?" he asked.

"If the catchers are found with dangerous weapons, they're fined. Other than that, not a lot, although we do find some support from the white folks. Mr. Douglass and Mr. Brown have helped us with that."

George Brown, editor of the *Globe* was a vocal abolitionist. Thaddeus had read many of his scathing editorials attacking the United States senator Henry Clay, the Fugitive Slave Act, separate schools, and anyone who opposed the Elgin settlement, a black community in the Western District established with the help of the Presbyterian Church. And the anti-slavery citizens of Toronto were galvanized into action when Frederick Douglass, a leading figure in the American abolitionist movement, addressed them at the newly built St. Lawrence Hall, their support demonstrated by a stream of letters to the aforesaid Mr. Brown's editorial page. Still, Thaddeus reflected, it was one thing to be part of a cheering crowd or to write a letter, another to actively intervene in an attempted kidnapping, as Luke had done. Not for the first time, he was filled with admiration for his son. Betsy had done a grand job of raising the boy.

"Mr. Douglass and Mr. Brown are fine for the speechifying," the man went on, "but the Blackburns are the ones who really help us here. Them and Mr. Abbott."

Thaddeus wasn't familiar with the names. "Mr. Abbott?"

"He's coloured, like us, but rich. He owns all sorts of buildings around here. The Blackburns own the cabs and they do everything they can to make it easier for the newcomers. They make it easier for everybody."

There was pride in the man's voice. "The coloureds don't ask for anything," Christie had said. They didn't need to, Thaddeus realized, because they helped each other.

Thaddeus thanked the men for their time and then he and Morgan walked along Richmond Street. Thanks to Dr. Christie's directions, they soon found the building that housed the dissecting rooms. It was, as Christie had commented, an awkward, squat structure made of brick.

"What are you going to say?" Morgan wanted to know. "You can hardly ask them outright if they've been cutting up stolen bodies."

"That's one of the reasons I brought you with me, Morgan. You're Keeper at the Burying Ground. I can say that we're trying to locate lost relatives, so the bodies in question can be moved to the Necropolis."

"Even though it's not the truth?"

Morgan was right. It wasn't the truth, but Thaddeus could think of no other approach. Finally, he said, "Well, if we *could* find their relatives, we could ask them if they want the bodies moved, couldn't we?"

"I suppose," Morgan said, although he looked skeptical.

"Otherwise, they're apt to shoo us away without telling us anything."

Morgan nodded, which Thaddeus took to be agreement. He knocked on the door. When there was no answer, he knocked again. After a long interval, the door opened just wide enough for a young man to peer out through the crack.

"Are you the physician in charge?" Thaddeus asked.

"No. I'm just a student."

"Might we ask you some questions?"

"I don't know anything," the young man said.

"I'm Thaddeus Lewis and this is Mr. Spicer, who is Keeper at the Strangers' Burying Ground in Yorkville. We're trying to locate some records regarding …"

"Abraham Jenkins and Isaiah Marshall." Morgan supplied the names, which had momentarily escaped Thaddeus, much to his annoyance.

"Yes. We believe they were … that is, we believe they might have come from here before they made their way to the cemetery."

"I don't know anything about records," the student said.

"Could you tell us who might?"

"I don't know," the student said. "I don't know anything about anything." And he shut the door.

"Well, he's made his ignorance abundantly evident," Thaddeus remarked. "At least he admits it. I'm afraid Dr. Christie was correct. We'll get no information here. Well, on to the next place. Let's see if we can find the African Chapel."

"Why isn't the African Church part of your circuit?" Morgan asked as they walked back along Richmond Street.

Thaddeus sighed. "Because of divisions within the Methodist Church." It wasn't a pretty history and he disliked telling it. "The American church officially took an anti-slavery stance, but they watered down their opposition in deference to the members who were wealthy southern landowners. Even so, things came to a head and the church split in two, north against south. And in spite of official policy, the northern congregations didn't exactly extend a welcome to its coloured members. There were coloured ministers, but they were allowed to preach only to coloured congregations, things like that."

"It seems to me the Methodist Church is mighty fussy about who it lets preach," Morgan said.

"Well, yes," Thaddeus had to admit, "it is, isn't it? In any event, the coloured congregation got fed up and formed their own Methodist Church."

"And they brought it here with them?"

"Yes, but a long time ago, when we were all still organized under the American conference. When we established our own governance there was some attempt to include the African Church, but it didn't ever seem to go anywhere and they were left on their own." As he said this, Thaddeus realized that he didn't really understand why this had happened. Maybe it was the pride of having their own church that kept them separate. Maybe. But given what he knew about people, it was far more likely that they were made to feel unwelcome, just like they had been in the States.

The African Methodist Episcopal Chapel was a small building set well back from the street, and again there were warning posters displayed at each side of the locked door. And again, within a few moments, a tall, grey-haired man appeared behind them, followed by two others, one of them waving a poker.

"Can we help you with something?" the first man asked, the challenge in his voice in contrast to the politeness of his question.

"We are here with an inquiry," Thaddeus said, tipping his hat, "but I must admit that I've been curious about this church for some time. I am a minister with the Canadian Methodist

Episcopal Church and I'm currently stationed on the Yonge Street Circuit. I know that your church is separate from ours, but I can't help but think that we have much in common."

"And what would that be?" the tall man said. "Other than our names?"

"I know that two unexpected visitors at your door must seem alarming," Thaddeus replied. "If I show you my appointment book, will you accept that I am who I claim to be?"

The tall man nodded, slightly and just once.

Thaddeus fished the small booklet out of his pocket and handed it over. He hoped it would be enough to gain him entry to the chapel as he had no other means of identification. The man looked it over and handed it back, but he made no move to dismiss the other two men, who continued to watch with suspicion as Thaddeus explained their mission to discover something of Isaiah Marshall.

The man's face relaxed a little at mention of the name. "Isaiah Marshall. He's been dead a long time."

"He has. That's one of the things we find so puzzling about what has happened. Did you know him?"

"We have never been a large community, although our numbers have grown in recent times, so that I no longer know everyone who lives here. But yes, I do remember Isaiah Marshall. He was a carpenter."

"Was he a member of this church?"

"No, I don't recall ever seeing him here. He was a private man and kept to himself mostly."

"Do you know if he had any family?"

The tall man shook his head. "Not that I'm aware of. I don't know where he came from either, whether he was free-born or a traveller. I do remember that he was a very fine carpenter. A cabinetmaker, really, except that he'd take the rough and ready jobs as well."

The man gave the information freely enough, but there was a guarded undertone to the response. There was something more that this man did not wish to share. Marshall had "kept to himself," he said, but offered no reason for it. It seemed an odd thing in such a small, close-knit community. Thaddeus waited, but the silence stretched out unbroken.

"Thank you," he said finally when it became clear that no more would be forthcoming. "I'm sorry to have bothered you Mr. ....?"

"I'm John," the man said. "John Finch."

"Thank you, Mr. Finch."

He turned to go and motioned Morgan to follow. He was curious about this church, but it was clear that their presence was unwelcome. He would impose himself no further.

But as they were walking down the path, the man with the poker asked, "They took this Isaiah's body? Why would someone do that?"

"No," Thaddeus replied. "They had no interest in the body itself. Whoever did it opened the coffin and threw Isaiah aside."

The man frowned. "So it doesn't have anything to do with the kidnappers?"

"I don't think so," Thaddeus replied, "although I admit I hadn't considered that possibility. The first grave that was opened contained a white man. At least we think he was."

"Oh." The man thought about this for a moment and then looked shyly at Thaddeus. "I thought maybe they were digging up coloured bones and using them to claim the bounty somehow."

Morgan spoke for the first time since they had arrived at the church. "I don't see how they could. Once the flesh has worn away, there's no difference between the bones of a coloured man and that of a white man. They're all the same underneath the skin."

Thaddeus knew that Morgan was speaking literally, his knowledge gained from his experience as a sexton, but the answer seemed to please the man, for he smiled.

"You're right, brother. We're all God's children."

The exchange seemed to have dispelled the tension entirely, so Thaddeus ventured another question.

"Where do you bury members of your congregation?" he asked. There seemed to be no graveyard attached to the church. Not enough land, he realized.

"Generally, they are laid to rest in the Strangers' Ground," Finch said. "Not because they are strangers, but because there is nowhere else to take them. The families who can afford it put up marble stones so the souls of their loved ones know they're remembered."

"The records seem to indicate that Mr. Marshall was indigent. And he had a plain stone marker."

"So it's unlikely that he was buried with anything of value," Mr. Finch said. "Is that what you mean?"

"Yes. You see our dilemma. The graves were opened for neither the contents nor the bodies themselves."

"I wish I could be more help to you, Mr. Lewis, but I remember very little about Mr. Marshall other than his occupation and the fact that he was rather odd. I must admit that I hadn't thought of him for years until you brought up his name. You could ask at the Baptist Church. Someone there might remember more."

"We've spoken with them already. Unfortunately no one there remembered him at all. We'll have to find some other line of inquiry. Thank you again. And someday I'll come back and see your church, if I may."

"Of course," Finch said. "Any Sunday. We welcome everyone."

Chapter 13

As it turned out, Luke had no difficulty finding an excuse to avoid social interaction with Perry and the Van Hansels. The medical practice turned very busy the next week, occupying the full attention of both physicians.

Luke was in the office, his nose buried in a copy of *The Pathfinder*, plucked randomly from the shelves of books in Dr. Christie's parlour. He was delighted to realize that the Inland Sea in Cooper's novel was, in fact, Lake Ontario. He had never before read a story that featured a geography that was so close to home. Ben's shelves had contained mostly English and French titles, classical works, or books translated from German.

When a knock came at the door, he was surprised to open it to find Andrew Holden, the man whose toe he had amputated as the result of an accident with an axe, standing there. He had seen Holden exactly twice since, both times in order to change the bandage on the stump. The man had grumbled and complained on both occasions.

"Why'd you take if off, Doc?" he'd said. "I'll have the devil of a time walking without it. Couldn't you have sewn it back on?"

"No, I couldn't have," Luke said. "The nerves were completely severed. If I'd tried to put it back it would have turned septic and you'd have lost the entire leg."

After he deemed that the wound was healing and no further visits were necessary, Luke expected not ever to see the grumbling Holden again.

"You'll want Dr. Christie," he said.

"I'll take Christie if I have to," Holden replied, "but I'd sooner have you. It's the youngest. He's got a fever."

Luke grabbed his satchel and followed the limping man down the street. They were met at the door of the cottage by Holden's wife, who held a mewling three-year-old wrapped in a blanket. The child had been well until the previous week, she said, when he began to run a slight fever. Over the course of the last few days he had become increasingly unwell, lethargic with an occasional nosebleed.

"I thought it was just summer complaint," the woman said. "Now I'm not so sure."

Luke left the child in his mother's arms while he made his examination. He could tell by laying a hand on the boy's forehead that he was spiking a high fever, and when he peeled back the blanket, he found rosy splotches on the child's chest. He had hoped that the mother was right and that the boy had contracted one of the many minor intestinal complaints that seemed to rise out of nowhere and subside just as quickly, but as Luke counted up the symptoms he was seeing he became certain that he was looking at a case of typhoid fever. Just to be sure he reached for the trumpet-like stethoscope that would allow him to better hear a heartbeat. There it was — a slow thump, thump, thump — too slow for a three-year-old. And when he moved the trumpet to the child's abdomen, the little boy flexed his knees in pain and batted the instrument away.

"What is it?" the woman asked anxiously when she saw the concerned look on Luke's face.

"I'm afraid it might be typhoid," he replied. It was the first of the season that he had seen, but he knew it wouldn't be the last. Typhoid fever was the summer scourge of the city and its outlying regions. Many doctors blamed it on the miasma that emanated from the outflow of Toronto's sewer, which emptied its vile, sludgy mess of human waste, animal dung, and butcher's blood into the lake. The vapours, they claimed, spread out over the city whenever the wind blew and contaminated not only the air, but any surrounding water as well.

Yorkville had no reliable water supply of its own, so most of its residents used the city water drawn directly from the lake, in some cases from close to the offending sewer mouth. Odd that water should be such a problem in an area so close to an inland sea, Luke thought, and one that during most of the year was intersected by numerous creeks and one large river.

He reached for his fleam. Typhoid was caused by a congestion of the blood, and by removing some of the offending matter, the patient's veins would run free again. The child screamed when he inserted the instrument, and continued to wail as the blood flowed into the basin Luke held beneath the punctured arm. He removed only a small quantity, no more than a quarter cup. That was enough for so small a body.

"You should make up a broth of beef tea," Luke instructed Mrs. Holden when he was finished. "See if he will take a little of it. And barley water, as well, as often as you can get him to drink. Don't wrap him in a blanket like that, he's hot enough as it is, and you might sponge him down with a little cool water a few times a day. We need to get his fever down. I'll leave you some calomel as well."

"Is he going to die?" she asked.

"That I don't know," Luke said. "If he gets through the next few days, he may do well enough. We'll have to wait and see."

He knew they were expecting him to say something about the child being in God's hands, and that they should pray for his recovery, but in Luke's limited experience this seldom did much good, and he would not offer false hope.

"I'll come back this evening," he told them. He could hope that this was an isolated case, but feared that it was only the beginning of the season of misery, and in this he was soon proved correct. He was called to see two more patients with similar symptoms that afternoon, three the next day, and the numbers increased after that until even Dr. Christie was forced to leave the house to help with the workload.

The more patients they saw, the more the disease seemed to spread, until Luke began to feel as though he were back in Kingston, tending to the Irish emigrants who had flooded, sick and starving, into the city. This epidemic, however, could not be blamed on emigrants. It had been a light season for ocean crossings. Timber droghers no longer plied the Atlantic in the same numbers, and the laws regulating shipboard conditions for passengers were tightened. The Irish were no longer streaming into Canada. They chose, instead, to go to the United States, where they thought there was a better opportunity to scramble out of their poverty.

In spite of the severity of the typhoid outbreak, Luke was gratified to find that many patients asked for him personally. He was making a mark, apparently. People had confidence in his skills, although in many cases he wasn't sure why some patients recovered and others succumbed so quickly. He did begin to wonder about the efficacy of bleeding. He generally preferred to be conservative with this treatment. Some physicians drew copious amounts of blood from their patients, but to Luke it had never made much sense to unduly weaken an already weak body. He continued to wield his fleam, but took smaller and smaller amounts when he did so. He could see no discernible difference in the outcome. The broths and teas he prescribed seemed to be a better help.

He and Christie were in constant attendance on their patients for ten days, snatching food when they could, napping for only an hour or two until they were called out again. The pace began to take its toll on the older man.

"Thank heaven you're here, Luke," he said at one point. "I couldn't have handled this by myself."

In a hasty conversation over a hurried breakfast, Luke asked Thaddeus if conditions were similar north of the city.

"Not anything like here," Thaddeus said. "A few cases in Eglington, I hear. One or two in York Mills. Nothing north of there. Or at least I haven't heard about it if there are."

Luke was puzzled. His father's report more or less supported the theory that a miasma from the city sewer had spread a cloud of contagion through the air, even as far as Yorkville, but had dissipated before it reached much farther. Yet, if contaminated air was the culprit, why weren't there any cases at all in the more northerly villages? And why wasn't everyone in Yorkville sick?

"Where do the villages get their water from?" Luke asked.

"I don't really know for sure," Thaddeus said. "Daniel Cummer has a lovely spring-fed well in a willow grove and it rarely goes dry, but I don't know if that's true for the rest of the wells at the settlement. And, of course, almost everyone in Thorne's Hill drinks from Holy Ann's well."

"They don't buy from the city supply?"

"I shouldn't think so. They're much too far away. Why do you ask?"

"I'm not sure. Just trying to figure something out, I guess. You certainly seem to have escaped contagion."

In fact, now that he had a chance to have a close look at him, Luke realized that Thaddeus seemed hale and fit. He was tanned from his hours on the road and no longer moved with the stiffness that had plagued him in recent years. The air of melancholy that had hung over him for so long had disappeared. All in all, he seemed to be in tremendous spirits.

"Oh me," Thaddeus said. "I'm a tough old bird. It would take more than fever to get me down. By the way, I'll be staying at the Spicers' for the next couple of nights. I promised to relieve Morgan. He's been trying to keep watch. I expect he could use a good night's sleep for once."

"None of them have been sick, have they?" Luke asked. He suddenly realized that he hadn't been called to the Spicer house, a fact that might have surprised him if he had noticed it before. Of course, they might rely on some other physician in the area. There was no reason to think that they should suddenly transfer their custom just because Luke's father knew them.

But Thaddeus confirmed that the Spicer family was well in the extreme, except for Morgan's lack of sleep. Luke was even more mystified. The incidences of typhoid were so hit and miss. One household could be struck down while their neighbours remained unscathed. Even within individual families the disease was selective, some members showing no symptoms at all while others were in a state of significant morbidity. Everyone had to breathe. It couldn't be the air.

"Where do the Spicers get their water from?" he asked.

"I have no idea. Why all the questions about water?"

Luke shrugged. "You're not the only one with a puzzle."

He tried to mentally map the spread of sickness, but could come up with no coherent pattern that would allow him to pinpoint the locus of the disease.

In any event, he had no time to give it any further thought, at least that day. He had at least twenty homes to visit. One of them was the Holden house, where, much to his relief, the three-year-old child seemed to be on the mend. Although still feverish, his temperature was not nearly as high as it had been, he no longer flexed his legs and cried when Luke touched his abdomen, and, best of all, his heartbeat had returned to something more approaching normal. In fact, it was all his mother could do to restrain him from climbing out of bed to play with the small black kitten that chased dust motes around the kitchen.

"I don't think he needs anything more than rest at this point. Keep giving him as much barley water as he will take, and try him with a little porridge tomorrow, but I really think he'll be fine."

Mrs. Holden burst into tears at the news. "Thank you, Dr. Lewis, thank you," she said. "We've lost three already. I don't think I could bear losing a fourth."

Andrew Holden had a big grin on his face. "Well, now, you did a lot better with this than with my toe, didn't you? No lopping things off this time."

"Andrew! Stop grumbling about your toe!" Mrs. Holden said. Then she turned to Luke. "Pay him no mind. He likes to tease you to your face, but he's been singing your praises to everyone else."

Luke was pleased to hear this, but he had been getting the measure of Holden anyway. He would talk to him just like he talked to his brothers. Or to the Irish. "This is dreadful," he said. "I've left you with nothing at all to bury. You'd better let me cut off another toe."

Holden grinned and waved at him to go away. "Get out, you quack! You've done enough damage already."

Luke's pleasure at the successful outcome of this case buoyed him as he worked his way through the streets of

Yorkville. Some patients were better. Others were still very ill. Only time would tell with most of them, but his efforts appeared to be doing some good.

He was hailed just as he was walking past the cottage where he had treated the old woman with cancer. It was the granddaughter, pallid and sickly looking. The entire Johnson family was ill, she said. Could Dr. Lewis please look at them?

Mrs. Johnson had only a mild case of fever, Luke judged. Her daughter was sicker, but the girl's temperature was starting to come down. The most dramatically afflicted was the young man, Caleb, the boy who had wrestled with his conscience so desperately over the question of his urges. He was delirious, his abdomen was distended, his arms flailed and he kept throwing the blankets off the cot that was set up once more in the parlour. Or maybe it had never been taken away, Luke thought. It hadn't been that long since the old woman had died.

"He's been sick for a while," Luke commented.

Mrs. Johnson nodded. "I didn't call you right away. I thought it was just a summer fever and we all seemed to be getting over it." She hesitated for a moment before she disclosed what Luke knew was the real reason she hadn't called him sooner. "We still haven't paid Dr. Christie for my mother's sickness."

"Don't worry about that right now." As much as Christie moaned about patients not paying bills, Luke was sure that he would never refuse to see someone because of an unpaid account, and that there were many sums on his books that would likely never be cleared. "What have you given him so far?"

"Just some oriental balsam."

Oriental balsam was a proprietary medicine readily available to whoever chose to buy it, and in Luke's opinion its purchase was a waste of good money. Its manufacturers claimed efficacy in cases of stomach pain, nausea, chlorosis, pallor, and apathy. Its principal ingredient was alcohol.

"Don't give him any more," he said to the woman. "I'll leave you some calomel."

He repeated the prescribed measures for all three of the Johnsons, opening their veins and removing various quantities of blood, and advised barley water, gruel, or beef tea. He was certain the woman would recover, and reasonably sure that the girl would, as well, but he was very worried about the condition of the boy. His abdominal pain appeared to be excruciating.

Luke opened his case and fingered the small bottle of pure opium extract that he always carried. He wondered about giving just a small dose. Just enough to take the edge off the pain Caleb was feeling, and to help calm the bowel, but the boy was already delirious and opium might well speed him into insensibility. Luke debated for a moment, but then shoved the bottle back into his bag. Caleb would have to battle the pain on his own while his body fought the disease. Luke knew, however, that he would have to be honest about the boy's chances of recovery.

"It's the typhoid fever that has everyone else down," he said to Mrs. Johnson. "I'm afraid your son has a very serious case of it."

The woman's shoulders sagged. "I was counting on him. My husband died two years ago, and then I had Mother to look after. The boy's been a great comfort."

And the only one bringing any money into the house, Luke guessed. This family would be in dire straits indeed if he died.

"I'm sorry," he said. "I've done what I can. I'm afraid the rest is up to him. He's young and we can only hope that he has the strength to fight it off. I'll come back this evening and let a little more blood. That may help."

The next few patients he saw seemed to be recovering, although one or two of them were still in danger of lapsing into the muttering delirium that signalled dire complications. He doggedly worked his way around the village, his buoyant mood gone. He became all too aware of how tired he was, and how helpless he felt when there was nothing more he could do than hand out the same old bromides of bleeding and calomel.

When he arrived back at Christie's, a small boy was waiting anxiously by the door.

"Mrs. Johnson sent me. She said to tell you to come quick."

Luke followed him down the street. When they arrived at the Johnson's cottage, he turned to the boy. "Don't go far. I may need you to take another message."

"I live just there." He pointed to the cottage next door. "I'll wait in case you need me."

Caleb Johnson was no longer muttering or fighting with his blankets. He was lying perfectly still, his breathing laboured. As soon as Luke entered the Johnsons' parlour, he knew that the final stages of the disease had been reached, and much sooner than expected. The boy must have been sick for far longer than the mother had reported. Or perhaps he had hidden it as long as he could.

Luke exited the cottage and whistled for the neighbour boy.

"Can you take a message back to Dr. Christie's for me?" he asked, handing over a coin. "Ring at the front door, and when the housekeeper answers tell her that I might be quite some time here. Tell her to let Dr. Christie know. Have you got that?"

The boy nodded.

"You may have to ring a number of times before she answers, but don't give up until she opens the door."

He nodded again and disappeared down the street.

Returning to the cottage, Luke shooed Mrs. Johnson and her daughter back to their beds. "Get what sleep you can," he said. "You both need it. I'll sit with him. I'll call you if anything changes."

He settled down on a chair at the parlour table. It could be a long night, he knew. The dying went when they were ready and it was surprising how often they clung to life long after one would have expected their bodies to finally give up. There was little hope of any other outcome in this case. All the portents were there — the distended abdomen, the unremitting fever, the lapse into unconsciousness.

His mind went back to the conversation with Caleb and his instruction that soon the boy's demons would be laid to rest by marriage. It seemed foolish advice in retrospect. He should have told the boy not to worry about it, to do whatever he felt necessary to set his adolescent nature to rest. Who would it harm? Certainly not Caleb, as it turned out.

And then, with a start, he realized that he could apply much the same advice to himself. For all he knew he could be the one lying on a deathbed tomorrow, or next week, or in a month. He could have been infected with typhoid at any time during his rounds of the last weeks. If not typhoid, then something else that could jump from patient to doctor — cholera, dysentery, consumption. It had been consumption that killed Ben. Was it even now lurking in Luke's own body, ready to burst out of hiding and carry him away in gushes of bloody sputum and running sweat?

He had sat by Ben's side, too. It had been during the last part of his second year of school when he finally admitted to himself that Ben was consumptive. He had noted the persistent cough, of course, and the hectic red flush that formed on Ben's thin face, but then, during the particularly damp winter of that year, Ben began throwing the quilts from the bed at night and would often sit bolt upright, sweating profusely and complaining of something gnawing away in his chest. His eyes grew brighter even as his body grew thinner.

A few weeks later, after a violent bout of coughing that left him shaky and breathless, Ben was no longer able to hide the blood on the handkerchief he held against his mouth.

"I'm not long for this world," he said then. "You know, you seemed like a miracle when you walked into my shop. Forgive me, Luke, but I knew this time was coming and I didn't want to die alone."

There was a reprieve the following summer, and in spite of what Luke knew of the disease, he harboured a hope that Ben might recover yet. But as winter once again unleashed its cold fury on the city, the disease returned with a vengeance.

Ben began to walk with a hunched-over gait, as if his spine no longer had strength to support him, and all the time the cough grew worse. Instead of lovingly dusting books and straightening shelves, Ben spent his days by the stove, wrapped in a blanket, rising only to look after a customer's needs. Luke took over as much of the work as he could, but by then he was in his first year of walking the wards, putting in long days of physically and mentally demanding work, constantly challenged by the surgeons to make a diagnosis, suggest a treatment, offer a cure. Nights were spent tending Ben, and Luke grew tired beyond belief.

He became so alarmed that he prevailed upon one of the surgeons at Montreal General to attend. Professor Brown was a brusque, impatient man who intimidated even the other doctors, but Luke knew from watching him that he was the best physician available. Even his expertise wasn't enough, however.

"This man is dying," he said after a cursory look at Ben. "A first-year student could have told you that. Honestly, Lewis, even you should have been able to figure it out."

"I did," Luke replied. "I just didn't want to believe it."

He paid Brown's hefty fee from the till and thanked him for coming.

"I'll expect to see you in the wards tomorrow, regardless," Brown said as he left.

Luke nodded, but he had no intention of leaving Ben's side. He sat with him by the stove, surrounded by his beloved books, until a final, violent hemorrhage ended it two days later.

Luke searched through Ben's personal effects, but he could find no mention of family, no relative he could contact, no one who should be notified. He had left enough money to provide for burial and a small stone, but little more.

Luke had many months of school left, and debated how he was going to complete them. He couldn't work in the hospital every day and keep the shop open as well. In the end, he contacted several of the booksellers along St. Vincent Street and sold Ben's entire stock to the highest bidder. It broke his heart, but it provided enough money, just, to allow him to complete his degree.

It had been hard after that, as hard as when he'd first arrived in Montreal. He rented another small closet of a room and tried to concentrate on his studies, but he longed for the companionship of a shared meal and the comfort of a shared bed. Hardest of all was that he could confide his grief to no one.

He would have stayed with Ben forever. But Ben was gone. And in the unlikely event that he ever found someone who could take Ben's place, he doubted that such an intimate arrangement would ever again be possible. He had resolved to return to the Huron, but his brother's farm was so remote that in the four years he had been there, Luke had seldom met anyone but neighbours. And on the rare occasions when a stranger wandered their way, the entire community knew about it the next day. There was no such thing as a secret along the Huron tract. If he went back, it would be to a solitary life.

He found that he was no longer so ready to accept this, and yet his alternatives were few in number. He wished, not for the first time, that he had his father's faith in an afterlife to guide him, that there would, indeed, be a reward in heaven if he resisted temptation in this life. But he had no such faith. Thaddeus had taken comfort in the Lord, but he had had the luxury of a shared lifetime with a beloved wife to help sustain it.

Luke knew that some men married anyway, not only to satisfy propriety and deflect suspicion, but, he suspected, for the simple comfort of having a home and companion, no matter how odd the circumstances might be. Perry's father was looking for a wife for his second son, or so Perry said, and he seemed resigned to the fact that sooner or later he would have to agree. Luke himself couldn't imagine it. He had met plenty of women whom he admired, but none who stirred him. Lavinia Van Hansel was pretty enough, in a fragile china-doll way. Cherub Ebenezer was the most stunning human being he had ever seen. The Irish girl in Kingston, Mary, had been a courageous and high-spirited girl who would have taken him in a heartbeat had he given her any hope at all. He appreciated their beauty as one might prize a finely carved statue or an exquisitely painted picture, but he did not want to possess them. How could he enter into a marriage with any woman when it would be nothing but a half-hearted fraud?

There was always Perry, he supposed, who made no secret of his interest. Perry, or someone from the taverns he frequented. But Luke found the prospect of canvassing the taprooms in search of a stranger profoundly distasteful. That wasn't what he wanted. He wanted Ben. But Ben was gone.

Luke had rebuffed Perry, shoved him away, and yet when he let himself think about Perry as a person and not as a threat, Luke realized that he quite liked the man. He was amusing. Charming company. He could never take Ben's place, of course, but Luke was tired of being lonely and fed up with feeling sorry for himself.

And Perry was a Biddulph. Dr. Christie had encouraged Luke to foster friendships with the well-heeled. He could scarcely object if he started spending time with Perry. But without the cocoon of an out-of-the-way bookshop, he would have to be very careful. After all, he lived in someone else's house, with his father a regular visitor. Yorkville was a very small village. And he had the reputation of Dr. Christie's practice to uphold. No hint must ever reach the ears of his patients in Yorkville. Or of Dr. Christie. Or, most importantly, of Thaddeus.

It could never be like it was with Ben, but maybe it would be better than being alone.

As he continued to talk himself into giving Perry a chance, Luke's head drooped lower, until sometime later — he could tell it was later by the position of the moon in the sky — he awoke with a start. Caleb had shifted his position and gasped. Blinking, Luke went to him, hoping against hope that this was a sign that he was fighting off the infection. Even as he reached the boy's side, he knew it was a forlorn hope, and when he examined his patient, he found that the boy's breathing was shallower than it had been earlier in the evening. It wouldn't be long now.

He made his way to the kitchen, where Mrs. Johnson was sleeping on the daybed. He gently shook her awake.

"I think you should come now," he said.

Her face crumpled, but she rose and followed him to the parlour, where she knelt beside her son and held his hand. They watched for another ten minutes, and then it was over.

Chapter 14

It began to rain the next morning, at first just a few drops here and there as the dry air soaked up most of the moisture before it could reach the ground, but early in the afternoon it turned into a steady drizzle that built into a downpour as the day wore on.

"Most welcome," Thaddeus remarked at the supper table that evening, when Christie grumbled about making rounds in such damp weather. "The farmers have been frantic. This may be enough to save their crops. It would be grand if it rained like this for a couple of days and filled up all the wells. I've seen people taking water from the millponds, even though they're covered in green muck."

"I think we'd see a lot less illness if the air was washed clean," Luke remarked.

"In my opinion, Toronto's sewer is the problem," Christie said. "They should stop the carters from drawing right at the mouth. Or at least make them wait until there's an offshore breeze so the vapours don't contaminate their loads. On the other hand, I suppose I'd barely have a practice at all if it weren't for these periodic epidemics. Not that our patients will be in any great hurry to pay." He gloomily stabbed at the fish fillet that Mrs. Dunphy had served them.

"Speaking of which," Luke said, "the Johnson boy didn't make it. He died last night."

Christie's face softened. "Yes, I got the message that you were sitting with him. Poor Mrs. Johnson has the worst luck, hasn't she? First her husband, then the old lady, now her son. She'll have a tough go without him."

"She didn't call us in soon enough. She hesitated over it because she owes you too much money already."

"Really?" Christie shook his head. "Now that's just foolishness. I've told her before that I won't press her. She can pay when and if she's able."

"Too much pride, I expect. She was embarrassed by it."

"Now you see, that's why we need a better class of clientele."

"Why?" Thaddeus said. "So you can make more money from them?"

"Yes. I can charge the rich ones more and the poor ones less." Christie glared at Luke. "Now you see, that's why I want you to cultivate this Biddulph chap. To help the Mrs. Johnsons of the world."

"Oh," Luke said, "I didn't understand before." He smiled. "I'll certainly do my best to chivvy him along."

"Honestly," Christie grumbled, picking a small bone from his fish, "You didn't think it was for my own benefit, did you? They can send all the toffs to the hangman for all I care, as long as I get to relieve them of a little cash along the way."

"It is easier for a camel to go through the eye of a needle than for a rich man to enter the kingdom of God," Thaddeus observed.

"That's a point you really should make more often," Christie said. "It would make my job easier."

Luke was still smiling, although when he realized that his father was watching him, he ducked his head and appeared to be entirely absorbed by his fillet.

Thaddeus was puzzled by Luke's willingness to fall in with Christie's agenda. They agreed that the Van Hansels must be avoided, yet it was at the Van Hansels that Luke had made this Biddulph fellow's acquaintance. Perhaps the connection wasn't terribly close, but they certainly travelled in the same circles. How could Luke see one without seeing the other? He'd have to ask him about it later, when Christie wasn't around.

"By the way," Thaddeus said, "I'll be spending the night at the Keeper's Lodge again. I offered to take another watch so Morgan can get some sleep."

"Have there been any more incidents?" Christie asked, as he shoved his plate aside and plucked a newspaper from the pile at the end of the table. "I must admit we've been so busy I'd forgotten about your puzzle."

"No, no more. But I don't know if that's because they haven't tried, or because Morgan's been so vigilant. Have you heard anything from your colleague at the hospital? I didn't ask before because I knew you were so busy."

"Haven't heard a word. Mind you, they've been just as busy in the city, so I expect he hasn't had a spare moment to deal with it. No other clues on your end?"

"Not really," Thaddeus admitted. "I'm working on a theory that there will be no attempt made during a full moon or in the days immediately before or following it, and that the same would hold for a new moon. But I'm not very confident in the prediction."

"I see," Christie said, nodding. "Not during a full moon because there's too much light, and not during a new moon because there's too little. Is that your reasoning?"

"Yes. But if the rain stops tonight and the moon breaks through the cloud, conditions could be ideal for another attempt."

"Well, I don't know if it's pertinent to your situation or not, but I ran across an interesting item in the paper this morning." Christie rooted through the mound of newspapers that had accumulated at the end of the dining table until he located the issue he was looking for. He handed a copy of the *Toronto Patriot* across the table to Thaddeus. "Page three, I believe. Peculiar discovery at St. James. Found by one of the construction crews."

Thaddeus scanned the item, then began to read aloud:

The sexton at St. James-the-Lesser Cemetery made the alarming discovery of a double-occupied coffin this week, through the circumstance of the construction currently being undertaken at St. James Cathedral. Masons were in the process of extending a footing for the new chancel when they found an unmarked gravesite.

St. James Cathedral was destroyed in a devastating fire two years ago, but its attendant cemetery was closed in 1844 due to the unfortunate circumstance of it having become filled to capacity. The bodies interred there were transferred to the cemetery of St. James-the-Lesser on Parliament Street. Evidently, not all of the graves were moved at this time, however, as labourers report having found several anonymous graves as a result of their construction efforts.

In the process of the reinterment of the latest find, the sexton at St. James-the-Lesser discovered a recently disturbed grave in an isolated section of the cemetery. He reports that the coffin had been pried open, revealing the strange condition of it having provided a last resting place for not one individual as is customary, but for two.

Thaddeus stopped for a moment and glanced at Luke, who was listening intently, then resumed reading:

The gruesome discovery recalls an incident in 1847, during the dreadful Irish emigration of that year, when a cart overturned, spilling out a coffin, and revealing that there were two bodies inside. An enquiry was called into the management of the Toronto fever hospital and the carters involved in the transfer of fever victims at the time, however the subsequent investigation failed to reveal the culprits involved.

It is not known if the two events are connected, or the reasons for the recent disturbance of the coffin at St. James-the-Lesser.

Thaddeus already knew the culprits who had been involved: Phillip Van Hansel — "Hands" — and his extensive network of underworld cronies.

"Do you think the two are connected?" Christie asked.

"I don't know," Thaddeus said. "But whenever I run across a coincidence like this, I sit up and take notice. There's really no way to tell unless we keep our eyes open." He saw no reason to confide his knowledge of the matter to Christie. The fewer people who knew about his connection with Hands, the better. He glanced at the top of the newspaper. "This item is from four days ago, but even so I think I'll go to St. James-the-Lesser tomorrow and ask if the sexton has any more information. In any event, I thought I should let you know where I'll be tonight, just so you don't wake up in alarm when you find me missing in the middle of the night."

Luke laughed. "No one ever knows where you are. Nobody worries about it anymore."

"I suppose that's true. But still ..." He was a little taken aback. It was true that, in the past, he had often deviated from his round of appointments in order to pursue a line of inquiry, and he supposed that no one would find it surprising if he did it again, but he liked to think that someone might be concerned if his absence became too prolonged.

"Thank you for apprising me of your whereabouts, Mr. Lewis," Christie said with mock solemnity. "I should have been sick with worry otherwise. Oh — and should another grave be disturbed tonight, would you please come and get me? I'd really love to see the body."

"I can only hope that it will be at four o'clock in the morning then."

Mrs. Dunphy brought in the dessert before Christie could respond with an appropriate retort.

* * *

Thaddeus shared a cup of tea with Morgan while Sally finished washing the supper dishes. The twins helped to dry them and put them back on the cupboard shelf. The tiny Spicer kitchen seemed very crowded with so many bodies in it, but Thaddeus found that he enjoyed the bustle around him. The twins no longer unnerved him as badly as when he first met them. They had grown used to him, too, he supposed. At any rate, they no longer stood and stared at him in silence.

Thaddeus looked at his friend. Morgan looked dreadful. His eyes were red-rimmed and his cheeks hollow.

"He's been working all day in the rain," Sally said. "He's about done in."

"There's a burial tomorrow. I had to make sure everything would be ready," Morgan said. "You can't leave it until the last moment."

Thaddeus felt that he was really far too old to be sitting up all night, but he realized that Spicer was at the end of his tether and was glad that he had offered to take that night's watch.

As soon as the kitchen chores were finished, Sally directed the twins to say good night to Thaddeus.

"Good night, Mr. Lewis," they chorused, and one of them smiled shyly at him.

Morgan stood to follow Sally out of the room. "If you'll excuse me for a few minutes, I'll just go and hear the children's prayers."

Soon Thaddeus heard childish voices reciting familiar words:

Now I lay me down to sleep,
I pray the Lord my soul to keep,
His Love to guard me through the night.
And wake me in the morning's light.

It was the first prayer his own children said, and one of the tasks he always looked forward to when he was at home was the hearing of prayers and the tucking in of children. He had been at home far too seldom, he realized now. Betsy had been left to raise the family and he had missed too many bedtimes.

"Do you really think something might happen tonight?" Morgan asked when he reappeared in the kitchen.

Thaddeus was no longer sure that it would. The rain had subsided to an intermittent drizzle, but the cloud bank that covered the moon had not dispersed and there was every likelihood of more rain to come.

"I don't know. It may be too dark. We'll see. But a grave was opened at St. James-the-Lesser a few days ago, and it may have something to do with what's been happening here. At the very least I think we should go and talk to the sexton."

"St. James isn't that far. I'd have time to go in the morning."

Sally bustled back downstairs and filled the teapot, then said goodnight to them and disappeared again. Yawning, Morgan rose to follow.

"Call me if you see anything," he said.

"I might, if I can't handle it myself. Otherwise I'll leave you to your bed. You look like you need all the sleep you can get."

Morgan nodded and stumbled after Sally. Thaddeus gave them a few minutes to settle themselves, then he doused the lamp. It would be easier to see the graveyard if his eyes were already accustomed to the darkness. He pulled the hard wooden chair closer to the window and settled in as well as he could for the long watch ahead.

He had expected to be uncomfortable in this position, but he found that he could still see through the window if he tipped the chair against the wall and rested his feet against the edge of the sink. Even this would have set his old bones creaking a few weeks ago, but there was no protest from his knee as he balanced his weight with it. He must be growing hardier with his return to the old travelling life, he thought. The extra activity was loosening him up, making him stronger.

Even as he thought it, he knew it was nonsense. He had been no less active at the hotel where there was a constant climbing of stairs and lugging of baggage. He had limped through his duties longing for an opportunity to sit down as soon as possible. Even the first weeks of riding the Yonge Street Circuit had made him, at times, acutely uncomfortable from the constant jarring ride over rutted roads.

The discomfort continued even when he returned to Christie's house and sank gratefully into his bed. Nothing had changed, he realized, until he visited Holy Ann's well. One drink of water from it and he began feeling better by the time he reached the next village. But that couldn't be. That would be a miracle, just like Holy Ann's admirers claimed. God was capable of many wondrous things, but Thaddeus's Methodist soul had difficulty believing that He would use so papal a thing as a holy well to accomplish them. Shrines and saints and splinters of the true cross were not acceptable to a reasoned faith.

More likely that it was a return to the challenge of saving souls that invigorated him, even though his efforts were being so poorly rewarded. Or perhaps it was the thrill of once again solving a perplexing mystery. Of being useful. He was willing to credit any of these agencies before he would start believing in the miracles of Holy Ann.

He was suddenly startled out of his absorption by a faint rattling at the door. Slowly he tilted the front legs of his chair back to the floor and lowered his feet, tensed to spring in case it was an intruder. He fixed his gaze on the door and held his breath to listen for a repetition of the sound he had heard. Nothing. It must have been the wind picking up, he decided, or the scratching of a small animal.

Then, as he watched, the bolt slowly rose out of the iron cleat and the door opened just a crack. He willed the gap to widen, just a few inches more, so that he could reach it in time to see who it was.

The prowler must have been listening as carefully as he. Either that or Thaddeus was more visible than he thought, for suddenly he heard a gasp. He leapt to his feet and flung the door open, but there was no one there. Then he heard the sound of running footsteps. He gave chase around the corner of the cottage, but by the time he reached the front walk, the would-be trespasser had disappeared.

He stood peering up and down the street for a few minutes, but he could see no evidence to indicate which way the intruder had run. He walked first in one direction, then in the other, listening and watching for anything out of the ordinary, but he could hear no more footsteps, no creaking from the wheels of a wagon or cart, no clip of a horse's hoof striking the hard-packed surface of the road. There was nothing to see but a small sleepy village bedded down for a rainy summer's night.

Slowly he turned around and went back to the cottage. He resumed his watchful position by the window, but he was sure that there would be no further disturbance that night. Whoever it was had been trying to get into the cottage, not the graves, and having been surprised in the act, it was unlikely he would return. With that decided, Thaddeus settled down in his chair and prepared to get whatever sleep he could.

* * *

The next morning Morgan became extremely upset when Thaddeus told him what had transpired during the night.

"Someone tried to break into the cottage itself? We could all have been attacked in our beds!"

"I don't think so. He was being very cautious, and as soon as he realized I was there, he abandoned the effort."

"He? One person, then?"

"I'm reasonably sure there was just one. I heard only one set of footsteps running away." But even as he said it he realized that he could be mistaken. Sounds echoed strangely when the clouds were low. "I suppose it might have been a burglar, although that seems unlikely." There was little in the Keeper's Lodge that would be worth the effort of stealing, although Thaddeus supposed that a burglar would have no way of knowing that until he got inside.

"Do you think it has anything to do with the graves?" Morgan asked.

"I don't know. But if it does, there's only one thing he could have been after."

"The ledger. But why?"

"Maybe our culprit wasn't sure where to dig next and hoped to find a clue that would point him in the right direction. Let's look at it again. We must have missed something."

Morgan fetched the leather-bound book from the shelf in the corner. Together he and Thaddeus leafed through the columned pages, but no more information offered itself up.

"I don't understand," Morgan said. "Whoever opened those two graves knew exactly where they wanted to dig. Why would they need to look at the records? There's nothing here but names and dates of death."

Thaddeus was just as perplexed. He was sure that Phillip Van Hansel was responsible for the double occupancy of the coffin at St. James-the-Lesser. He would be willing to believe that it was Van Hansel who had dug it up for some reason. But he couldn't make any connection between Hands and the graves at the Burying Ground. And why would Hands want the ledger, if that was indeed what the intruder had been after. Maybe the attempted break-in was completely unrelated. Maybe it was a burglar, as Morgan had first assumed.

It was a short walk to Parliament Street where St. James-the-Lesser Cemetery had been established to provide a pleasant vista over the valley carved by the Don River. The grounds had opened less than ten years previously, and its designers followed the newly fashionable plan of making graveyards pleasant and park-like. Mature trees were left in place all along the walkways, with grassy stretches of lawn between the plots. It was a far more welcoming place than the Strangers' Burying Ground, where the graves were laid out in regimented rows as close together as it was possible to arrange them.

Morgan was visibly impressed. "This is a lovely place. Much nicer than my cemetery." And then the import of his own words struck him. "I guess that's why they want to move all my poor strangers," he said with a wistful tone to his voice.

"No, that's not why," Thaddeus said. "It's because the village wants the land, not because it would be a nicer place for the bodies of the departed. And even if the surroundings are better, I doubt anyone looks after the residents as well as you do."

"Do you think they know?"

"That anybody cares? Yes, I think they do. I think they like it, that someone is looking after their bones." Morgan looked a little more cheerful then.

The more prominent Anglicans among the departed occupied resting places in the highest sections of the cemetery, under shady trees close to the entrance, their marble monuments intersected by snaking walkways.

As they walked through the grounds Thaddeus realized why it had taken the St. James sexton so long to discover the opened grave — the site they were looking for was tucked into a neglected-looking part of the cemetery, hidden by the slope of land above it: easy pickings for a resurrectionist, hidden from the main gates and the more established section of the graveyard.

There was little to see when they finally found the grave, just fresh mounds of earth over two adjacent plots. One mound covered the newly moved coffin from St. James Cathedral. It had no marker as yet — the cathedral records would have to be searched in order to discover who it was, Thaddeus supposed. After all, it had lain forgotten for some time.

The second grave was marked by a plain square stone set into the ground at the head of the mound: *William Miller b. 1824 d. August 13, 1847.*

He might have been a fever victim, given the date. A Protestant and a member of the Church of Ireland, otherwise the local Anglicans would not have buried him in their ground. Poor William, only twenty-three years of age, buried with a stranger in a strange land. And what of his coffin-mate? There was not even a name on a plain marker to indicate who he or she had been.

"Do you think this has anything to do with our graves?" Morgan asked.

"I find the date provocative," Thaddeus said. "It fits with our timeframe. And I think I know how two bodies ended up in the same grave, but I don't know much beyond that."

Morgan looked at him speculatively, knowing there was more to the story. When no more came, he said, "You know, you couldn't find Isaac Simms until you told me what was going on."

Years previously Isaac Simms had murdered five young girls, and Thaddeus had been at a loss to track him down until he confided in Morgan. Then they had chased him down together and Thaddeus had to admit that he couldn't have done it without Morgan's help.

"You're right. I should tell you," Thaddeus said. "But it's a very long story and it concerns not only me, but Luke as well. Let's talk to the sexton to see if he knows anything more. Then we'll decide whether or not it has anything to do with our puzzle. If it does, I'll fill you in."

They walked back to the main gates and knocked at a cottage that seemed to be connected with the cemetery. The door was opened by a man who wore a surly look on his face.

"If you're here to gawk at the coffin with the extra body, you can just turn around and go home again," he said. "It's been all covered up and there's nothing to see."

"No, we don't need to see the coffin," Thaddeus replied. "We just need to know whether or not there have been any other graves tampered with."

The question took the man by surprise. "Others?" he said. "Why would there be others? One was bad enough."

Morgan stepped forward. "I'm the Keeper over at the Burying Ground. We've had some troubles there, as well. We're trying to figure out what's going on."

"Oh. Sorry," the man said, "I've been plagued by ghouls ever since that article appeared in *The Patriot*. You'd think people would have better things to do."

"Do you have any idea when it happened?" Thaddeus asked.

"It must have been a night or two before we moved the coffin from the cathedral. I'd have noticed it sooner otherwise. They didn't even bother trying to hide what they'd done. Just dug it up and left it."

"It's not likely that it was bodysnatchers, then?"

"Well, no — they didn't take the body, did they?"

"And who, exactly, was William Miller? Do you know?"

The sexton shrugged. "Fever victim, according to the record, but there's not much information besides that. I don't know anything about the second one in the coffin. Took me aback, that one did."

"I can just imagine," Thaddeus said. "If there are any more disturbances, I wonder if you could let Mr. Spicer know?"

"Of course."

Thaddeus thanked the man for the information and he and Morgan walked back through the cemetery gates. Once out on the street again, he stopped, lost in thought, while Morgan hovered impatiently beside him.

Thaddeus knew that it was Hands who was, at least indirectly, responsible for burying extra bodies in coffins in 1847, although he hadn't expected to find one of these double-occupancies in an Anglican cemetery. William Miller had certainly not been given a very desirable plot. But that would stand to reason, if he was an immigrant. Not really part of the local establishment, but not so foreign that burial could be denied.

On the other hand, it was possible, Thaddeus supposed, that Miller wasn't an immigrant at all, but a local citizen. Many of them volunteered in the fever sheds in 1847. Many of them were stricken with typhus and died as a result. Their deaths occurred in their own homes, though, and they had no doubt been surrounded by concerned relatives and comfortable surroundings. A funeral cortege with a crowd of mourners would have accompanied them to their final destinations. How could an extra body be slipped into a coffin when so much attention was focused on the official occupant?

No, the subterfuge would be far easier to pull off if the Anglican William Miller was an immigrant. But even if he was, there was still no apparent explanation for his having been dug up again.

Thaddeus knew that the majority of the bodies carted away from the fever hospitals and sheds had been poor Irish Catholics and that they were buried at their own churches. Not the new cathedral, St. Michael's, which had not yet been completed in 1847. They would have been taken to the old church, St. Paul's. If he was to make any connection between Hands's old tricks and the current strange occurrences at the Burying Ground, he should start by asking questions at the Catholic church.

"Well?" Morgan asked. "What do you think?"

"I'm not sure. But at some point I'd like to visit St. Paul's Cemetery to ask a few questions there."

"Why?"

"Because I know for a fact that at St. Paul's there are more occupants in coffins than there ought to be. I want to know if they're being dug up as well."

"How do you know all this?"

Thaddeus eyed Morgan as he weighed the risks of telling him about the encounter with Hands Van Hansel. The last thing he wanted was to put any of the Spicers in danger. On the other hand, Morgan had a point. The young man had proved himself in the Simms case. Thaddeus was sure he could trust him now.

"You must keep this to yourself," he said. "And I won't tell you the name of the man involved. Not because I lack confidence in you, but because it's safer that way."

When Morgan nodded, Thaddeus related the bare details of the story — the double coffins; the skirmish in the yard that resulted in two men dead over the corpse of an Irish girl; the wounding of a man who had since become a very powerful figure in Toronto.

"I still don't know whether or not it has anything to do with what has been happening at the Strangers' Ground, but it seems an odd coincidence that four bodies that were all buried at more or less the same time have now been disinterred."

"I would agree," Morgan said, "except that both of my burials were singles. And if this man was in the business of stuffing coffins, why would he want to have them opened again? The whole point of putting things in the earth is so they don't see the light of day again."

It was a valid point, and one that Thaddeus had no answer for. "I don't really know, Morgan," he said finally. "To tell the truth, I'm grasping at straws." But he wasn't. Not really. He felt as though he had found an entry into a maze, and now all that remained was to follow the twists and turns that would lead him to the end.

* * *

As soon as they reached the Keeper's Lodge, Morgan ducked inside to fetch a tie and to clean the mud from his boots in preparation for the afternoon burial. Thaddeus was debating whether or not he should carry on to St. Paul's alone when he saw a familiar figure coming along the street toward him.

"I thought I should come for the committal," Luke said when he reached his father. "It's the young man who died from typhoid. It's a funny thing, you know, when you think about being a doctor, you always think in terms of saving patients, not losing them."

"I'm sure you did everything you could."

"I did. But there wasn't enough that I *could* do."

Thaddeus fell in beside his son. They weren't so different, he and Luke. They both felt their failures too keenly. St. Paul's could wait.

They walked to the back of the cemetery where the gaping hole that Morgan had dug was waiting to be filled.

"Where have you been?" Luke asked while they waited. "I half-expected you at breakfast."

"Asking questions. We went to St. James-the-Lesser this morning, but the grave was filled in and the sexton didn't have much to tell us."

"Ah yes. The double burial. Do you think the disturbances are related?"

"Not that I can see. You and I both know who doubled up the coffin, but that doesn't mean the same person dug it up. Besides, someone tried to break into the lodge last night."

"A thief?"

"There's nothing worth taking. I think they were after the cemetery records." Thaddeus shrugged. "Or maybe I'd just like to think that. It still doesn't get us any closer to finding out who the culprits are." He glanced at the front gates. "Here they come."

A cart turned in at the cemetery and rolled slowly along the laneway until it pulled level to where Luke and Thaddeus were standing. This was no black hearse with fine horses and drapings of crepe, but a plain wagon that would have served as well to haul water or hay. Nor was there a cortege of mourners in funeral finery trailing behind it, just a preacher and a straggle of neighbours. Two of the men in this group stopped to comfort the weeping mother. She said something to them. They nodded and went to the back of the wagon.

"Perhaps we should make ourselves useful," Thaddeus said. "I don't think there are enough able-bodied men in the group to act as pallbearers."

"You're right," Luke said. "One of them is Andrew Holden. He has a bad foot."

Morgan joined them as they walked to the wagon and helped to slide the coffin from the bed, then shouldered it for the measured walk to the grave.

After they had helped lower the coffin into the ground, all three of them stepped back behind the mourners. They were there out of respect, and would give room to those who truly grieved.

The minister was a little long-winded, Thaddeus thought. He had always tried to keep the graveside committals short, so it wasn't too hard on the family. Certainly the mother looked as though she could stand little more, but then Luke had told him that she was ill as well. As the service dragged on, Thaddeus realized that he would not now have time to walk down to St. Paul's cemetery as he had intended. And he would be leaving in the morning to meet his appointments. His questions would have to wait until his return.

He wasn't sure that there would be any answers then, either. The coffin at St. James pointed in Phillip Van Hansel's direction, but little else did. It wouldn't surprise Thaddeus in the least if Hands turned out to be the culprit, but then he stopped to remind himself that he had a long history of believing in the guilt of people he didn't like.

Chapter 15

Luke needed an excuse to go into the city so that he could meet Perry. Three days of heavy rain had cleansed the air, and the epidemic that kept the practice busy finally burnt itself out. There were no new outbreaks, no more deaths, and now only a dozen or so convalescent patients still needed to be seen. Dr. Christie pronounced most of his patients cured, and with a sigh of relief, handed whoever remained over to Luke, who even then found that their care occupied only a part of his day. He had time on his hands again.

Even though Christie once again disappeared into the back part of the house for most of the day, Luke was sure that he would be happy enough to cover the practice for an evening, especially if it was for a social occasion that involved a member of the Biddulph family. But Luke wanted to find an activity that would provide a reasonable explanation for Perry's presence, just in case anyone asked questions about how they happened to be together. And, if Luke was honest with himself, one that would provide him with a graceful exit if he changed his mind at the last moment.

The St. Lawrence Hall, beside the new Toronto City Hall, was proving to be a popular place for entertainment, offering everything from concerts and anti-slavery lectures to accounts from travellers who had successfully returned from exotic excursions. Three days after Thaddeus left to plod back up Yonge Street, Luke saw that the newspapers were advertising a lecture by a Mr. Horace Winthrop, a British gentleman who had recently completed a journey through Egypt and the Middle East. It was scheduled for the following evening.

Surely no one would think anything of it if he attended such an educational offering. And the timing was perfect. Thaddeus was safely away from Yorkville. Otherwise, Luke knew, his father would want to go with him.

He dashed off a short note and put it in the morning mail: *Travel lecture at St. Lawrence Hall 7 p.m. Friday evening? Meet you at the door. Luke* — and was rewarded with an answer by return post: *See you there. Perry*

On the day of the lecture Luke was distracted and unfocused, still uncertain of the wisdom of his decision. Nevertheless, he waited until late in the afternoon to go to the barber's for a shave, and after supper he went upstairs to brush his coat and his shoes. Mrs. Dunphy had laundered and starched a fresh collar for him and he fastened it carefully to his best shirt. He brushed his hair back on both sides and wondered if he should have asked the barber for some pomade to stick it down with, then decided that it would have made him look too eager. Once dressed, he inspected himself in the mirror and came to the conclusion that he looked as presentable as it was possible for him to be. Then, hands shaking, he left the house and walked as far as Tollgate Road. Just as he reached the corner, a horse taxi trotted by. Luke flagged it down. Tonight he would treat himself to a private ride.

When he arrived at the entrance to the St. Lawrence Hall, Perry was waiting in front of the building, leaning nonchalantly against the post of a gas lamp, looking polished and dapper. He broke into a lopsided grin when he saw Luke.

"Wasn't sure you really meant it."

"Neither was I," Luke replied.

"Did you want to go inside?"

"I should for a while. Just so I can report on the lecture tomorrow."

They joined the line of people waiting to be admitted to the assembly hall. They were a fashionable group, the women's skirts wide and billowing, and despite the heat some of them wore brightly coloured Indian shawls wrapped around their shoulders. The men nearly all sported colourful waistcoats and extravagant cravats. Luke felt grey and nondescript in the midst of so much finery. Perhaps he should have asked for pomade after all.

The auditorium seemed a perfect complement for the elegance of its audience. A massive chandelier hung from a plastered medallion in the centre of the ceiling. Corniced windows and doors and pilasters lent a classical air to the space, while the raked gallery and the stage that thrust out into the room afforded an excellent view from any seat in the house.

They took chairs near the back and on the aisle. Luke was relieved to see that, although the hall was reasonably full, it was by no means sold out. He could see empty chairs scattered here and there throughout the rows. Their own empty seats would not be glaringly noticeable when they left.

The audience applauded when a bewhiskered gentleman walked up onto the stage and introduced himself as Mr. Winthrop. He carefully laid his notes on the lectern and then he began: "Your eyes, accustomed perhaps to the soothing green of field and wood, are dazzled by the intense rays of the sun, the horizon shimmering in the distance, and by the suffocating heat that envelops you like a shroud. Every movement is an effort, every breath a triumph wrested from the dry and desiccated air that insidiously siphons away the moisture in your nose and lungs. More than anything, this is the reality of Egypt."

The man had travelled from England, he said, in order to view the astounding pyramidal structures that thrust skyward from the Egyptian desert. These masses of chiselled rock were tombs for the pharaohs of Egypt, ancient rulers who raised monuments as a testament to their own greatness.

Luke was excruciatingly aware of Perry in the chair beside him, the scent of his hair oil, their elbows brushing on occasion as he shifted in his seat. He forced himself not to sneak sideways glances at the pointed profile, and to concentrate on the speaker's words, as Christie was sure to question him about the lecture at breakfast the next morning.

"We made our way to the site by riding on a camel, an uncommonly uncomfortable mode of travel. These ships of the desert are irritable creatures, and had we not had the assistance of the local Egyptian herders, I doubt that we should have been able to mount them. Mrs. Winthrop, in particular, suffered greatly."

The lecturer's wife had, apparently, travelled with her husband, and it was promised that later in the program this redoubtable lady would regale the audience with the difficulties of travelling in a foreign country in the genteel manner to which she was accustomed.

Sphinxes and sheiks, dunes and dhows. Luke sat impatiently through the next half-hour. Finally Mr. Winthrop announced a short break so that the good ladies and gentlemen in the audience might partake of refreshments, which were being served in an adjacent salon. Luke and Perry exited the hall.

"A drink?" Perry said when they reached the street. "I'm parched after all that talk about heat and sand."

Luke nodded. "A drink." If he was going to so cavalierly cast aside his previous resolutions he might just as well make it a good throw, he decided. Perhaps a glass of gin would steady his nerves. He followed as Perry walked north.

Again, they dodged down a small street off Yonge and twisted and turned through a warren of alleys until they reached a building with a scarred wooden door. One side of the frame showed the same peculiar scratching that Luke had noticed before.

Perry pointed to a mark. "That's the sign that you're safe. You won't run into trouble here."

"Are there many of these places?"

"Only a few. But enough."

Perry held open the door and beckoned him into the tavern where they found a table in a dark corner.

"Beer?"

"No," Luke said. "I think I'd like something stronger."

"Whisky's the stuff, then." He asked the tavern keeper for two whiskies and brought them back to the table.

Luke sipped his tentatively, wrinkling his nose at the smell and almost gagging at the strong, burning taste, but when he swallowed it down it made his insides feel warm. Another sip and he could feel himself relaxing.

Perry was uncharacteristically quiet. Luke cast about for something to say that would ease the tension that had built between them.

"So what does the sign mean? The one on the door?"

"It's a reference to the classical Greek story of Orestes and Pylades."

"I'm afraid I'm not familiar with it," Luke confessed.

"They were raised as brothers, but became much more, if you know what I mean. The sign is an "O" and a "P" intertwined." With a finger he traced the shape on the scarred surface of the table, then narrowed his eyes and began speaking what Luke understood was a quotation from somewhere.

"And while the barbarians were standing round in a circle Orestes fell down and lay on the ground, seized by his usual mania, while Pylades wiped away the foam, tended his body and covered him with his well-woven cloak acting not only like a lover but like a father. For when from boyhood a serious love has grown up and it becomes adult at the age of reason, the long-loved object returns reciprocal affection, and it is hard to determine which is the lover of which. For as from a mirror the affection of the lover is reflected in the beloved."

Perry's mouth twisted into a wry smile. "One of the few things I remember from a mythology class taught by a particularly sadistic schoolmaster. He was supposed to have been teaching us about Odysseus and the Trojan War, but decided to depart from the curriculum. It was only after he tried to bugger my brother Theo that I realized why."

"What happened to him? Did your brother report him?"

Perry looked surprised. "Of course not. Theo was far too embarrassed to breathe a word to anyone but me. But I followed the old bastard one day. That's how I discovered this place. I didn't know then how useful the information would be."

"So the schoolmaster scratched the sign on the door?"

"It must have been him. It's a pretty obscure story, and those particular details are usually glossed over in favour of a description of how Orestes killed his mother, which is apparently a far more acceptable tale for impressionable young minds. I doubt that many of the men who frequent these places know what the symbol really stands for, but they've come to recognize what it means. Around here, at any rate, it means that you're in snug company."

Luke's knowledge of the history of Greece and Rome was non-existent. Mythology was the stuff of private boarding schools, of money and grand homes. His education had consisted of reading, writing, and arithmetic until he'd decided to go to medical school, where the emphasis was on memorizing anatomical names and pharmaceutical applications. He was suddenly aware of what a different world Perry Biddulph came from, and it made him feel shy and gauche. He groped for an intelligent comment and finally decided on a subject he was familiar with.

"So this Orestes — why did he 'fall down to the ground with his usual mania'? Did he have epilepsy?"

Perry threw back his head and laughed. "Trust a physician to zero in on clinical description and ignore the moral innuendo. It does sound like epilepsy, doesn't it? Julius Caesar had it, too." He took a long sip from the glass in front of him, then looked up, his face serious, his black eyes fixed on Luke's face. "It doesn't have to be me, you know, although I'd like that. I could show you how to meet someone else."

With this humble and generous offering, and the effects of another sip of whisky, Luke finally made up his mind to forge ahead. He looked across the table at Perry and smiled.

"No, I want it to be you. You've been nothing but kind to me since I met you, and …" He was so unfamiliar with the language of courtship that he was having difficulty finding the words he wanted. Kindness wasn't what he meant. "And I like you very much. I'd like to know you better. I think I can trust you …" Again he fumbled over the sentence. This wasn't a piece of horse-trading, he thought, the deal to be sealed with a handshake. Why couldn't he say what he meant?

Perry galloped to his rescue. "Trust? I'm not sure I've ever been the recipient of anyone's trust before. But don't worry; I'll do my best to be worthy. I do understand what's at stake. And I like you, too, Luke."

They downed their drinks and Perry rose from his chair. Luke was entirely unsure what was expected next, but he followed Perry back out to the warren of alleys.

"It's a lovely evening," Perry said, "C'mon. I'll show you the sights." And then he led the way across a handful of streets until they reached Molly Wood's Bush.

Chapter 16

The first few days of Thaddeus's circuit were miserable. The heavy rain turned sections of the road into quagmire, and although he tried to spur his underfed pony into something more than a resigned plod to get through them, the animal was leery of the slippery footing and balked several times. Thaddeus was forced to climb down from his buggy and lead the animal through the boggy mess, the mud soaking him to the knees. Even when the pony could be persuaded into forward motion and he could ride again, the rain dripped down both sides of his hat and ran down the back of his neck. And on top of everything else, his knee started to ache again.

It was with great relief that he reached Cummer's Settlement. In light of the increased attendance at his last Sunday service, he had scheduled two extra classes and he was gratified that there was reasonable attendance at both. He was again invited to an excellent meal and a comfortable bed, and Mrs. Cummer managed to brush most of the dried mud from his trousers, although Thaddeus wasn't sure if she was concerned for his welfare, or merely anxious to keep the dirt from her spotless kitchen.

He was in a much better mood the following morning when the day dawned clear. The extra meetings at Cummer's Settlement had disrupted his schedule somewhat, and he needed to make good time in order to reach Newtonbrook for a women's class. But even the pony seemed to be in better spirits and stepped at what was, for it, a lively pace. He was on time for the meeting, and was pleased to see that one of the women had brought her aunt with her, swelling the ranks to a grand total of five. It was progress. Slow progress, but something to build on.

Once again, however, there was no one at the wagoner's house in Thorne's Hill. He drove the buggy back out to the main street and hesitated, but only for a moment. He would drink again from Holy Ann's well, he decided, even though he in no way subscribed to the belief that it was Holy Ann helping his knee. It was just good water, that was all.

By the time Thaddeus reached the limit of his circuit and started back toward Yorkville, the late summer sun was once again making the road shimmer with heat, and he could see thunderheads building in the west. He had hoped to complete his last evening meeting and push on to Christie's, but he was sure a storm was building. He would ask his host for a bed, he decided, and return to Yorkville the next day.

* * *

Luke hadn't intended to see Perry again so soon, but after their first rendezvous, he found himself agreeing to meet a few nights later. It was on this second evening, as they were walking back to Yonge Street in search of a cab, that Perry suddenly blurted out that Lavinia Van Hansel was anxious to see Luke again. "She asked me to tell you," he said.

"Why does she want to see me?"

"I don't know. She wouldn't say. She's just told me to tell you."

"But I don't want to see her."

"I know. But I promised to pass the message along."

Tell her I'm busy."

They walked in silence for a few minutes and Luke assumed the matter was closed until Perry said, "I'm sorry, I know you don't like Lavinia, but couldn't you just meet with her and see what she wants?"

"I don't have anything she wants."

"Maybe you could tell her that in person."

"No."

"For me?" Perry's voice took on a wheedling tone that Luke found puzzling.

"No."

"Please?"

"I don't understand," Luke said. "Why do I need to see her? Just tell her I'm not coming"

"She thinks you can help her. I can't find what she's looking for. For some reason, she thinks you can."

"How could I help her? I don't know anything."

"Couldn't you just tell her that yourself? It wouldn't take long." It was clear that Perry wasn't prepared to let the matter go.

"Why is this so important to you?" Luke stopped walking abruptly. There could be only one reason that it was important. "Is she putting pressure on you to get to me? You're supposed to deliver me up so she can get something out of me?"

"Well, she asked me to ask. 'Deliver you up' is a little strong."

"And if you can't get me to play along, she'll tell your father all your nasty little secrets. Is that it?"

Perry shrugged. "More or less. After all, that's how she works."

"And what happens if I refuse?"

"I was hoping you'd help me out, Luke. I don't think it's a lot to ask."

Then Luke was struck by a thought so cold he could barely find his next words. "Is … is that what this is all about? Has been right from the start?"

"No!" Perry said. "Of course not."

Luke's head was spinning. "I thought you just wanted to be with me."

"I do!"

But the reason for Perry's persistence was beginning to make sinister sense to Luke. "I should have known. You made such a point of rushing over to me that night at Lavinia's party."

"Luke! No!" Perry protested. "That's not how it is at all."

"And then you came running as fast as I called." Luke felt a wave of anger rising up over his dismay. "You'll do anything to keep your hands in your father's pockets, won't you Perry? Who else are you willing to go off into the woods with if it'll get you what you want?"

He could tell by the look on Perry's face that the words stung.

"Do you really think I'd do that? Is that the kind of person you think I am?"

"I don't know what else to think, Perry. It's the only explanation I can come up with."

Their raised voices were starting to draw stares from passing pedestrians, but Perry didn't appear to care who overheard him.

"You can go to the devil, Luke Lewis," he shouted. "Go on — run back to your stupid little village and leave me alone. I'm sorry I ever met you." He turned and strode angrily down the street. Equally angry, Luke set off in the opposite direction.

Anger kept him walking, in spite of the fact that an omnibus and two horse cabs rumbled by. What a fool he'd been, to think that Perry could have any genuine interest in someone like him. He'd been blackmailed into seeing Luke, that much was clear, and like the small-town dupe he was, Luke had walked right into the trap. Well, Lavinia could go to the hangman for all he cared. And so could Perry.

He could only be thankful, he supposed, that he hadn't told Perry anything about his prior encounter with Phillip Van Hansel. What price would Lavinia exact if she knew that he'd been present the night an Irish girl shot her husband? Not only present, but helped spirit the girl away after, far beyond the reach of any vengeance Hands might take? Or that Luke's father had written a letter that directed suspicion Van Hansel's way? If Lavinia knew that, Luke would be vulnerable to whatever threat she chose to employ.

And then he realized that she had no need of that knowledge. She already had an effective threat she could use against him. The same one she was using on Perry. Blackmail was too easy when the target was so open.

What an idiot I am, to think that I could get away with this. Cherub had followed him after Lavinia's tea party, he was sure of it. She could have followed him to his tryst with Perry as well. Or, for all he knew, Perry had told Lavinia all about it, the three of them sniggering about him over tea in the parlour. One word to Christie was all it would take. One word to Christie and another to Thaddeus and Luke's life would be in ruins.

So would Perry's, he realized, if he had been telling Luke the truth. And as angry as he was, Luke couldn't wish that to happen. He had liked Perry, right from the first. If he didn't like him, why would he now be so angry?

Because he had been used, he told himself, in spite of what Perry claimed. And then unbidden, Perry's protests came back to him. *That's not how it is at all*, he said. But how else could it be?

It could be like it was with Ben, came the unwelcome argument. Luke had been a poor student, cold and penniless. Ben gave him food and shelter and friendship just when Luke needed it most. To someone who hadn't known them, would it appear that Luke was nothing but an opportunist? It might well have, he realized.

And then it occurred to him that Perry didn't understand the implications of what he was asking. He didn't know the danger the Van Hansels posed. He didn't know, because Luke hadn't told him.

He should have given Perry the benefit of the doubt, or at the very least an opportunity to explain himself. Instead, Luke lost his temper and let his bruised feelings guide his tongue. He had been vile to Perry, his words to him inexcusable. *What's wrong with me?* he thought as he continued walking north. *I can be up to my chin in blood and muck and filth and keep a cool head, but whenever I have to deal with my own feelings I fall to pieces.*

By the time he reached Tollgate Road, Luke was thoroughly miserable. *Go back to your stupid little village* Perry had shouted at him. Luke would. And then he would stay there. But in order to stay there safely, he would have to find out what Lavinia wanted.

All she had asked Perry to do was to arrange a meeting. Luke couldn't imagine what she would ask of him, but if this concession was enough to extricate him from the mess he'd gotten himself into, he would go and hear her out.

Chapter 17

With remarkable ill timing, Lavinia suggested that Luke meet her at the Van Hansel house on the same day that Thaddeus was more or less due back in Yorkville, although his schedule tended to be erratic and subject to sudden change. When Luke woke that morning he was relieved to discover that his father hadn't returned yet, and hoped that he wouldn't make an appearance until later in the day. If he didn't have to dodge Thaddeus, he wouldn't need to find excuses. They had agreed that they would avoid the Van Hansels, and he had no way of explaining to his father why he was going against that decision without revealing at least part of the reason.

Nor, he decided, would he inform Dr. Christie that he was going into the city. Now that the summer epidemic had burned itself out, there really wasn't a great deal of work to get through in a day. Should an emergency arise while Luke was gone, Christie could take care of it, although if there was a sudden accident or illness Luke would have to think of some way to account for his absence. But he couldn't run the risk that Christie might mention something to Thaddeus.

He had only two patients to call on that morning — Mrs. Cory, who as a teetotaler required a script for her evening's dose of brandy, and an old man who caught a summer cold that had turned into pneumonia. The latter's condition was exacerbated, Luke was sure, by the fact that he had been employed at the brickyard for more than twenty-five years and no doubt had breathed more than his share of fine brick dust. He prescribed some extract of belladonna and instructed the man's wife to set him up in a chair by an open window.

"Keep him wrapped up, but let him sit upright. There's a lovely breeze. The fresh air can only help him."

The woman looked dubious, but she would probably do as he instructed. After all, he was the doctor. He wished he could direct the rest of his affairs as easily. Just a word and everyone would do what he wanted.

It was still only eleven o'clock when Luke arrived back at Christie's. Desperate for a diversion, he wandered into the parlour and grabbed a book from the jumble of titles lying unshelved on the table. *A Compendium of Gods and Heroes from Greek Mythology*, he read. Intrigued in spite of his worries, he took the book through to the office with him. Ever since Perry had told him the tale of Orestes and Pylades he had been meaning to ask more about it. Well, he wouldn't be able to ask now, would he? He'd have to look it up for himself.

He might have known that Dr. Christie would have a relevant book on the matter. Christie had apparently received much the same sort of education as Perry had, and no doubt was familiar with the story, although it was unlikely that the same construction would have been put on it.

Luke could find no reference to it in the book. It was apparently not a popular tale. Perry said as much, he remembered.

There were, however, a number of other interesting stories: Prometheus, who stole fire and was punished for it by having an eagle set to an eternal feasting on his liver; Pandora, who opened the lid on the woes of the world; the great Trojan War and the journey of Odysseus. As Luke skimmed through the book he found numerous instances where the gods had descended to earth and by force or by guile had impregnated beautiful women to give rise to a race of heroes. Here and there he found veiled references to love, or more likely, he thought, lust, between men, but nowhere could he find any reference to Orestes and Pylades. Their story had been omitted from this particular edition.

He flipped to the front of the book and found a subtitle that he failed to notice before: *Greek Mythology for Senior Classes.* This was a school text, designed for innocent eyes. Perry's schoolmaster had been teaching far beyond the usual curriculum and with an obvious purpose in mind. And even though he hadn't found what he was looking for, the stories were fascinating and Luke continued to browse through the book, sampling the text here and there, skimming over pages to get the sense of each story. He had reached the end of the book when he discovered a thin paper in pamphlet form stuck between the endpapers. *The Lives and Adventures of John Cottington, Alias Mul-Sack.*

Curious, he pulled the booklet out and began to read:

Did you ever hear the like,
Or ever hear the fame,
Of five women barbers,
Who lived in Drury Lane?

Drury Lane, Luke assumed from the context, was an insalubrious part of the City of London. Mul-Sack had been apprenticed as a chimneysweep at a young age, a position that he ran away from before his term was up. He had learned the trade, he reasoned, and could set up easily on his own. He was so successful that he began to pass himself off as a gentleman: "No liquor but sack, forsooth, would go down with him, and that too must always be mulled to make it more pleasant."

He acquired his nickname because of this habit, the story claimed. But what Luke read next made him nearly drop the paper. Mul-Sack was drinking in an unfamiliar tavern one evening when he spied what he thought was a very beautiful woman. He approached her, but she declined his attentions, insisting that only matrimony would suffice to gain her interest. Mul-Sack agreed, and off they went to their wedding. It was only that night in the marriage bed that Mul-Sack discovered that he had espoused himself to a hermaphrodite by the name of Aniseed Robin. Robin was well known in Drury Lane. Children chased him through the streets, throwing stones and lumps of manure at him. And contrite as he, or she, was, it was all too much for Mul-Sack, who after that took to a life of crime.

Luke hurried through the rest of the story, but could find no further mention of Aniseed Robin, only that Mul-Sack was eventually arrested in a riot in Drury Lane, in which five "Amazons" took it upon themselves to punish a wayward wife in a "highly barbarous" manner, and that Mul-Sack ended his life on the gibbet, brought finally to justice for theft, pickpocketing, and highway robbery.

At the end of the tale, Luke carefully replaced the pamphlet and returned the book to the parlour, where he sat down heavily in a chair and tried to determine what, if anything, the tale signified.

The facts surrounding Mul-Sack's life of crime were straightforward enough. When Luke first saw the skeleton in the office, Christie openly referred to it by the highwayman's name and described how he had acquired the corpse. He made no secret of his keen interest in the subject of corpses. He had recounted a famous case of grave robbing and murder in Scotland and had expressed a wish to view the next victim that turned up at the Strangers' Burying Ground. Although slightly odd, Luke supposed that it was not an entirely aberrant interest for a physician, and it was in no way strange that Christie told him the story to explain the presence of the skeleton.

Luke tried to recall everything he could about the conversation of that first day. Christie summarized the tale in a few short sentences, referring to Mul-Sack only as "a famous highwayman." He had then gone on to relate how he acquired the bones. Perhaps he hadn't considered Mul-Sack's strange marriage relevant to the conversation. He hadn't mentioned the five Amazons of Drury Lane either.

But what if there was more to it than that? What if, in his brusque Christie*ish* way, he assumed that Luke knew the story already, and concocted a reference to Mul-Sack in order to serve notice that he knew all about Luke and would brook no improprieties?

And then a second thought occurred to him that was so amusing it bubbled up through his anxieties and made him laugh out loud: Christie and corpses and the terrible smell that emanated at times from the nether regions of the house. Was it possible that he was not content with one skeleton, but was in the hunt for more? Was he the culprit who had been robbing the graveyards of their decomposed bodies?

He must remember to share this thought with his father, who would be amused at the notion of the elderly doctor creeping out at midnight to maraud in the local cemetery: Christie, who became short of breath when hurried and was disinclined to leave the house under the best of circumstances.

And then another, more sobering thought struck Luke. What if Christie had been tendering a bargain? What if the culprit really was Christie and he was offering his silence on Luke's proclivities in exchange for Luke's silence on his own?

But the bargain had been offered far too subtly, he realized, for either of them to be sure it was struck at all. Still, it was a tantalizing theory. Luke had not paid much attention to Morgan Spicer's graveyard puzzle and didn't know what his father had managed to discover so far. In fact, when he thought about it, Luke realized that he had not been paying much attention to his father either. He would trot out his preposterous notion of Christie as bone digger, he decided. It would be a peace offering that Luke and Thaddeus could laugh about together.

There was still no sign of Thaddeus when Luke went in to the dining room for his dinner. He could safely meet with Lavinia Van Hansel, and by the time he returned to Yorkville, his father would probably be back as well. Luke would tell him then.

* * *

There appeared to be no one around when Thaddeus reached Christie's house the next day. The noontime dinner was long over and the dishes cleared away from the dining room table, although the smell of cooking seemed to linger in the room. In search of Luke, he knocked at the office door. When no one answered, he tentatively opened it, but there was no one there. The boy must be out seeing patients. Thaddeus had no idea where Christie might be. He wondered if Mrs. Dunphy was in the kitchen, but he hesitated to barge into her domain. Thaddeus had been made more than welcome in this house, and had been encouraged to consider it his home, but he still felt like a boarder and was loath to trespass into the rooms that he hadn't been specifically invited to use. He returned to the front hall and called out a hello.

Mrs. Dunphy appeared at the top of the stairs, broom in hand.

"Oh, Mr. Lewis, you're back again, are you? All is well?"

"Yes, thank you, but I'm feeling a little peckish. No, don't come down," he said as Mrs. Dunphy prepared to descend. "I want only a slice of bread or two and I can get it myself, if that's all right with you."

"Well, of course it's all right," Mrs. Dunphy said. "Help yourself to whatever you need. The bread is in a box in the pantry. You'll find some cheddar wrapped in a cloth beside it as well, if you'd like it. And push the kettle over onto stove while you're there. I'll be ready for a cup when I'm finished here."

Thaddeus went through to the kitchen and located the bread box in the pantry. He lopped himself a couple of thick slices and helped himself to a wedge of cheese. He looked for somewhere to set his makeshift dinner while he filled the kettle. There was an old pine table and four chairs in the centre of the kitchen, but the tabletop was mostly occupied by something wrapped up in a greasy-looking tarp.

As he set his food on one corner of the table, he became aware of a musty smell emanating from the bundle, and then he noticed a dark stain that had seeped through the tarp and left a stain in the pine. He filled the kettle and set it on the stove. Then he hesitated. The contents of the bundle were really none of his business, but the odour and the stain were so peculiar that he was curious. Gingerly, he peeled back the layers of canvas to find a long, thin, flayed carcass. Whatever it had been, its pelt had been skinned away to reveal the muscles and vessels beneath it.

He could only guess at what it had been. Weasel? Otter? But why on earth would Mrs. Dunphy have a skinned otter sitting on her kitchen table?

"It's a marten." Thaddeus jumped at the sound of the voice. "Oh good, you remembered to put the kettle on."

"I'm sorry, I didn't mean to pry," Thaddeus said. "It's just that I noticed the smell."

Mrs. Dunphy snorted. "Oh, that's nothing. Wait until he boils it. I try to make him do it outside. The smell is dreadful if he does it in here." She seemed completely unconcerned by his macabre discovery.

"Where did it come from?"

"Someone brought it to Stewart — Dr. Christie," she said. "He likes to boil things down and look at the bones. Should I bring you a cup of tea when it's ready?"

"Thank you. That would be lovely." He retrieved his bread and cheese and retired to the dining room in confusion. He'd had no idea that Dr. Christie was in the habit of cooking animals so he could "look at the bones" as Mrs. Dunphy put it. Who would want to do that? And he didn't confine his efforts to animals, apparently. After all, there was the peculiar skeleton in the office that he was so proud of having reconstructed himself.

Was it possible that Thaddeus had been chasing the wrong notion all along?

Christie certainly expressed a keen interest in the contents of the coffins at the Burying Ground and had grilled Luke about the appearance of Isaiah Marshall's skeleton. He instructed Thaddeus to "keep an eye out" for any interesting bones at the Dissecting Rooms. Whoever unearthed the bodies at the Burying Ground seemed to take no interest in the corpses themselves. They had been pulled out of their graves and thrown aside. But what if the advanced state of their decay merely made them difficult to remove, and the perpetrators left them behind only because they were interrupted in mid-snatch?

Morgan said quite specifically that there were two intruders in the graveyard. If one of them was Christie, who could the other man have been? Unless it wasn't a man, but Mrs. Dunphy. When he stopped to think about it, Thaddeus realized that the doctor and his housekeeper had a very odd relationship. Mrs. Dunphy seemed to function as an equal to Christie. She certainly had no reservations about yelling back when he bellowed at her, in a way that would be inappropriate in most households. She refused to answer doors or bells. She referred to Christie as "Stewart," then corrected herself. She was a large woman. Could she have been mistaken for a man in the dark?

Then again, she seemed unconcerned with Thaddeus's inadvertent discovery of the marten carcass. Nor had she attempted to keep him out of the kitchen when he asked about getting something to eat. Whatever Christie was up to, she obviously found it in no way odd.

He thought back to the night of the second incident at the Burying Ground when Morgan pounded on the front door in such a panic. It had been Christie who answered. Thaddeus heard him stumble down the stairs and open the door, and he was standing in front of it bleary-eyed and in his nightclothes when Thaddeus followed. Morgan had been in close pursuit of the intruders. Christie could not possibly have run from the cemetery to his house, gone upstairs, changed his clothes, and come back downstairs in the time that had elapsed. But what if there had not been two men that night, but only one? Morgan saw "one of them," he said, just as he'd slipped into the street. Maybe he assumed that there were two intruders because he had seen two before. Could Christie have sent Mrs. Dunphy off on her own to dig up the second grave?

Thaddeus shook his head. This was fanciful in the extreme. He was seeing patterns where none existed. If Christie wanted bodies to boil, surely he could just present himself at the dissecting rooms and ask for the ones they had finished with. Resurrectionists still plied a lucrative trade because of the shortage of cadavers, in spite of the legislation that made unclaimed bodies available for medical study. But what happened to these illegal corpses when the anatomists were finished with them? Someone must take them somewhere. And Christie had a contact at the general hospital. He probably knew someone at the medical school as well.

It would make no sense for him to risk raiding a graveyard when he could more easily obtain bodies elsewhere. But, Thaddeus thought, nothing about this puzzle made sense.

He would talk to Luke, he decided, and get his son's reaction to the notion of Christie as bodysnatcher. Luke seemed disinterested in Morgan Spicer's puzzle and disinclined to speculate on how to solve it, but surely his curiosity would be piqued by Christie's macabre activities.

But, Thaddeus decided, there was no point in waiting around for Luke to turn up. He could be gone all day. He was a busy man, after all, with patients to see. He wasn't in a position to make himself available whenever his father might have something to discuss with him. Thaddeus couldn't expect his son to be the same confidant his wife had been. He wasn't Betsy.

He shook off the melancholy thought. In the meantime, he decided, he'd follow his first instincts and find out what he could at St. Paul's Cemetery, even though he was less and less convinced that any answers lay there. He rose and left the house, forgetting that Mrs. Dunphy had promised to bring him tea.

He collected Morgan at the Burying Ground and together they walked along the Concession Road to Parliament, then turned south toward Queen Street. A month or so ago, Thaddeus realized, this much walking would have jangled loose the shards that floated around in his knee and set him wincing with each step. Now he kept a brisk pace and ignored the omnibuses as they rattled by. His knee felt fine.

St. Paul's Cathedral was in what was commonly referred to as "Corktown," a neighbourhood for the Irish workers who found employment in the nearby brickyards and breweries. Shabby and insubstantial cottages had begun to replace the makeshift sheds and lean-tos that huddled along the banks of the Don River, a sign, Thaddeus supposed, that the Irish were establishing some kind of permanence in the city, whether the staid citizens of Toronto were in favour of their presence or not.

The cemetery was located at the east side of the red-brick St. Paul's Church. They could find no one about, either in the grounds or in the church itself, until a door opened at the rear of the building and children came spilling out into the yard. There must be a school here, as well, Thaddeus thought, and the children have finished their lessons for the day. A young, pleasant-looking priest followed them into the yard.

"May I be of assistance?" he asked, the lilt in his voice betraying his Irish origins. Thaddeus was reminded suddenly of Father Higgins, the Irish priest who had died of typhus in Kingston.

Again, Thaddeus introduced Morgan as Keeper of the Burying Ground in order to provide a justification for his questions, then briefly outlined the events that had brought them to St. Paul's.

The priest looked puzzled. "Our cemetery is no longer open. It filled up far too fast with fever victims back in '47. Everyone goes to St. Michael's Cathedral now."

"The graves that were opened at the Strangers' Ground weren't recent," Thaddeus said. "They date from several years past. It's a very odd thing, and we thought it would be worth-while to ask if the same thing were happening here."

The priest shook his head. "If there had been such a dese-cration, I'm sure I would have heard about it. As far as I'm aware, all of our souls are sleeping peacefully."

Thaddeus thanked the man for his trouble and walked away, almost certain that it was not Phillip Van Hansel who was digging up graves. If Hands was involved, there should be disturbances at St. Paul's similar in nature to those at St. James-the-Lesser and the Burying Ground. St. Paul's was where most of the dead from the fever hospital had ended up. It was where most of the double burials would have taken place. Christie made a far more likely suspect.

It began to drizzle again as Thaddeus and Morgan walked back toward Yorkville, and by the time they reached the Keeper's Lodge they were both sodden.

"Come in," Morgan said, "Sally will make us some tea and rustle up something for us to eat."

Thaddeus was wet and hungry and he found Morgan's offer tempting, but he was anxious to talk to Luke and won-dered if he should go straight back to Christie's. On the other hand, Thaddeus supposed, he could scarcely share his suspi-cions about Christie at the man's own supper table. And there was no guarantee that Luke would even be there, now that he'd found friends in the city. Perhaps it was better to take his welcome where it was surest. He followed Morgan into the lodge and was met with broad smiles from both Sally and the mob of identical children.

Chapter 18

"You've been avoiding us, Dr. Lewis. I hope we haven't offended you in any way." Lavinia poured a cup of tea into a thin porcelain cup. Luke expected her to hand it to him, but instead she took it herself and settled back into her chair, leaving him standing across the table from her. Like a servant, he thought. Or a supplicant.

Cherub sat in the corner near the shelf of whatnots that Perry had made so much fun of. Her face was in shadow, and he might have missed her altogether had it not been that the whites of her eyes flashed as he entered the room.

"I've been very busy," he said in response to Lavinia's question. "There was an outbreak of typhoid in Yorkville and it was all Dr. Christie and I could do to keep up with it."

"Yes, I heard there was a great deal of illness around this summer. However, the contagion appears to have passed on. And you seem to have no difficulty finding time to spend with Perry Biddulph."

Luke's stomach instantly turned into a queasy mass. There was the threat. Now what was the price?

"You know, Luke, I was intrigued when I first met you," Lavinia went on. "I always find that doctors are fascinating people to know, and you're such a good-looking one." She reached forward to extract another cube of sugar from the silver bowl in front of her. "And then I met Dr. Christie, who struck me as an extremely interesting man indeed." She slowly stirred the sugar into her tea. "When he first came barging into the parlour wearing that incredibly fouled apron, I was convinced that he was a *useful* physician, if you know what I mean. Alas, I've since discovered that this is not the case. Your Dr. Christie is nearly as upright as he appears, although he does have a habit of bilking his well-to-do patients."

It took Luke a moment to understand what was implied by the word *useful*, but then he realized that Christie's appearance that day must have seemed extremely suspicious. There were some doctors, he knew, who could be persuaded to help a young girl out of a predicament. There were some doctors who made a practice of it. Christie was not one of these. No stream of women appeared at his office door. No patient was ever shown into the back part of the house, to emerge white-faced and shaky a few hours later. And then it occurred to him to question how someone like Lavinia Van Hansel would even know about what some girls asked of doctors.

She was looking at him with amusement. "You're wondering how I have knowledge of such things."

"Well, yes. I mean, you're the respectable wife of a ... businessman. I'm surprised you've even heard of it."

She took a sip of her tea, and savoured it for a moment before she replied. "It's like this, Luke. Since I know your secrets, I'm sure it will do no harm to share a few of mine."

Is that what she wants? Luke thought. *A tame doctor? Somewhere to send whores when Fowler's Solution fails them?* He felt sick. This was worse than anything he had imagined.

But what she said next surprised him. "First of all, you should know that I absolutely detest my husband."

"But ... you're married to him."

"Wives often detest their husbands. And there's rather a lot about Phillip to detest."

"Why did you marry him then? Or did you not find out about him until after?" Marry in haste, repent at leisure was the old adage, and the thing about old adages, Luke knew, was that there was often good advice in them.

"Oh no, I knew all about him, and so did my father." She set her teacup down on the table and looked at him squarely.

"It's a long, sad tale, and one that is repeated all too often. My grandfather made a great deal of money. My father managed to lose it all in a number of distinctly *un*enterprising enterprises. Best way out of the mess, of course, is to auction the daughter to the highest bidder."

"Even though your father knew Van Hansel was a thug?" Luke wanted to call the insult back as soon as he uttered it, but Lavinia seemed to take no offence to it.

"He was a thug with money. Make no mistake, Luke, I was bought and sold every bit as much as Cherub would have been had you not rescued her that day." Her thin eyebrows arched. "However, I am surprised that you know about Phillip. I thought he covered his tracks more effectively than that."

"It's a long story," Luke said. "And no slight intended, but what is he getting out of your father's arrangement? I suspect he has plenty of women, if that's what he wants."

Lavinia poured herself a second cup of tea. "Respectability. Introduction to the proper circles. A way to make a connection with old money." She shrugged. "We weren't precisely top of the heap, you understand, but father did know a few people. None of whom would ever let their daughters within fifty feet of Phillip Van Hansel if they could help it. I was the best he could do in the patronage game."

"And you went along with it?"

"Yes, I did what my father wanted. What choice did I have? But I made it my business to find out everything I could about Phillip's business. I know all about the brothels and the bribery and the fraud. The blackmail. The violence and intimidation. I can't quite prove murder, but I have no doubt that it happened. I know everything there is to know about my husband except for one thing. I don't know where he's hidden his money. And I need money, Luke, so I can get away from him."

"I have no money. I can't help you."

"I know that," she said with a wave of her hand. "It's my husband's money I want. I've earned it." And just for a moment bitter lines showed around her rosebud mouth.

"Can't you just divorce him?" Divorce was uncommon, but Luke had heard of a few cases where marriages had been dissolved.

Lavinia sighed. "That's not an easy thing to do in this country. It requires an act of parliament. One must prove cruelty or abandonment, and of course the personal lives of both parties are laid bare for the entire legislature to see — and for the public to read about in the newspapers."

"Wouldn't that be a good way to get at him? Let everyone know what he is?"

"Let's just say that it wouldn't serve either of our interests. It's easier in the States — they actually have a divorce law — and that's where most people go. But I wouldn't be able to take Cherub with me. She was nearly snatched off the streets of Toronto. She wouldn't last long on the streets of New York. And I won't leave her here where Phillip can get at her. He has a long reach — and a grudgeful nature."

Hands doesn't like it when he's crossed. The steamer captain had said that in Kingston. And so had the Irish girl who had been so desperate to get away from him. Luke had no difficulty believing it.

"Besides," Lavinia went on, "at the end of it all I'd be left with nothing. A man's property is his own. A wife has little claim on it."

"I'm very sorry for your difficulties," Luke said, "but I don't understand what it is you want from me."

"I didn't understand it myself for the longest time. You just sort of turned up, and I thought I'd wait to see how you could make yourself useful. But then you disappeared again."

"I was aware of your husband's activities, and I must confess they made me extremely uneasy. I thought it best if I didn't pursue our acquaintanceship."

Her lip curled a little. "Really? So your reluctance to exploit a friendship with the Van Hansels was on the basis of moral misgivings? Rather ironic for a molly."

The epithet stung, but in a way helped Luke, because it made him angry. If Lavinia could be blunt, so could he.

"When I first met you I didn't know that your husband's name was Van Hansel," he said. "I knew him only as Hands. It wasn't until the night of your party that I realized who I was dealing with. And I had good reason to avoid meeting him again."

"So that's why you left through the garden doors," Lavinia said. "And here I thought it was love at first sight. Perry's been a bit of a disappointment, you know, in spite of the fact that he's a Biddulph. Of course, I didn't realize when I first met him that he was such a naughty little black sheep."

So Perry hadn't set him up after all, if Lavinia's words were to be believed. She'd noticed Luke follow Perry into the garden, but she hadn't engineered it. Luke's accusation had been completely and contemptibly wrong.

"Leave Perry out of it," he said. "What do you want?"

Her eyes widened in mock surprise. "Oh, so you *are* in love. Lucky Perry." She set her teacup down and leaned forward in a confiding pose. "You have to understand about Phillip. He trusts no one. Not even me. And especially not banks. He found himself in a bit of trouble a few years ago. He'd perpetrated a fraud in connection with the fever hospital."

"By doubling up on the bodies that went in coffins," Luke said. "Someone at the hospital was claiming a per diem payment for patients who had long since died."

Lavinia's eyes narrowed. "You really do know a great deal about him, don't you? No wonder you wanted nothing to do with us."

Cherub spoke for the first time since Luke had entered the room. "Be careful," she said in a soft voice. "You have no idea what danger you're in."

Lavinia ignored her. "Since you already know the whys and wherefores, you'll also know that Anthony Hawke was appointed to investigate the matter. Hawke is like a bulldog when he has a job to do. Phillip was sure the trail would lead to him. He was in a panic. So he buried his money where he thought no one would ever look for it."

"With the double bodies in the coffins?" Luke guessed. "But now that the trouble's blown over, he's started to retrieve it." That would explain the disturbance at St. James-the-Lesser, he realized, but what about at the Strangers' Burying Ground? There were only single bodies there.

Lavinia confirmed his guess. "Yes, he's digging it all up again. The government is guaranteeing the return on railroad bonds. There's a large fortune to be made, if you have a small fortune to begin with. He's borrowed as much as he can, but it's not enough. He needs every cent he can lay his hands on. That's why he's moving so fast, taking chances. He's grown careless. So careless that he left a book where I could find it. I made a copy."

She pulled a small green account book from the folds of her dress.

"But the majority of the fever victims at the hospital would have been taken to the Catholic cemetery at St. Paul's," Luke said. "And a lot of them would have been buried all at once, in mass graves. He wouldn't be able to get at those very easily." That was the way it had happened in Kingston. There was no reason to believe that it would have been any different in Toronto.

"As far as I can tell he didn't use St. Paul's to hide his money," Lavinia said. "He chose other places instead. Some of them are double burials, some of them aren't. But every grave contains an emigrant, or an indigent, or a person with no family. They're all people nobody cared about. There would be no one to complain if the body was disturbed later, you see. No one to raise an alarm or demand an investigation."

No one but Morgan Spicer, Luke thought.

"He must have reasoned that he could retrieve his money over time, and that the disturbances would be attributed to vandals or resurrection men. He didn't anticipate that he would ever need it all at once." She handed him the book. "See what you can make of it."

Luke opened the book. There were only a few pages with writing on them, but a few pages were enough. He was astounded at the amounts listed. He had thought that each grave might contain a small bag of notes and coins — pounds and shillings — none of it amounting to more than a few hundred. The book detailed thousands and thousands in British pounds sterling and American dollars. He could decipher the initials Van Hansel used to denote some of the cemeteries — *SJ* was obviously St. James-the-Lesser; *M* was probably Methodist, although there was no indication of which particular Methodist cemetery was being referenced. And yes, there was *SB* — Strangers' Burying Ground — but he realized that he could understand the code only because he already knew what some of the letters referred to. Otherwise they were meaningless. He could only guess at the other initials that had been inked in beside each entry. He pointed to one that had an *E* beside it.

"Does this mean 'Emigrant'?" he asked.

"I think it must. And I think *V* is for vagrant. *W* is for whore."

"And *M*?"

"Molly, I expect. I just tried to think of every variety of outcast I could and guessed it from there."

Luke winced a little at the term *outcast*, but he couldn't fault her reasoning.

"The trouble is," she went on, "even if you know what the letters stand for, there's no indication of where to go from there. The book tells me where and how many and how much, but it doesn't tell me how to find the individual graves. There's some other part of his code that isn't in the book."

"And you thought that Perry could help you figure out where the mollies are?"

She shrugged. "I thought there might be some clue in Wood's Bush. Or he might hear something at one of the taverns he goes to. He's been singularly unsuccessful."

Luke was a loss. "How do you think I can help you with this, if Perry can't? I'm not nearly as connected in the city as he is. I've been here only a short time."

"You live in Yorkville. Manufacture some excuse to get a look at the records at the Burying Ground. See if there's a clue there."

Luke already knew there wasn't, or his father would surely have mentioned it. He stopped himself from blurting this out just in time. There was no point in giving his hand away.

"And don't wait too long," Lavinia said. "Phillip will be back for the rest of his money sooner rather than later. This is my best chance, Luke. Otherwise Cherub and I will never get away. I need you to find a way to get to the money."

"I see," he said. "And if I don't, you'll tell Dr. Christie all about me, is that it?"

"Well, of course I will," she said in a low voice. "And I'll do worse besides. I'll take Perry down with you."

* * *

Luke decided to start walking back to Yorkville, in spite of the fact that there was a fine mizzle in the air and that he had already been gone far too long. He needed the time to think through the bizarre conversation with Lavinia Van Hansel. His mind was in turmoil with the implications of what she had told him and what she had asked him to do. Her message was clear: figure it out, or both he and Perry would be dragged into the dirt. Maybe even end up in prison. *So you are in love*, Lavinia had sneered. Luke had thrown away any chance at that, but maybe he could at least manage to keep poor, feckless Perry from drowning in the mud.

And what would Luke himself do if he failed to deliver? He didn't know. But even more to the point, what would Hands do if he found out what his wife was up to? And that the Lewises were within such easy reach? *Hands doesn't like it when he's crossed. He'd hunt me down to the ends of the earth.* Lavinia was threatening exposure. She couldn't know that for Luke the stakes were far higher than that.

He was nearly at the city limits when one particular of her conversation struck him. At no point had she mentioned Thaddeus. This thought was enough to make him halt suddenly, with the result that a young woman carrying a basket of vegetables nearly fell in an attempt to avoid the suddenly stationary object in her path. He apologized profusely, but she only glared at him and went on.

He began walking again, slowly. Was it possible that Lavinia didn't know about Thaddeus? He supposed it was. Thaddeus was off on his circuit most of the time. He usually stayed at Christie's for only a day or two until he set off again. Even if Cherub had been sent to spy on Luke, her timing would have to be precise for her to realize that there was an extra occupant in the Christie house. And if Lavinia didn't know, Hands couldn't find out.

He felt a little better with this realization. At least he could be fairly certain that his father was in no danger, but how strange it was that Morgan Spicer's puzzle had led them straight into the very situation that Luke and Thaddeus wanted so badly to avoid. Luke was sure that solving the mystery at the Burying Ground was nothing more than an intellectual exercise for Thaddeus, a way to use his powers of observation and deductive reasoning as an antidote to the frustrating task of ministering to an unrewarding circuit. As a result Luke had not paid much attention to his efforts. In fact, he'd barely spoken to his father about it. The little he did know had come from casual mealtime conversations. Now he wondered if his father had uncovered anything that would prove useful to Lavinia. He needed to talk to Thaddeus.

Feeling easier in his mind now that he had determined a course of action, Luke boarded an omnibus that took him the rest of the way to Yorkville. Just as he disembarked at the main intersection the skies opened and the rain began to fall heavily. He ran for the nearby Keeper's Lodge, hoping he could wait out the downpour there.

"Oh, your father's in the kitchen," Sally said when she answered his knock. "Come in out of the rain. Please, come back to the kitchen and have a seat." She shooed a twin off one of the stools that had been pulled up to the table.

"Oh good," Thaddeus said, when he saw who it was. "We need to talk to you."

"And I to you." Luke's eyes slid over to Morgan, who was looking even more unkempt and weedy than ever. Of course, Thaddeus said he had been staying up at night keeping a watch over the cemetery. "I'm not sure where to start."

"First things first," Sally said. "Would you care for a cup of tea?"

"That would be grand, thanks, Mrs. Spicer. I hope my father hasn't drunk up all your supply."

"He's paid for it with his good company," she returned.

And then, while he idly watched Sally refill the kettle at the kitchen pump, he found himself asking, "Where do you get your water, by the way?"

She looked puzzled. "A carter fills up the cistern every month or so. It comes with the house."

"Forgive my curiosity. I'm just trying to figure out what caused all the sickness we've had." The mind is an astounding thing, he thought. In spite of everything else he had to think about, it was still grappling with the question of what caused the typhoid outbreak in Yorkville.

"Our water must be fine," Sally said. "None of us fell ill."

Luke tucked this piece of information away to puzzle over later and returned to marshalling his thoughts into something coherent to say to his father.

Thaddeus jumped in before he could get the first word out. "I need to talk to you about Christie. I think he may have something to do with the graves being opened."

Sally frowned at him, indicating the children with a nod of her head.

"Matthew, Mark, Ruth, Rebecca, I think you should go play in the parlour now," Morgan said.

One of the girls removed her thumb from her mouth. "But we want to play with Mr. Lewis," she said.

"Go on now," Sally said. "Do what your father says. You can look at the big Bible with the pictures in it if you like."

The twins crowded down the hall. Looking at a picture book was evidently a great treat.

"Remind me to bring some books down from Christie's for them," Thaddeus said to Luke. "He's got more than he knows what to do with. I'm sure he won't mind if I borrow a few."

"I'm sure it would be fine," Luke said. He was grateful for the interruption in the conversation. He'd forgotten that he, too, had briefly, if not seriously, wondered if Christie was involved. But he wasn't sure how to respond to his father's statement.

"I went through to the kitchen, to get something to eat," Thaddeus went on as soon as he was sure the children were out of earshot. "There was a skinned marten carcass on the table. Mrs. Dunphy came in while I was there, but she didn't seem to think there was anything out of the ordinary about it. She told me he boils things down, for the bones."

"Well, that would explain the fumes that stink up the house sometimes," Luke said. "But I can't imagine that he would go so far as to exhume bodies just to get bones."

"But what about the skeleton in the consulting room? Where did that come from?"

"He's had it for years. He got it in Edinburgh."

"Are skeletons things that are easy to come by there?" Morgan asked.

"Well, no," Luke replied. "He did boil it down himself, but he told me that he took it from the medical school. It had already been well-dissected and they were done with it."

"Well, there you go," Thaddeus said. "He obviously has no qualms about working with old bodies."

"But if he boils down old bodies, what's he doing with the bones?" Morgan asked.

"Maybe he wires them together like the one in the office and sells them," Thaddeus said. "He can't be the only doctor who wants a skeleton. And he's always complaining about money."

Luke hadn't expected to defend Christie. The old doctor's activities might be very strange in nature, but they had nothing to do with what was happening at the Strangers' Burying Ground. But Luke could think of no way of convincing Thaddeus of Christie's innocence without disclosing his source. Finally he said, "I really don't think it was Christie. How would he have managed it? And he hates leaving the house."

"We're working on a theory that Mrs. Dunphy is involved," Morgan said.

"She is rather a large woman," Thaddeus pointed out. "She could easily be mistaken for a man, especially if she dressed as one. It wouldn't be the first time we know of that someone has masqueraded as the opposite gender."

"But …" Luke said. He was desperate to turn this conversation away from the preposterous notion of Christie as grave robber and toward any other clues that Thaddeus had uncovered, but Spicer and his father had seized on their explanation with far too much enthusiasm to let it go easily. "I'm sure it's not Christie," Luke said again. "Have you found any other avenues to explore? You were off to see the coffin at St. James-the-Lesser, if I remember correctly."

"Ah yes, the double burial," Thaddeus said. "Well, we know who's responsible for that, don't we? We went over to the cemetery at St. Paul's as well, but we found nothing that would tie the gentleman in question to the disturbances that took place here."

Luke's eyes widened at the casual, albeit anonymous mention of Hands in front of Spicer. Thaddeus noticed his look.

"Oh, it's all right. I filled Morgan in on the general thrust of the story. And as it turns out, there's little evidence that the man is involved anyway."

"I'm not so sure," Luke said. "I don't understand who else could be bothered to dig up the double graves."

"But that doesn't explain what's been happening here," Morgan said. "My bodies were buried by the county and there's only one in each grave. Unless …" he stopped for a moment to think and then he said, "unless the coffins came from the same place and that's the connection."

"Who has the contract to supply coffins to York County?"

"Several of the cabinetmakers. It depends on where the bodies are coming from. Sometimes it's Williams, sometimes it's Striker and Plews. Other times it's Fraser and Hess."

"We followed the wagon to a cabinetmaker's that night," Luke said to Thaddeus. "Wasn't the name on the gate Fraser and Hess?"

"It was somebody and somebody," Thaddeus said, his eyes narrowing as he tried to recall the sign.

"So if all of the coffins in question were supplied by Fraser and Hess, wouldn't that point to …"

"Our nefarious friend," Thaddeus said quickly. Luke understood that he had protected the Spicers by not supplying the identities that went with the story, but he was getting dizzy from trying to express his thoughts without using names or giving anything away. He hoped that his question about coffin supply would result in another look at the cemetery ledger. Armed with the knowledge of who was responsible, he might find some clue as to which graves had been targeted.

His hopes were dashed when Morgan said, "There's no mention in the records of where the bodies came from, much less the coffins. I'm sure there's a record of contracts, but that's the sort of thing that's handled by the Board of Trustees."

"Is there any way you could ask them?"

"I'm not sure it would help us much," Thaddeus said. "Even if we tie the bodies here to the double burial at James-the-Lesser, there's still nothing to tell us why they're now being dug up."

"Didn't the man at the African church — Mr. Finch — say that Isaiah Marshall was a carpenter?" Morgan said. "I wonder if he worked for Fraser and Hess."

"Yes, he did say that. He also said that Marshall kept to himself. And there was something else about him that Finch didn't want to tell us."

"Maybe … our friend … was hiding something besides bodies. And maybe Marshall helped him hide it," Luke said. "And whatever it was, the gentleman in question needs to get it back."

Thaddeus thought about this for a moment, then shook his head. "No, I don't see it. The beauty of putting extra bodies in the coffins is that no one would ever be likely to unearth them. He'd never be found out."

"But that would be true for anything else he wanted to hide, wouldn't it?" Morgan said. "And it would explain why he had no interest in the bodies themselves."

"But not why he suddenly decided to open all these graves. Even if there was something else hidden in the coffins, something that he now wants to retrieve, it would be incredibly foolish to dig so many up over such a short period of time. One grave now and then is easily attributable to resurrectionists. Three graves in a handful of weeks is bound to attract someone's attention."

"But only yours and mine," Morgan pointed out. "And yours only because I told you about it. The constable I spoke to wasn't concerned at all. And I wrote a letter to the Board of Trustees, but I haven't heard a thing from any of them. It hasn't attracted much attention at all."

"That's true," Thaddeus admitted. "You may have something there. So where does that leave us?"

"It's either a criminal conspiracy, or Dr. Christie has lost his mind," Morgan said.

"I still think Christie makes the most sense. It's the simplest explanation. And after all, he offered to write to his colleague at the hospital, but we haven't heard a word. I'm wondering now if he even sent the letter."

It was time to put paid to the Christie theory, Luke decided. That was the only way he would ever be able to get his father to focus on Hands.

"I don't agree with you," Luke said. "I don't think it's Christie at all. And I'll prove it."

Thaddeus looked at him with surprise. "How will you do that?"

"I'll ask him."

Chapter 19

There was no point in taking anything but a direct approach. Luke knew that it would be impossible for him to get into the back of the house undetected. Now that his presence was no longer required to see to patients, Christie again spent most of his day either in the dining room or somewhere in the kitchen regions. There was also Mrs. Dunphy to dodge. Other than the times she dumped plates of food on the table, Luke seldom saw her, and he assumed that she spent the bulk of her time in the kitchen — this was confirmed on several occasions when he heard her voice in admonishment to something Christie had shouted at her. Only occasionally would he run across her in another part of the house, duster or broom in hand. There was little likelihood of there being a time when Christie was absent while Mrs. Dunphy was cleaning.

But armed with the knowledge that, whatever Christie was doing, it had nothing to do with the events at the Burying Ground, Luke saw no reason why he shouldn't just walk into the kitchen and see for himself. All he needed was an excuse to seek Christie out. Thaddeus wanted books for the Spicer twins. Luke would make an appropriate selection or two from Christie's shelves and ask to borrow them.

The next morning he dawdled at his breakfast and then made an excuse to go back upstairs where he waited until he heard Christie and Thaddeus get up from the table. Coming back downstairs again he passed Mrs. Dunphy, who had her broom and duster in hand. Just as well to have her out of the way, Luke thought, although his father said that she seemed unconcerned about his discovery of the marten on the kitchen table.

He walked through the dining room to the parlour. He would be unlikely to find any books that were specifically for children on the shelves, but he knew that there were numerous volumes put out by the Edinburgh Cabinet Library. He had read a number of them himself, particularly enjoying the tales of polar exploration and an account of the travels of Marco Polo.

Thaddeus was sitting in the parlour, staring at a piece of paper.

"It appears that Dr. Christie wrote to his colleague after all," he said when Luke appeared at the door. He waved the letter he held in his hand. "This came in the morning mail. It confirms that both Abraham Jenkins and Isaiah Marshall died in hospital and that both their bodies were sent for dissection when no one claimed them. There's not much information beyond that. I'm not sure that it helps much."

"It helps exonerate Christie," Luke pointed out. "And I intend to clear him entirely."

He ran his finger along the spines of books, head tilted to read the titles. Halfway along the row he found *Lives and Voyages of Drake, Cavendish and Dampier, Including a History of the Buccaneers*. Perfect. The twins could play at swashbuckling pirates. And then he found another small volume tucked behind two of the adjacent books: *The Tales of Aesop*. The perfect moral counter to rapine on the high seas.

"I'll ask if you can take these to the Spicers," he said to Thaddeus. "Wait here and I'll fill you in on what I find."

Books in hand, Luke walked through to the kitchen, but to his surprise there was no sign of Christie. There was no tell-tale carcass on the table, either, although the trace of a musky smell lingered in the room.

He opened a door to his right. It was the pantry, full of jars of preserves and vegetables set on racks. He returned to the kitchen. There was another door to his left, but he knew that it led to the office. It was this door that Christie had burst through the day Luke had been so immersed in a book that he hadn't heard the Holden boy knocking. There was a third door on the rear wall, which under ordinary circumstances he would have assumed led to the large lean-to woodshed at the rear of the house, and beyond that to the small yard outside. The shed was no longer needed for wood, he knew, since Christie had switched to coal, the fuel delivered once a month by a rumbling cart that dumped its black load directly into the cellar through a ground-floor hatch. He opened the door. The use to which Christie had converted his shed was astonishing.

The room was full of bones. Not bones like the ones that had been disturbed at the Strangers' Burying Ground, stained and worn from their time in the earth. These bones were uniformly white and carefully reassembled, their relationships charted, their joint articulations noted and recreated, and then displayed as if the flesh and muscle had magically melted away, the organs banished and the fundamental nature of each animal laid bare. He recognized a rat, a frog, a rabbit. A bird, which from its size Luke knew must be an eagle, perched on a rafter, its wings spread wide. A tiny turtle skeleton clung to its shell, the long spine of a snake spread its S shape across a polished wooden board; a bat hung from wires in the ceiling, the leathery wings gone, only the elongated fingers spread out as if it were in mid-flight. Each animal had been meticulously pared down to its essential being, its identity evident at a glance, but minus the fur and the skin and the sinew that masked its structure.

Evident in all but one case, that is. One skeleton was only half-assembled, its head attached to its backbone, but a wooden packing case had been substituted for its hindquarters. It was impossible at this juncture to tell what it was, except that Luke felt that there was something familiar in the way the back curved, something recognizable in the head, even though the teeth had not yet been returned to the jaw.

"It's a pig," said a voice from over by the large window that had been set into the back wall of the shed. Luke whirled to find Dr. Christie smiling out from behind an easel. "Hard to tell when they're only half put together, isn't it? Believe it or not, domestic animals are harder to come by than wild ones. Hunters and trappers often bring me carcasses, but pigs go straight to the butcher. I was lucky that this one sickened and died of something-or-other first. The butcher said it wasn't fit to eat."

"I'm sorry to intrude," Luke said, "but I wondered if I could borrow these books for the Spicer twins."

"Of course," Christie said. "And it's no intrusion, no intrusion at all. If I'd known you were interested, I'd have shown you long since. Fascinating hobby, the putting together of bones. You learn so much. Started with old Mul-Sack, been going ever since, whenever I got the time."

Luke walked over to the hanging bat. "It's incredible, isn't it?" he said. "The bones look like fingers."

Christie beamed. "They do, don't they? Nature is a wondrous thing. It was delicate work, getting them down correctly. Tell me what you think of the finished product." He nodded toward a workbench that ran along one side of the shed. "I did it recently. It should be at the top."

Puzzled, Luke walked over to a pile of large papers that were stacked neatly on one corner of the bench. He selected the topmost and turned it over, and there was the bat, its skeletal remains faithfully depicted in pen and ink. It was a fastidious work, each articulation clear, each small joint transcribed. In spite of the fact that flesh and muscle were absent, it looked to Luke as though it could fly off the page.

He turned over the next paper and there was the turtle, then the snake, the rabbit, and all the other animals that had been boiled to bone.

"These are beautiful," he said.

"I rather think the rabbit is a bit of a failure. I didn't get her back together in quite the right way. Didn't really capture the way she moves. I'll have another go at it. They're easy enough to come by."

"But…." Luke wasn't sure what he wanted to say. Why seemed a foolish thing to ask. He could understand why. He had the same fascination with the structures that lay under the flesh. It was the reason, really, that he decided to become a doctor.

"I know, it seems a very odd occupation, doesn't it? But I've been fascinated for years. I'm trying to convince myself that the sketches are good enough to be published some day, perhaps in a folio or some such arrangement."

"I would be fascinated by such a book," Luke said.

"Really? Do you think so? Very kind of you to say. More success with the actual bones, I think, than with the illustrations. The trick, of course, is not to over-boil the carcasses.

They can sometimes turn to mush. And then, of course, I like to whiten them up with magnesium carbonate before I put them back together again. Makes a nicer display, I think, and helps disperse any oil still left in them."

"I wondered why you asked me to get such a large supply from the apothecary."

"Oh yes, I suppose I should have explained," Christie said. "Had you asked, I would have. But you didn't seem very curious, not even about poor old Mul-Sack, so I didn't pursue it."

Mul-Sack and Aniseed Robin. His intention in seeking out Christie had been to prove that he was no grave robber, but maybe Luke could discover the significance of the highwayman's story as well. He willed his hands not to shake.

"To tell you the truth," he said, "Mul-Sack kind of bothers me."

"What? Really? Oh, my dear boy, he's not there to bother you. He's there to bother me."

"I'm not sure what you mean."

Christie stared at Luke for a moment, then seemed to make up his mind to speak. "I'm glad you came in here this morning, Luke. There's something I've been meaning to talk to you about for some time, but I wasn't just sure how to approach it. Bit of a delicate subject, if you know what I mean."

Luke's hands seemed to have taken on a life of their own. He placed the illustrations back on the bench so the shaking wouldn't be so noticeable.

Christie sighed. "I don't tell many people this story, and it's painful for me to talk about it, but I think you'll understand when you hear it. Mrs. Dunphy is my cousin, you know. She very kindly came here to look after my household when my dear wife died. Flora — Mrs. Dunphy that is — had a younger brother, Alan. The Gods must have been in a jocular mood when they created Alan and Flora. You may have noticed, Luke, that she is rather an unprepossessing woman — no, much as I love her, it's true," he said when Luke made a polite sound of disagreement. "And as big and clumsy and homely as poor Flora is, Alan was her opposite: handsome and graceful and full of life. We all grew up together. They were my brother and sister, in my eyes. As he grew into a man, Alan was coveted by every young woman who met him, but it was impossible to be put out by this because he was such a modest and good-natured chap. And, as it turned out, he hadn't the least interest in girls."

Luke thought he was going to be sick. He clenched the side of the bench with both hands and bowed his head so that he could catch a breath.

Christie appeared not to notice. "I never gave it much thought until he came to the university. I was older and occupied with my studies. I didn't look after him as I should have. He was found out one night and his fellow students stripped him naked and doused him in a cattle trough — harmless enough, I suppose, though humiliating. But his life was a misery from that night on. Everywhere he went he was sniggered at and whispered about. His professors would barely acknowledge his existence. A couple of times he was caught by some of the ruffians in the town and beaten rather badly. It was too much for him."

"What happened?" Luke's question was a whisper. He already knew what had happened.

"I did nothing," Christie went on. "I was afraid that the taint would rub off on me. I had only a year and a bit to finish my studies and I thought that if anyone knew that Alan was my cousin, I, too, would be beaten in the town and shunned at the university. So I ignored him. And then one night he went to his rooms and hanged himself. A month later I acquired Mul-Sack. I boiled him down and put his bones back together in such a way that he would always remind me that bigotry can only lead to a bad end. But most of all I keep him around to remind me of my own treachery."

"The pointing finger," Luke said. "I thought it was pointing at me."

"Really? Oh, I am sorry. I didn't realize you would take it that way. But don't worry, I know all about you."

Luke willed himself to keep breathing while he waited for Christie's next words.

"I've known from the start," Christie said. "Your Professor Brown, at the university, was no friend to you. When you expressed an interest in joining this practice he wrote me a rather nasty letter. He claimed that you were unsuitable for the position due to your suspect morals, and that it was well known in the city that you were in an unnatural relationship with a local bookseller. He did his very best to scuttle your career before it even started."

It had been a mistake to call in Brown. Luke had known it at the time, but he had been so distraught over Ben that he would have done anything to try to save him.

"As soon as I received that letter, I decided that you were the one I wanted. You were by no means the most qualified applicant. Some of your classmates had sterling recommendations and far better marks. But I took it as an opportunity to atone, at least a little, for what I failed to do for Alan."

Luke was astonished. He didn't know what to say. Finally he stammered out an almost inaudible and completely inadequate "Thank you."

"Oh, it's nothing to do with you, boy, although I must admit that so far I'm not sorry about my choice. I've been watching you. You've proved yourself to be a good doctor. People like you. No, the thing that really decided it was the way Brown did his filthy business behind your back. Cowards like that should be hanged."

This last, ludicrously typical addendum to the most generous thing anyone had ever done for him released a torrent of pent-up tension and anxiety in Luke. He began to laugh, and he couldn't stop it, any more than he had ever been able to control the shaking of his hands.

Christie looked at him with puzzlement.

"I'm sorry," Luke said. "I just didn't expect this. Do you want to know why I came in here this morning? Because my father thinks that you're the one who has been digging up the graves at the Burying Ground. I said I'd prove him wrong, but I didn't know that he was as wrong as it's possible to be."

"Me? He thought it was me?"

"Aided and abetted by Mrs. Dunphy, dressed as a man."

Christie began to laugh then, too. "Brilliant!" he said. "Flora dressed up as a bone digger. Oh my goodness, the mental image that conjures up is priceless." Then he subsided somewhat and added, "You mustn't ever tell her. She's all too aware that she's an ugly duckling."

"I won't breathe a word," Luke promised.

"Yes, I think enough has been said on all counts, don't you? We both know where we stand. Now, are you going to hang around here all morning or do you have some patients to see?"

Luke smiled. "I'll leave you to it."

But just as he reached the door, Christie spoke again. "Mind you, what you do about telling your father is up to you." And then he settled himself happily at the easel again, humming a tune to himself, off-key and punctuated by the occasional "dum-de-de-dum."

* * *

Thaddeus was in the dining room pretending to read a newspaper. He looked up when Luke came from the kitchen.

"Well?" he whispered.

"It's not Christie," Luke said. "Go see for yourself." And then he grabbed his leather satchel and walked out the door, leaving Thaddeus sitting open-mouthed at the table.

Chapter 20

It had been grey and cloudy, threatening rain all day, and that evening, just as Mrs. Dunphy served up a plate of sausages and fried potatoes, Luke heard a patter against the window as a sprinkle of raindrops began to fall. As he reached for a sausage, his father said "I think I should go to the Burying Ground tonight."

"Do you have some sort of presentiment or something?" Luke asked.

"No. It's just that there's a half-moon tonight, and it's cloudy. I'd like to test my lunar cycle theory."

"It's more than cloudy," Luke said. "It's actively raining."

Thaddeus looked unconcerned. "Oh, don't worry, this is just a shower. It'll clear up later."

"Maybe I'll come with you," Luke said. He would tag along with his father and try to get a look at the cemetery ledger, although neither Thaddeus nor Morgan Spicer seemed to think that there was anything to see other than the simple recording of burials.

"The more the merrier," Thaddeus said. He looked pleased. "Would you like to come along as well, sir?" he said to Dr. Christie.

"Oh, I shouldn't think so," Christie said. "Don't fancy standing around in the rain. Unless, of course, another grave is dug up in spite of your efforts. If that occurs, you might come and get me so I can have a look."

"I think one human skeleton is enough for anybody."

"Oh, don't worry, I don't intend to spirit it away. I just want to look. I've always felt that I didn't get the shoulder articulation quite right on poor old Mul-Sack."

"We'll let you know," Luke said. It was amazing how much more comfortable he felt with Christie after their startling conversation among the bones. He had been shy about joining the mealtime banter before. Now he felt perfectly at ease with it. Part of the reason, he realized, was that the most worrying of his problems was resolved. He could disregard Lavinia's threat, at least as far as he was personally concerned. He felt, for the first time, that he had the advantage in the situation, and he was determined to use it, somehow, to extricate Perry. Luke once again felt a stab of guilt and regret at the accusation he had made, but he could see no clear way to undo it. He could only, like Christie, atone after the fact.

Thaddeus was correct in his weather prediction. By the time they were ready to leave, the rain had stopped, although the sky was still dark and cloudy. They were only a few steps down the street when Luke saw Andrew Holden limping toward them. He grinned when he saw Luke.

"Oh look, it's the quack out for an evening stroll."

Thaddeus looked surprised at the flippancy of the greeting, but Luke grinned at Holden in return. "Andrew Holden, this is my father, Thaddeus Lewis."

"Pleased to meet you, sir. I'd shake your hand, but mine got a little muddy finding this fellow." He showed them what he was carrying. It was a dead salamander, quite a large one, blue-black with irregular splotches of yellow splashed across its back and tail.

"It's beautiful," Luke said. "Where did you get it?"

"Down by the brewery pond," Holden said. "He was lying in some brush. I reckon a hawk or something got him and then dropped him. He was already dead when I found him."

"You're not going to eat him, are you? Salamander stew for supper?"

"Hmmm, I hadn't thought of that. But I reckon he's not too tasty. I'll take him to Christie instead."

"Do you supply Dr. Christie with a lot of animals?" Thaddeus asked.

"We all do," Holden said, "but it's getting harder to find things he'll pay for. He never wants the same thing twice. I sold him a big bullfrog in the spring, but then it got so dry everything disappeared. I spent a lot of time grubbing around in the pond looking for things, but all I got was muddy."

"Glad to hear that business has picked up," Luke said. "And you'll make Christie's day with that fellow."

"Your Dr. Christie certainly has a fascination with bones, doesn't he?" Thaddeus said when they had walked on.

"He probably should have been a surgeon, or a scientist or something, rather than a jack-of-all-trades doctor in a small town," Luke said. "A waste, really. He's so knowledgeable."

"Quite incredible. I've never seen anything like it."

"Did he show you the drawings he made?"

"Yes, and I think his plan to publish them is sound. There's a new interest in the mechanics of how the world works. The Great Exhibition proved that. On the other hand, it's too bad that his pastime is so innocent. Christie as a grave robber would have provided an easy solution to Morgan's puzzle. I'm not sure where this leaves us in terms of finding the culprit. Of course, if it had been Christie, the consequences would have been a bit awkward for you, wouldn't they?"

"To say the least," Luke replied. "And for you, as well. Do you think Mr. Spicer would mind if I had a look at the cemetery ledger?"

"I don't think you'll find anything there," Thaddeus said. "We've been over it and over it."

"I'm sure you have," Luke said. "I don't really expect to find anything. But you never know, sometimes a second eye can pick out something that the first missed." *Especially when the second eye already knew what was going on*, he thought. *Surely there's something there that will lead to the right graves.*

Sally answered the door. "I chased Morgan off to bed already," she said. "The grass has grown up so much with the rain it's taken him three days to cut it. He's about done in. I'll get the twins settled, then I'll come and sit with you."

Thaddeus stopped her as she turned to go. "May we have another look at the ledger while we wait?

"Of course." She went to the cupboard and fetched it down. "I'll be very happy if you manage to find something. I've had enough of this nonsense. Morgan is wearing himself out."

"There you go," Thaddeus said, handing the book to Luke. "Do your worst."

"What was the name of the first one again?" he asked.

"Abraham Jenkins. It's quite a long way in. The records go all the way back to when the cemetery first opened.

Luke flipped forward until he found the name. Date of death, cause of death, date of burial. Nothing more.

"And the second?"

"Isaiah Marshall."

He found it a few entries later. Again, nothing but a few sketchy details of his death. He scanned the names listed between the two. Nothing. He flipped the pages backward. Nothing. He leafed forward a few pages. Nothing. There were no tell-tale initials beside any of the names. Nothing that would tie any of the deaths to the name Van Hansel. Nothing that would tell him where Hands had hidden his fortune. He closed the ledger.

"Well?" Thaddeus said.

"Nothing that I can see." He shrugged. "I thought it might be worth looking." He was disappointed that he could see no clue that his father might have missed, although he supposed he shouldn't be surprised. Morgan and Thaddeus would have searched it thoroughly long since. "So what is your plan? Do we just sit here until something happens?"

"Would you prefer to sit outside in the rain?"

"I don't think it's actually raining anymore. We might stand a better chance of catching someone if we were in the graveyard."

"We might stand a better chance of scaring them off, too," Thaddeus pointed out. "Besides, if anything happens tonight, it won't be until later, when it's dark. It was nearly twelve the night someone tried to get into the cottage."

Luke had forgotten about the attempted break-in at the Keeper's Lodge. It must have been Lavinia, hoping to steal away the ledger. Or more likely Cherub, who seemed willing to do whatever Lavinia asked of her.

"We could take turns watching," Luke said. He knew that as much as Thaddeus was itching to solve the puzzle Morgan had sent his way, he would grumble at sitting in a damp graveyard for hours. "Why don't we go outside now while there's still a little light, and decide on the best place to wait?"

It was as good an excuse as any he could think of to search the graveyard for something that might help Lavinia.

If he found nothing, there was little more he could do. He would have to report that he had done his best and hope it was enough. She had blackmailed Perry, and when he failed, she turned her attention to Luke. If he failed, he could only hope that she would look elsewhere.

"I suppose we could wander around for a while," Thaddeus said, and then his resolve seemed to firm up. "Yes, that makes sense."

They rose from the table and went outside. The rain had stopped and sunlight began to break through the dispersing clouds. Luke stood and surveyed the Burying Ground. Unlike the newer cemeteries there was little shelter, just row after row of graves, shoehorned closely together. There were a few trees growing along the back fence, but other than those, the chapel or the cottage itself were the only features large enough to effectively hide a man.

"Which way do you suppose they'll come, if they come at all?" Luke asked.

"It would make most sense to climb the fence at the back, where the buildings would screen you," Thaddeus said. "Although they did come through the front gates the second time."

"Then this side of the chapel would provide the best shelter. It would hide you no matter which way they came."

"Agreed. Now let's go back inside. You can take the first watch later."

"I'll just look around a bit, then I'll join you."

Thaddeus returned to the cottage. Luke set off down the pathway, making a show of stopping to look around now and again, just in case his father was watching out the window. There wasn't a great deal to see. Here and there a family had put up a marble headstone, but the majority of the markers were plain slabs of granite with the barest of details inscribed on them. He reached a point halfway down the grounds and ambled over to the mound of earth that still lay raw over the Jenkins grave. Morgan had replaced the marker when he reburied the body, but Luke could find nothing that differentiated it from any of the stones beside it. He wandered through the graveyard until he came to Isaiah Marshall's grave.

He could see nothing there that was out of the ordinary either. His investigation appeared to have reached an end. Disappointed, he rounded the row to walk back to the lodge. Just as he turned, a shaft of sunlight briefly lit the back of Marshall's stone, illuminating a small scratch in the granite. It was barely noticeable, just a small mark a few inches from the bottom, something that at first glance could well have been ascribed to the scrape of a shovel. And that would have been hidden by grass before Morgan had ruthlessly scythed it to the ground. Luke bent down for a closer look, and once he saw it clearly, he was astonished that no one had noticed it before. It was a tiny, entwined *O* and *P*. The same mark that was on the doorframes of the taverns Perry had taken him to; the same mark that was a recognized symbol of welcome for men like him. He stood up, then bent to look again. It was unmistakable.

Had Isaiah Marshall been like Luke, a man who had to hide in the shadows? An *outcast*? Marshall had been a carpenter. Had he worked for Fraser and Hess, who in turn worked for Van Hansel? Had Hands known all about Marshall, and used his coffin as a treasury, confident that no one would come questioning if someone were to dig it up one night? It made sense. And how many more like Marshall were buried here?

Luke wanted to run up and down the rows to check the backs of the stones, but mindful that Thaddeus might be watching, he forced himself to move slowly. He couldn't waste too much time, though — the sun was starting to slip below the horizon. It would soon be too dark to see clearly. Then he realized that the old-fashioned layout of the Burying Ground would work to his advantage. The graves were arranged in strict rows, the coffins buried in the order in which they had arrived. Anthony Hawke's investigation into the embezzlement of funds at the Toronto Fever Hospital had begun in 1847, and with no conclusions reached, petered out sometime in 1848. Hands would have no need to hide his money so thoroughly once the investigation drew to a close. Luke need only examine the stones that were planted in 1847 or 1848 in order to discover if there were any more marked graves. And they were all laid out in tidy rows for him.

As he walked from Isaiah Marshall to Abraham Jenkins he looked closely, not at the etched fronts of the markers he passed, but at the backs of the opposite row. Nothing, nothing, nothing ... then another faint scratch. He stopped. This was not the *O* and *P* he had seen before — it was an arrow-like icon. He didn't know what it meant, but, like the other, it seemed to have been deliberately carved. The name on the stone was Amelia Quinn. A female. One of the poor girls who had been forced into a brothel and had died there of disease or despair? It seemed likely.

He found two more like it by the time he reached Abraham Jenkins's grave, and took careful note of the names.

He stooped to examine the back of Jenkins's stone. Here he found a faint squiggled line, a crude representation of a snake or a worm slithering across the ground. It meant nothing to him, but he would wager that it correlated somehow with the list that Lavinia had copied.

Beyond Jenkins, another molly, an additional whore, and two more snakes. Did the symbol stand for vagrant, perhaps? And then the dates on the stones began to read 1849. He stopped walking and counted up the marks he had found.

There were eight in all; eight graves with substantial amounts of money hidden in the coffins. His years of memorizing lists of medicines, of learning the names of organs and bones, and the signs and symptoms of disease stood him in good stead now. He fixed the names and locations of each grave in his mind and repeated the list several times over until he was sure that he could retrieve them at a future date.

But then he wondered if he should retrieve them at all. If he delivered them up to Lavinia, would she really leave Perry alone? Would she and Cherub dig up the money and leave the country, never to be heard of again? Or would she merely present him with another demand, another extortion, another threat? Without doubt, the safest course of action would be to keep the secret to himself. If Hands ever discovered what Lavinia was up to, the trail would lead straight to Yorkville and Thaddeus. Luke would save Perry if he could, but not if it put his father in danger. He would have to do some careful thinking before he did anything at all.

He went back to the lodge where Sally had joined Thaddeus at the table.

"What do you think?" Thaddeus asked.

"I think the best place to wait is by the chapel."

"Agreed. You can go first."

Luke could see that his father had settled comfortably with the teapot. In fact, Thaddeus seemed supremely comfortable with his new pastime of drinking tea in the Spicer kitchen whenever he could. Luke was sorry that he had been so little company for Thaddeus since they'd come to Yorkville. There had been so many difficulties, so many preoccupations. But these were being cleared away, one by one, and Luke resolved that from then on he would make more time for his father. Time was something he would now have with the epidemic over. And with no Perry to distract him.

Sally went to bed at ten. "If anything happens, give a shout," she said. "Morgan will be disappointed if he misses any excitement."

"I'll try, but I can't promise. A shout would warn intruders, as well," Thaddeus pointed out.

"Yes, I suppose it would, wouldn't it?" She sighed. "Poor Morgan, he's been so overwrought by this whole thing. You'd think someone was trying to walk off with one of the twins, the way he's been carrying on."

"We'll do our best to alert him if anything happens," Luke promised.

Shortly after eleven o'clock, Thaddeus dragged his chair over to the window. "I'll watch from here," he said. "You can go outside."

The last thing Luke felt like doing was sitting in the damp grass, but he supposed that having suggested the idea of posting a guard in the graveyard, the least he could do was to play out the charade. He grabbed the old fustian overcoat he had brought with him and walked out to the chapel, hunkering down in the lee of it as best he could. Lavinia said that Hands would be along for his money sooner rather than later, but Luke doubted that anything would happen on the one evening he had decided to lie in wait. He pulled his hat down over his head as far as he could and pushed the collar of his coat up to protect the back of his neck against the damp chill of the August night.

While he waited, his mind wandered around and through the events of the past few days. They had been momentous, on any number of counts. He no longer had to fear that some strange intelligence would reach Dr. Christie's ears and endanger not only his employment, but his future prospects. He had solved Morgan Spicer's puzzle, and Lavinia Van Hansel's as well. Quite by accident, of course, and he could scarcely tell anyone about it or claim the victory, but it was an accomplishment nonetheless. On the other hand, he had once again embroiled himself and his father in the affairs of one of Toronto's most dangerous men and managed to destroy a friendship that had barely begun. The life of a village doctor was proving to be anything but uneventful.

As he waited, Luke felt himself drifting into a half-conscious doze, his thoughts darting here and there until, unexpectedly, they settled on the causes of typhoid fever. He knew the outbreak in Yorkville had to be related to the summer's drought, and although current medical convention pointed a finger at Toronto's sewer, the facts as Luke knew them didn't quite fit this theory. The Spicers used city water regularly, yet none of them had fallen ill. The Christie household did as well; in fact, most of the citizens of Yorkville were dependent on Toronto water. Not so in the villages farther north. Most people there had wells. Not all of them were inexhaustible like the one in Daniel Cummer's willow grove, and Thaddeus said that he had seen people taking water from the millponds. But there had been far fewer cases of typhoid in the north.

What were the other sources of water in Yorkville? There were any number of streams and creeks that meandered across the escarpment, Luke knew, but they had dried away to nothing in the drought. When they were running they spilled into the ravines below and from there to the waters of the Don River — except where they were held up by the dam that created the pond by the brewery. The pond that Andrew Holden had grubbed through, looking for specimens to sell to Christie.

Luke's first patient had been Andrew Holden's son.

We all supply him, Andrew had said. *I sold him a big bull-frog in the spring.* Had Andrew been infected with typhoid at the pond and somehow carried it to his son? But then why hadn't Andrew himself fallen ill? Had Caleb Johnson gone hunting there, too? Caleb had been his mother's only source of income. It stood to reason that he would try to bring in a few extra coins by catering to the local doctor's eccentric hobby.

The miasmic fumes from every privy and commode and fouled creek, and even from the decomposing bodies of the Burying Ground itself, must somehow be carried down through the layers of rock to concentrate in the pond below. Was it possible to be infected just by dabbling in polluted water? Luke's medical training told him that this was nonsense. Infection was carried through the air, not the water. Still, he thought, Christie should tell his hunters to stay away from the pond, just in case. Tell them to look for something besides toads and salamanders.

And then his mind finally grew weary of problems and he slept.

He had no idea how much time passed, except that when he came fully to again, the moon was shining through a thin veil of clouds. He looked around at the bizarre shadows cast by the swaying branches and the marble gravestones. These were almost perfect conditions for a covert midnight raid.

And then, as if he had conjured it, he saw a light bobbing by the cemetery's northern boundary fence.

He rolled over onto his knees and glanced at the window of the lodge. There was no way to tell if Thaddeus was watching, and no way to creep to the back door without running the risk of alerting the intruders. Luke would wait to make a move, he decided, until they got a little closer. Then he could only hope that his father hadn't simply fallen asleep in his chair.

The light disappeared and for a moment he thought he'd been mistaken, that it was simply someone walking along the side of the building adjacent to the Burying Ground. Then, as the moon broke fully free from a cloud, he could just make out two figures creeping into the graveyard. They had needed the lantern, he realized, to provide light to climb the fence.

He watched as the two worked their way across the vacant section of ground, and then they veered suddenly and he lost sight of them. Moving as carefully as he could so as not to make any noise that might signal his presence, he rose to his feet and stepped to the other side of the chapel. He had trouble locating the figures again in the darkness until he caught a glint of light from the shuttered lantern. They were stopped at a grave not far from Isaiah Marshall's, in a row where Luke had found three stones with marks scratched on the back. He listened for the sound of shovel striking earth, but the wind had risen and the rustle of leaves masked any noise the men made. It would be easy digging tonight. The ground was soft and sodden from the recent rain.

He glanced back at the lodge in time to see the door open slightly. Thaddeus was awake after all, and judging from his caution, he had seen the lantern, as well, but his view of the trespassers' current position would be blocked by the chapel. Luke stepped back until he was sure he was out of sight, then waved his arm at Thaddeus. He was unsure what to do. If they rushed at the men now, they were likely to be outrun, and the opportunity to apprehend them would be lost. He debated creeping over to the lodge to consult with his father, but then he would run the risk of being seen. He glanced at the lodge again. Thaddeus was motioning him to move to the rear of the chapel. Luke sidled along the stone wall until he reached the corner of the rear wall. From this position he would be able to more effectively cut off the intruders, should they bolt the same way they had come. Luke wasn't sure what his father had in mind, but he crouched, tensed and alert. He would be ready for whatever it was.

Now he could hear the faint *scritch scritch* of a shovel, then a muttered oath, followed by the hissed admonition, "Shut your trap, Cuddy."

After long minutes of watching, Luke had to step back from the corner and stretch his limbs, cramped already from his inadvertent doze and made worse by his hunched position by the wall. Then he peeked around the corner again as he heard the dull thud of the shovel striking wood. He glanced at the lodge door, but could discern no signal from Thaddeus. Surely his father would make a move soon. The grave robbers were well and truly caught in the act now.

Then, as the moon rose a little higher in the sky, Luke saw someone climb over the fence that separated the cemetery from the Tollgate Road. He shot a glance at the intruders. Only the head and shoulders of one of them was visible. He was well down in the hole he'd dug. The other stood over him, but his attention was fixed on the metal box that his accomplice was handing up to him and he didn't notice that someone was creeping toward him through the shadows cast by the stone monuments.

It was Morgan Spicer. Thaddeus must have sent him out the front door of the lodge to make his way along the front of the Burying Ground. As Luke watched, Morgan snaked stealthily closer, until he was no more than twenty feet from the grave. Suddenly he jumped up and shouted. The man holding the lantern dropped it and ran toward the back fence, the other scrambling out of the grave to follow him. Luke broke into a barreling sprint across the graveyard, vaulting headstones as he ran. When he shouted, the intruders realized he was on a course to intercept them and they abruptly changed direction, running for the west corner of the grounds. Morgan anticipated this move and was there to cut them off. And then suddenly Thaddeus appeared from behind the chapel, blocking their exit to the south.

The men circled around Morgan, hoping still to reach the western fence, but in the dark and their hurry, they failed to see the mound of earth that was heaped up over Caleb Johnson's grave. One of them tripped over the end of it and tumbled to the ground. The other stopped to help him to his feet.

The man's head was down, focused on lifting his partner, and he didn't see Thaddeus running at him from one side, or anticipate the bone-jarring tackle that knocked him flying. Luke ran forward, too, ready to jump on either of the culprits should they attempt to rise.

But the men lay there, blinking and confused by the sudden ambush.

"Who are you?" Morgan demanded. "Why are you digging up my graves?"

Thaddeus grabbed the lantern, unshuttering it to cast full light on the men's faces. One of them was Hands, just as Luke expected, but he was taken aback to realize that he knew the other as well. It was the same man who had been in the cabinet-maker's yard the night Hands was shot, the same man who had chased the Lewises halfway across Toronto. The man on whom Luke sicced a guard dog so they could get away. The scars were still there on his face — ugly, sunken welts that had healed badly over the flesh that had been ripped away. Hands would not be the only one wanting revenge on the Lewises.

Hands looked in bewilderment from Thaddeus to Luke. It was Cuddy who recognized them. "I know you. I know you both!" His face settled into an angry sneer. "You're the two who set the dog on me. Hands and I have been looking for you. And here you are, fallen right into our laps."

"I think you've fallen into ours," Thaddeus pointed out. "We'll be sending for the constable now."

"I don't think so," Cuddy said. And then, before anyone could step forward to grab his arm, he pulled out a gun and waved it menacingly at Luke and Thaddeus. He scrambled to his feet, and then, still pointing the gun, reached down with one hand to pull his boss upright.

Van Hansel retrieved his hat and brushed the mud from his trousers before he fixed Thaddeus with an appraising stare. "It is you. Well, well, well. Where's the girl? The one who shot me?"

"Long gone," Thaddeus said. "I have no idea what happened to her."

She had fled across the border, Luke knew. Surely she was safe now, or was Hands's reach that long? He didn't know, but he would follow his father's lead and claim ignorance of her fate.

"We'll have to see if we can help your memory along a little," Hands said. "And I expect Cuddy wouldn't mind some time alone with the pair of you, as well. You quite ruined his good looks when you sicced that dog on him, you know. He may want a little revenge of his own. Turn around and walk slowly toward the gate."

Thaddeus appeared to stumble a little as he turned, and Luke reached out to steady him. Morgan had been standing to one side, seemingly forgotten, and as soon as Cuddy's attention was drawn by Thaddeus's movement, he rushed forward. But he was a little too far away to take Cuddy by surprise, and too small to knock him down. Hands caught at Morgan's jacket as he flew by. It was enough to send Spicer tumbling to the ground. Hands dropped on top of him, dug his knee into Morgan's stomach, and transferred the grip of his good hand to Morgan's throat.

"I've got him, Cuddy," Hands said. "You take care of the other two."

Cuddy waved the gun. "Start walking, and no funny business this time" he said. "Keep your hands where I can see them."

They had taken only a step or two when the night erupted with shouts. Luke heard Sally yell, "Get back here!" He heard the shrieks of small children. He heard Cuddy yell, "What the ..." And he heard Hands's roar at Morgan to hold still. After that everything seemed to happen at once. Four small children shot past the chapel, their white nightgowns billowing out behind them. They looked rather like angels, Luke thought, identical freckled angels spilling out from the tiny church to exact their vengeance on the mortals before them. Or demons, maybe, risen up from the depths of the graves. Either way, they presented an unsettling spectacle.

They ran past Thaddeus and barreled into Hands, their combined weight and the force of their attack nearly knocking him over. With only one functional arm, Van Hansel was finding it difficult to subdue the struggling Morgan, and had no hand free to counter the twins' attack. He kicked at them awkwardly, and one of them — Luke wasn't entirely sure which, but he thought it might have been one of the girls — grabbed Hands's leg below the knee, then lowered her head and sunk her teeth into his leg.

Cuddy shouted and pointed his gun in the direction of the melee. "Get away! Now!"

The double set of twins ignored him, intent on saving their father. Hands yelled and kicked again. This time his foot connected solidly with one of the boys. Sally shrieked and the boy howled, adding to the pandemonium.

And then, behind Van Hansel, Luke saw a slim figure slide out of the shadows and snatch the metal box that was lying unguarded on the grass: Cherub, who must have been watching from the edge of the cemetery. Hands turned and saw her, too, but he was off-balance from the twins' assault, and she raced over the short distance to the fence before he could regain his feet and give chase. She had to slow down in order to scale the barrier though, and this gave Hands time to reach her, with Cuddy not more than ten feet behind.

Van Hansel was just reaching for Cherub's foot when a shot rang out. Luke gasped. But it was not Cherub who fell to the ground. It was Hands.

Luke ran to the fallen body while Cuddy stood open-mouthed. Cherub dropped to the ground on the other side of the fence and stopped to look at the fallen man, but only for a moment. Then she fled down the street.

The bullet had struck Van Hansel in the back, and blood was spreading across his jacket from an ugly, ragged hole. Luke pulled out his handkerchief and wadded it into the wound to try to stop the bleeding. The shot had entered the body between two ribs, and was fired at such close range that he judged it had carried enough force to pierce the lung. He rolled Hands over onto his side and lifted him to a half-sitting position. As Luke feared, blood spewed from the man's mouth when he attempted to speak and his breath was shallow.

Cuddy seemed to recover his senses and raised his pistol again.

"Get a doctor, quick," he barked.

"I am a doctor," Luke said. "Don't point that thing at me."

Cuddy hesitated for a moment, uncertainty on his face, and let his arm fall to his side. Thaddeus made his move then. He leapt at Cuddy and grabbed his arm from behind, groping wildly for the gun as Cuddy raised it in a futile effort to aim it at his attacker.

Before either Morgan or Luke could scramble to his aid, Sally raced through the graveyard to the struggling pair, shovel in hand. She took a great sweeping swing at Cuddy's outstretched hand. The shovel connected solidly with his wrist, knocking the gun to the ground. It fired on impact.

Luke reflexively ducked behind Hands, but the bullet ricocheted harmlessly off a gravestone and embedded itself in the ground.

"Don't you ever, *ever* point a gun at my children again," Sally spat into Cuddy's confused face. Thaddeus managed to grab Cuddy's free hand and wrenched both of his arms behind him while Morgan shook off the profusion of children in his arms and ran to scoop up the fallen weapon.

"I've got him," Thaddeus said. "Morgan, go get the constable."

Morgan nodded and disappeared toward the front gates.

Luke returned his attention to the wounded man he held.

A gush of foamy blood spewed from Hands' mouth as he croaked out the words "My … money." He glared at Luke, took a long, shuddering breath, and then said, quite clearly, "You'll pay for this." The issuing of this threat apparently exhausted him. His eyes rolled back in his head, and his breathing became even more laboured. And then, with a last effort at speech that came out as nothing more than a gurgle, Phillip Van Hansel ceased to breathe entirely.

Chapter 21

Thaddeus took charge of the subsequent investigation by the befuddled local constable, who seemed to have difficulty grasping the details of what had occurred in the graveyard. The sound of gunfire had roused the people in the neighbouring houses, and several of the men, seeing Thaddeus's firm grip on Cuddy and the bloodied corpse in Luke's arms, jumped the fence to offer their assistance. They cheerfully, and none too gently, took charge of Cuddy, who hysterically protested his innocence.

"It was an accident! I swear! The gun went off by itself!"

The men paid no attention to him, other than to jerk his arm now and again when he grew too loud.

The constable arrived, red-faced and gasping, with his nightshirt trailing out of his trousers and his shoes untied, disturbed, no doubt, from a deep and complacent sleep. He surveyed the havoc in the graveyard with dismay.

"Just what the devil happened here?" he demanded.

"It was grave robbers," Morgan said, giving Thaddeus an opening to provide an uncomplicated version of the evening's events. He wasn't entirely sure he understood what had happened himself. Best to keep it simple, so the constable didn't get confused.

"I believe Mr. Spicer reported a similar occurrence a few weeks ago," Thaddeus said.

"Well, yes he did," the constable sputtered. "But my goodness, there's a man dead here. Do you want to tell me how that happened?"

The constable addressed this to Thaddeus, rather than Morgan, so Thaddeus quickly outlined what had happened as he understood it.

"After the first disturbance, which you, of course, know all about." The constable nodded. "Mr. Spicer began keeping watch at night hoping he could circumvent any further damage to the graves. Tonight I was keeping him company, as I have done on previous evenings. His vigilance paid off, as we noticed two men with shovels enter the graveyard, and as you can see," here Thaddeus pointed at the disinterred body that lay in the opened grave, "they were in the process of unearthing another corpse."

The constable took a step or two toward the body for a closer look, but quickly retreated when he detected the smell coming from it.

"We accosted the men, who attempted to run off," Thaddeus went on. "Unfortunately, one of them had a gun, which must have gone off while they ran. The second man was hit. I'm sure it was an accident."

"That's right," Cuddy growled. "It was an accident."

An accident that he hit his boss, Thaddeus thought. He had been aiming for whoever it was that had snatched the metal box and climbed over the fence. Thaddeus had no idea who this might be, and, until he knew more, he judged that it was best to omit this part of the story. He had no explanation for the presence of the third intruder. The important thing was to have Cuddy firmly in custody, and Thaddeus was reluctant to volunteer any information that might send the constable down any path other than the one he had been directed to.

"And who might you be, sir?" the constable asked, squinting up at him.

Thaddeus marshalled all the ministerial authority he could muster. "My name is Thaddeus Lewis. I am a minister for the Methodist Episcopal Church, currently assigned to the Yonge Street Circuit. Mr. Spicer is an old friend."

"I see," the constable said, and turned his doubtful gaze toward Luke. "And who might this be?"

"I'm a physician," Luke said.

The constable seemed content with this answer, assuming that Luke was there to attend to the wounded man and had not played an integral part in events. Thaddeus let the assumption stand. He would keep Luke out this, if he could. Hands was no longer a threat to the Lewises, but Cuddy had been looking for them, too. Thaddeus had no way of knowing if Cuddy had friends who would be willing to carry out a directive for revenge.

"Well," the constable said finally, "it'll be up to the coroner to sort it all out. And the magistrate after that." He turned to the men who held Cuddy. "Can you boys help get him to the jail?" and when they nodded, he led the way out of the graveyard, Cuddy struggling and protesting the whole way.

"It was an accident!" he cried. "I didn't mean to!"

"Doesn't matter whether you meant to or not," the constable said. "A man's dead, regardless. If you're lucky, you're on your way to jail. If you're not, it'll be the gibbet."

Morgan found two pieces of canvas, one to cover Van Hansel's body, the other for the corpse that had been exposed.

"Do you think they'll be all right for tonight?" he asked anxiously.

"I'm sure they will," Thaddeus said. "The coroner will be along soon to look at Hands's body. We'll keep an eye on them both until then, but we can do that from the cottage. I, for one, need to sit down. And Luke needs to clean himself up. Come on in."

"Hands?" Morgan asked. "Is that the gentleman you told me about? The one who was shot?"

"Yes."

Morgan nodded. "He was luckier the first time, wasn't he?"

When they entered the Spicer kitchen, Sally was heating milk on the stove. "I'll never get this crowd to bed again if they don't calm down," she said. "I'll make some tea, as well."

"I'd just as soon have some milk," Thaddeus said. "I need to calm down, too."

He sat at the table and one of the twins scrambled up into his lap while another leaned up against him. The remaining two climbed up onto their father.

Luke went to the kitchen pump and began sluicing Van Hansel's blood from his hands.

Thaddeus watched him for a few moments and then he said, "You know, every time I go anywhere with you, you end up covered in blood."

"And every time I go anywhere with you, you tackle someone to the ground. Are you all right? You were crippled for days after the last time."

Thaddeus seemed surprised, not so much by the question as by his own answer. "Yes, I'm fine. Even my knee is sound." And then he looked sheepish. "I'm not sure why, except that I've felt wonderful ever since I started drinking from Holy Ann's well. It seems clear to me that there's something special about the water, but I'm not sure I want to credit it."

"Holy Ann's well in Thorne's Hill?" Luke said, daubing at his coat with a cloth. "I doubt that has anything to do with it. A far better explanation is that you've also been drinking water from Daniel Cummer's well."

"I don't follow," Thaddeus said. "There's nothing special about Cummer's well except that it's spring-fed and never goes dry. And there's a grove of willows around it." His eyes widened as he grasped what Luke was implying. "It's the willow trees, isn't it? Their roots go down into the water table."

"It could have an effect," Luke said. "Although it's more likely that water has trickled through the leaves and branches into the well below. We have no idea, really, what lies in the ground."

"I can't believe I was almost so foolish as to believe in Holy Ann."

"I can't believe you were so foolish as to grapple with a man half your age. You're way too old for that kind of nonsense, you know."

Thaddeus was about to take offence when he realized that he was being teased.

"Oh, you," Sally said, slapping at Luke's shoulder. "You shouldn't talk to your father that way."

Luke grinned. "In any event, there are far easier ways to get willow tea. If you find it helps, I'd be happy to get some for you."

"Only old folks drink willow tea."

"My point exactly," Luke said.

In spite of his grumbling, Thaddeus welcomed the diversion in conversation. He didn't want to talk about what had happened in the Burying Ground until he had a chance to review the incident and try to fit all the pieces of the puzzle together. As he thought about it, though, he realized that he was still missing too many of them. There were many questions he wanted to ask, but they were better left until the children drank their possets and were herded back to bed. He wondered if they realized what they had witnessed. He hoped not. And then he felt a surge of admiration for the way they had rushed to their father's defence, as dangerous a thing as that was for them to do. He hoped that Sally would scold them mightily and then tell them how brave they had been.

The twin on his lap had finished only half of her mug of milk when her eyes started to droop. Sally picked her up and took the other by the hand to lead him upstairs. The remaining two followed, rubbing their eyes and yawning.

"Well," Thaddeus said when they had left the room, "that was an interesting evening. I'm still not sure what it was all about."

"It seems your first guess about the double burials was the right one," Morgan said.

"Yes, but I'm not sure why," Thaddeus said. "Obviously there was something hidden in the coffins that Hands wanted. But why did he start retrieving them all at once? And who ran away with the metal box?"

Morgan turned to Luke. "You said right from the start that it couldn't be Dr. Christie. Why were you so sure?"

Luke shrugged. "I guess it was a Holy Ann reaction," he said. "I just didn't want to credit it."

* * *

The next morning Dr. Christie insisted that Thaddeus escort him to the Burying Ground and arrange for him to view the unearthed corpse, in spite of the fact that Thaddeus was bone-weary and longing for bed. He and Morgan and Luke had spent the rest of the night sitting vigil over the bodies in the graveyard. He and Morgan spent the hours going over and over each event and each piece of evidence, but at the end of it all

Thaddeus felt he was no closer to solving the puzzle. Luke had little to say on the matter, appearing at times to doze off in his chair, but Thaddeus didn't know if this was because he had no insight to contribute, or if he was simply tired. It was unlikely that he was rattled by the experience of having a man die in his arms. It had happened to him before, and he was far better equipped to deal with it now. He was a doctor, after all, and no doubt had seen far worse during the course of his training. Still, it seemed a little odd that he was so silent about the affair.

As soon as they returned to Christie's the next morning, Luke went off in search of Mrs. Dunphy to ask if anything could be done to salvage his stained clothing, leaving Thaddeus as the sole object of Christie's badgering insistence on viewing the exhumed body.

When they arrived at the Burying Ground, Thaddeus realized that it was Morgan who appeared to have been most rattled by the events of the previous night. He was red-eyed and bleary, and seemed almost insensible to what was happening around him. Hands's body had been removed, the coroner having examined it and taken copious notes for the inquest that would be called. Morgan was given permission to rebury the other body, but he had only just taken up a shovel to do this when Christie arrived to waylay him.

"Dr. Christie wondered if he might have a look at the corpse," Thaddeus said. "He won't touch anything, but he thinks an examination of the bones might be useful."

Morgan agreed, and he and Thaddeus walked toward the front of the cemetery while Christie climbed down into the grave with every evidence of delight at having been afforded such a unique opportunity.

"One of the trustees showed up this morning," Morgan said when they reached the fence. "The board finally took notice of what was going on."

"Surely they recognize how diligent you've been," Thaddeus said. "No one else would have sat up all those nights to protect the graves."

"Oh yes, I'm a fine fellow," Morgan said. "Job well done and all that. But the trustee also took the opportunity to inform me that Yorkville is officially starting a petition to close the Burying Ground. He said he thought he should let me know, as he didn't think it would take long to get the required number of signatures. The board plans to start asking the families to remove bodies to the cemeteries of their choice." He sighed. "I'm going to have to move on soon, and I don't want to."

"I know, you and Sally are happy here, aren't you?"

"Yes, we are, but it's more than that. It's the job itself. Somehow it's not just work. It's something that needs to be done. I wanted to be a preacher because I thought it would make me important. But here … I don't know …" He screwed up his face and looked off into the distance as he tried to find the elusive words that would describe what he meant. "I'm not important here. But the bodies are, and they need someone to look after them."

"I know what you mean," Thaddeus said. Morgan's inelegant words described what Thaddeus himself often felt while riding a promising circuit. It was the feeling that was missing on Yonge Street, the idea that he was making a difference to people. Others had reached them before he had had a chance to, and now their spiritual needs were being met in new and different ways. Even Holy Ann was more of a success than he was. He would see it through, complete his appointment, but he had no idea what he was going to do after that.

He would be sorry if he could no longer spend time with the Spicers. He had been reminded again of the essential worth of the Morgan Spicers of the world, and he was finding pleasure in his interactions with Spicer's twins. He and Betsy had had so many children and lost nearly all of them, and now there were too few grandchildren to spoil. There was Martha, of course. But Martha was a young lady now and no longer needed him as much as she had when she was little. Other than that there were only the children of his eldest son, Will, and they were in distant Huron, too far for a casual visit. Thaddeus briefly wondered if he should go there, make an effort to get to know them, but he had never got on as well with Will as he did with Luke, and he didn't know if an extended visit to Huron would be entirely welcome.

"All I can say, Morgan, is that life changes, and you can never be sure what direction it will take. All you can do is trust in the Lord. *He revealeth the deep and secret things: he knoweth what is in the darkness and the light dwelleth with him.* We'll just have to wait and see what happens."

Morgan nodded, but he still looked glum.

They waited until Christie, humming happily to himself, had gleaned whatever information he wanted from the dead body, then, once again, Thaddeus rolled up his sleeves to help Morgan restore a grave.

* * *

Thaddeus stuck to his story at the inquest, with the result that Cuthbert Nelson, as Cuddy's full name turned out to be, was acquitted of criminal responsibility in the death of Phillip Van Hansel, in spite of the fact that Cuddy was a known criminal with prior arrests for assault, robbery, and public drunkenness, none of which, however, had ever resulted in a conviction.

The jury seemed unconcerned about the desecration of the grave, which was just as well, as Cuddy had no explanation for what he and Hands had been doing in the Burying Ground that night.

"No, I think this judgment is fair," Thaddeus said when Luke questioned whether they should have mentioned that Cuddy was, in fact, shooting at someone else when he hit Van Hansel by mistake. "After all, we have no idea who that someone else was, or what motives anyone had. Let it lie. With any luck, Cuddy will be grateful that we backed his story and forget about the incident with the dog."

The newspapers, however, were not prepared to be so generous and howled their dismay at the verdict. *The Daily Patriot* seemed particularly incensed by what they termed the "incompetence" of the jury in failing to ask a number of pertinent questions.

"What was a prominent businessman like Phillip Van Hansel doing in a remote graveyard with such a ruffian?" Dr. Christie read out at the breakfast table the day after the ruling was handed down. "One can only conclude that Nelson lured him there with the intent to murder, as evinced by his attempt to open a grave so that he could dispose of the body. No one with a sensible mind would countenance the notion that an upstanding citizen like Van Hansel would participate in a crime so odious as grave robbing. There are far more sinister elements to this tragic incident than were revealed at the inquest."

"Now that's a true statement," Thaddeus remarked. "Although I can't for the life of me figure out what they are."

"Odd business, to be sure," Christie said. "I'm not convinced we'll ever know the truth of the matter. And Spicer was so optimistic that you could sort it out for him."

"I don't seem to be able to sort out much of anything for poor Morgan," Thaddeus said. "I couldn't make him a preacher, I couldn't solve his puzzle, and I can't even give him any practical advice on what to do about his current difficulties."

"What difficulties?" Luke asked. "Now that the graves are safe, I thought his troubles would be over."

"The Board of Trustees at the Burying Ground has notified him that his position may be terminated soon. The village intends to circulate a petition to have the cemetery closed. The trustees will ask the families to move the bodies."

Christie was skeptical. "Not that nonsense again." He shook his head. "People can petition all they like, but nothing can happen until the legislature gives its approval. That will take years, if it happens at all. Not to mention the fundamental flaw in the scheme. It's a Potter's Field. Most of the bodies buried there have no family to move them. It could all be done at public expense, I suppose, but someone would have to vote funds for the purpose, and I can't see anyone being in favour of that. Tell Spicer to stop worrying."

"I suppose you're right," Thaddeus said. "I'll tell him. I hope it will cheer him up."

Chapter 22

Luke was sure that the majority of his problems were now neatly resolved. He was square with Christie and confident that his position as junior physician was secure. The old doctor didn't give much credence to Luke's theory that typhoid fever had come from the millpond, but at Luke's insistence, he did promise to keep his hunters away from the pond in the summertime, just in case.

He was also on a far more even keel with his father. Their latest adventure had restored some of the camaraderie Luke had felt when they'd been chasing the trail that first led them to Hands. He was finding mealtimes entertaining affairs when Thaddeus was in Yorkville. Now that he was no longer so preoccupied with his worries, he felt free to join the spiralling conversations and sometimes even managed to surprise the two older men with an observation or point of view that hadn't occurred to either of them.

The source of Lavinia Van Hansel's complaint — her husband — would no longer be an aggravation to her, and surely she would now find herself in comfortable enough circumstances, if the amounts secreted in the coffins were any indication. Van Hansel had been a rich man. Lavinia would now be a rich widow. She could do whatever she wanted. There was no longer any reason for her to manipulate Perry, or anyone else for that matter.

Luke still regretted his hasty words to Perry, but he concluded that there was no way to set it right again. There had not been a single word from him in the weeks since Van Hansel's death. Luke couldn't blame him for that. Not after the accusations that had been hurled. Even if Perry gave him an opportunity to explain, Luke wasn't sure that any explanation would be enough to justify what he'd said.

He tried, as much as possible, to put Perry out of his mind, but now that there was no epidemic to keep him occupied he found that he had only occasional cases to see in the morning and that his afternoons were by and large free. He began to understand why Christie was so absorbed in the reconstruction of skeletons. Luke had no intention of taking up so strange a hobby, but he needed to find something to do.

One afternoon, just after Mrs. Dunphy cleared away the dinner dishes and Christie disappeared into the shed, Luke wandered into the parlour and was looking idly through the shelves for something to read when he heard a knock at the front door.

When he opened it, he was surprised to find Cherub Ebenezer standing there.

"Dr. Lewis! I'm glad it's you who answered. I need to talk to you."

"By all means, come through to the office." He could think of no reason why Cherub would seek him out unless Lavinia had some new demand to make of him. He couldn't begin to think what it might be, but in spite of his understanding with Christie, he decided that it would be far better to keep their conversation private. He motioned her to a chair and took his place behind the desk.

"What do you want?"

She seemed not at all put out by his directness. "Did you find what we asked you to look for?"

"Yes, but I don't know why you need it. Surely the problem has been resolved?"

"Anything but. We need it more than ever. By the time the dust settles Lavinia will be lucky if she has the clothes on her back. The vultures will have picked them all away."

"I don't understand," Luke said. "Hands was rich. Lavinia should have plenty of money now, shouldn't she?"

"Yes, Phillip had a lot of money. But everything he had is tied up somehow. Concealed. So that no finger could ever be pointed at him should anyone come asking questions. He also borrowed a lot to invest in railroads. His creditors are calling in the loans. His partners will make sure that they get their share of what's left. Lavinia has no call on any of it."

Luke had no knowledge of business and how it worked, but he found it hard to believe that Lavinia would be left with nothing. "But surely there was some provision made," he said. "Hands can't have left her destitute."

"He didn't intend to. His will left her the use of the house and a yearly amount in maintenance, to be paid from the estate, with his brother Peter as the executor."

"Well, there you go then. She'll be all right, won't she? With her brother-in-law to look after her?"

"You really don't understand what the law does to women, do you, Luke?" Cherub said. "Anything Lavinia gets is on Peter's sufferance. And Peter Van Hansel is an avaricious bastard. If there's anything left of Phillip's estate, he'll take it."

"Can she not go to the courts? Isn't she entitled to a certain percentage or something?" Luke's knowledge of property law was even sketchier than his knowledge of business, but he couldn't believe that the widow of a wealthy man could be left in such dreadful straits.

"A percentage of nothing is still nothing," Cherub said. "Peter claims there's not enough money to pay her anything at all. I've been asked to leave. And he's already put the house up for sale. We need to know what you know, Luke."

Luke debated for only a moment before he realized that his course of action was clear. He could get rid of Lavinia Van Hansel with the stroke of a pen. And, for once, the expedient choice also happened to be, as far as he was concerned, the ethical one.

"I have the names from the Burying Ground. There were eight in all. Hands took two. You already have one. That leaves five. That should be enough, I would think." He grabbed a piece of paper and found a pen. He was pleased that he had no difficulty remembering the names and was able to write them down quickly. He handed the paper to Cherub, and the look of relief on her face confirmed the truth of her story. "How were you planning to get at them?" he asked.

She shrugged. "That part we haven't figured out yet. But at least now we know where to dig."

"You won't get away with digging up more than one, you know. There's been too much publicity in connection with Van Hansel's death. If any more graves are tampered with it will be reported in the newspapers and the Board of Trustees will have to investigate. After that, the Burying Ground would be watched far too closely."

She took a moment to digest this, then her voice took on an edge of panic as she realized the truth of what Luke was saying. "Are you suggesting we dig them up all at once? How do we do that?"

"If I tell you how to get them, do you promise me that you and Lavinia will go away?" he said. "And I don't mean 'go away' as in 'leave me alone.' I mean 'go away' as in you'll leave the country."

"That's an easy promise to make. That's what we want to do anyway. Life would be far easier for us in Europe."

"Then you should know that there's a petition to close the Burying Ground. The village wants the land. The trustees are asking families to move the graves."

Cherub's eyes grew wide. "So all we have to do is claim the bodies and take them somewhere else?"

"Yes. It will cost you a little to have them carted and you'll have to pay for cemetery plots somewhere else, but it won't amount to a lot. After all, you've already stolen one metal box full of money."

"But won't it look suspicious if we claim all five?"

Luke shook his head. "Split it up. Lavinia can sign for three of them, you for the other two."

"A coloured woman? Will they believe that they're mine?"

Luke smiled. "Who's to say different? One of the bodies that Hands dug up was a coloured man. Far more likely at the Burying Ground than at any other cemetery in the city, I'd say."

Her worried face relaxed a little, but Luke could tell that she was still puzzled by something.

"Don't worry," he said. "The village is anxious to have the ground closed. There won't be any argument. And none of the people you're carting away have any family to ask questions about what you're doing."

"It's not that," she said. "I just can't figure out why Hands went to all the bother of digging in the first place. He could have just marched in and offered to pay for the removal."

"There's been talk of closing the cemetery for years, but no one took it seriously until just recently. He might not have known about it. I was told once that he had his hands in everything, but he may have thought Yorkville wasn't worth reaching for."

"Thank you, Luke." She rose to leave, but just as she reached the door she turned to him, an odd expression on her handsome face. "You have no idea what this means to us. Or maybe you do. We're not so different, Lavinia and I, from you and Perry." And then she let herself out.

Luke was surprised at her revelation, but then he realized that he shouldn't have been. He should have seen it before. Poor Lavinia. He could almost feel sorry for her.

* * *

A week later, Luke had just finished checking on old Mrs. Cory and was walking down Yonge Street when he noticed Spicer and his father in the Burying Ground and a carter's dray rolling slowly along the laneway. Curious, he walked over to the cemetery and down the lane to discover Lavinia Van Hansel perched on the cart beside a very dirty and disreputable-looking driver, who jammed his hat down farther over his face when ordered to stop. As he drew closer, Luke saw that the strain of the last few weeks showed clearly on Lavinia's face. The lines around her mouth had deepened and there were new ones at the corners of her eyes. Her skin was still porcelain, but she no longer reminded him of a china doll.

"Dr. Lewis! How lovely to see you!" she said.

He nodded to her. "And you." He glanced at the wagon's load. There were three coffins stacked in the bed, jammed up against a large steamer trunk. "On your way to a funeral?"

"Oh," she said, with a wave of her hand, "my mother's family, you know. We'd quite lost track of them until we heard the Burying Ground was closing. I've purchased them a nice shady plot at the Necropolis."

"Excellent plan."

"Thank you, Luke."

"Pure self-interest."

"No," she said, "providing the names was self-interest. Offering the means of removal was an act of kindness."

Luke glanced over to where his father and Spicer were standing, and was relieved to see that they were too far away to overhear the conversation. "I've been the recipient of great kindnesses myself," he said. "My benefactors would also claim self-interest, I suppose, but they were kind nonetheless. You're welcome."

The driver shifted in his seat impatiently, drawing Luke's attention. There was something in the way he held the reins that seemed familiar. And then Luke realized that it was Perry, dressed up to look like a particularly slovenly carter. Lavinia had evidently exerted one last little bit of pressure and enlisted Perry to help her move the coffins. She didn't seem to find it odd that Perry had yet to speak to him. She must have been told that he and Luke had fallen out.

"You know, it's almost too bad I'm not staying in Toronto," Lavinia went on. "You're a fascinating man, Dr. Lewis. I would like to have known you better."

"And if that were the case, I would be running as fast as I could in the opposite direction," Luke said.

She smiled. "Just tell me one thing before I go, never to be seen again in this fair city. How did you know about my husband? You hadn't been here for more than a few weeks, and yet you already knew all about him."

Luke hadn't expected to see Lavinia Van Hansel again, and he certainly hadn't considered telling her about the night in the cabinetmaker's yard. Even though there was little danger in her knowing now, a part of him was still reluctant to give up the secret. Except that Perry was sitting there beside her. If he told Lavinia, Perry couldn't help but hear. Maybe it would make a difference, maybe it wouldn't. But it was probably the only opportunity Luke would ever have to explain himself.

"I was there the night your husband was shot," he said.

"Yes, I know. Cherub saw you in the graveyard."

"No, not that time. The *first* time."

She looked at him with astonishment and then she began to laugh, a deep chuckle that lit up her face and washed away the lines.

"You were *there*?" she said, looking at him with delight. "Oh my goodness, what are the chances? Tell me what happened. He wouldn't ever say. Was it you who shot him?"

"No, it wasn't me, but I was there. My father and I were trying to track down the family of an Irish emigrant girl whose parents died of fever. The trail led us to Toronto, where we discovered that the girl had been tricked into entering a brothel by people who worked for Hands. In the process of finding her, we also discovered that your husband was involved in any number of discreditable activities. There was the embezzlement of the liquor rations, the coffin-stuffing. And he raped a girl. As soon as she had a chance and a gun she took a shot at him."

"What happened to the girl afterward? Or do I want to know?"

"She got away. With our help. As far as I know she's in the States somewhere with the love of her life."

"Good for her," Lavinia said. "I'm glad."

Perry sat with his head down, his hat still covering his face. He hadn't moved, but Luke knew he was listening, could *feel* him listening.

"There's more," Luke said. He wanted to make sure that Perry understood exactly what the stakes had been. "My father wrote a letter to Anthony Hawke and told him everything we knew. That's the reason Hawke suspected your husband."

Perry's ludicrous hat tilted up just a bit as he shifted his head to hear.

"Your father is the older gentleman over there with the Keeper?" Lavinia asked. "He must be. You look just like him. And he's here in Yorkville as well?"

"Yes."

"Well, it's no wonder you went skulking out the garden door as soon as you saw Phillip at the house that night. You and your father would have been in a very precarious position if he had realized who you were. He never liked being crossed."

"I'd heard that."

"I don't know why you didn't tell me this before." And then she laughed at her own foolish words. "Well, yes, I do know. I'd have made your life miserable, wouldn't I?"

"Yes, you would have," Luke agreed.

"I'm only sorry the girl wasn't a better shot. It might have saved us all a great deal of trouble." She smiled down at him. "But it's all turned out as well as it could have, I suppose. I owe you, Luke Lewis."

"Just make sure you actually deliver these bodies. Otherwise the Keeper will be in a state."

"He's already made that perfectly clear." She frowned and shook her head. "Odd little man. Well, good luck, Dr. Lewis."

Perry had still not said a word.

Luke watched as the wagon rumbled away. He'd tried. That was all he could do. And then, just as the wagon turned the corner onto Tollgate Road, Perry suddenly ripped the shapeless hat off his head and looked back at him. He gave no sign, made no gesture, but for Luke, for now, it was enough.

He waited until the wagon was out of sight, then he continued walking across the Burying Ground to where Morgan and Thaddeus were standing beside a gaping hole. Spicer looked dreadful. He was sweaty and begrimed, his thin hair plastered against his head.

"Morgan's been digging for hours," Thaddeus said. "There's been five coffins moved already. Two yesterday and three just now."

"Are you sure your Dr. Christie knows what he's talking about?" Morgan asked, his forehead furrowed with worry. "It's only been a few weeks since they sent the letters out to the families and all these bodies have gone already."

"I wouldn't worry about it," Luke said. "I expect it's just an initial rush. The families who want to look after their loved ones would come right away, as soon as they were contacted. I think you'll see the response fall off dramatically after this, and then nothing will happen for a long time."

"Do you really think so?"

"I'm sure of it," Luke said firmly.

Thaddeus shot a questioning glance at him, so Luke changed the subject quickly. "I hope you weren't doing any of the digging."

"No, I merely supervised. My old joints are serving me well right now, but I won't ask that much of them. I saw you talking with Mrs. Biddulph. Is she the same family as your friend?"

"Mrs. Biddulph?" Luke said, and then he realized what Lavinia had done. She'd not only recruited Perry to play carter, she'd had him arrange the removals. The name Biddulph would carry weight with the Board of Trustees. They wouldn't think twice about granting permission to move so many graves at once, not if it was a Biddulph who was asking. "Ah, yes, Mrs. Biddulph. A distant relative, I believe."

"So where are you off to now?" Thaddeus asked.

"I've seen my patients for the day. I was just heading home."

"We're about to badger Sally for a cup of tea. And I promised the children I'd read them another chapter from *The Travels of Marco Polo*. Would you care to join us?"

"I'd love a cup of tea," Luke said. "But I should point out that it's not fair. The only things you would ever allow us to read when we were children were Bible stories."

"That's true enough," Thaddeus admitted as they began walking toward the cottage. "I don't know why I was such an old stick-in-the-mud." Then he grinned at his son. "Never mind. I'm making up for lost time."

Acknowledgements

The Toronto Strangers' Burying Ground was located on the northwest corner of Yonge Street and what later became known as Bloor Street — now some of the most expensive real estate in Canada. In 1855, the government of the United Province of Canada finally gave the cemetery's board of trustees permission to close it and sell the property, provided that all 6,685 graves were removed to other cemeteries. However, because no families could be contacted on behalf of approximately three thousand of the people who had been buried there, it wasn't until 1874 that all of the graves were finally moved to the Toronto Necropolis and Mount Pleasant Cemetery.

I am indebted to Jamie Bradburn, whose excellent article "Historicist: In Potter's Field" (*Torontoist*, October 29, 2011, St. Joseph Media) first drew my attention to the Strangers' Burying Ground, and to Hamish Copley's website, The Drummer's Revenge: LGBT History and Politics in Canada, which offered insight into attitudes toward homosexuality in mid-nineteenth-century Canada and detailed the story of Alexander Wood.

Louis-Hippolyte LaFontaine and Robert Baldwin by John Ralston Saul, part of the Extraordinary Canadians series (Penguin Group Canada, 2010), provided an account of the Montreal riots and the burning of the Parliament building; and *Black History in Early Toronto*, by Daniel G. Hill (*Polyphony*, Summer 1984: 28–30, Multicultural History Society of Ontario), described Toronto's black community in the 1850s.

Background material was drawn from "Body-Snatching in Ontario," by Royce MacGillivray: tspace.library.utoronto.ca/bitstream/1807/17619/2/body%20snatching%20Ontario%20CBMH.pdf; *Mrs. King: The Life and Times of Isabel Mackenzie King* by Charlotte Gray (Penguin Books Canada, 1997); *The Canadian County Atlas Digital Project* (McGill University); Derek Hayes's *Historical Atlas of Toronto* (Douglas & McIntyre, 2008); the website Lost River Walks, Toronto Green Community and Toronto Field Naturalists; *A Light on Medical Practice in 19th Century Canada: The Medical Manuscripts of Dr. John Mackieson of Charlottetown*, by David A.E. Shephard, MB (*Canadian Medical Association Journal* 1998: 159: 253–57); *Lucian: The History of Orestes and Pylades from Amores (2nd Century A.D.)*, translated by W.J. Baylis; *Toronto Called Back*, by Conyngham Crawford Taylor, printed for the author by William Briggs, Toronto, 1886; and the website for Niagara Apothecary: A Pharmacy Museum in Historic Niagara-on-the-Lake.

Many thanks to Matti Kopamees for locating books in the midst of chaos; to my agent, Robert Lecker, for his excellent advice; to my editor at Dundurn, Allison Hirst; and, as always, to Rob Kellough for his fortitude, but not for suggesting that Thaddeus be given the line "Luke, I am your father."

More Thaddeus Lewis Mysteries by Janet Kellough

On the Head of a Pin

Thaddeus Lewis, an itinerant "saddlebag" preacher, still mourns the mysterious death of his daughter Sarah as he rides to his new posting in Prince Edward County. When another girl in the area dies in a similar way, he realizes that the circumstances point to murder. But in the turmoil following the 1837 Rebellion, he can't get anyone to listen. Convinced there is a serial killer loose in Upper Canada, Lewis alone must track the culprit across a colony convulsed by dissension, invasion, and fear.

Sowing Poison

After many years, Nathan Elliott returns to Wellington, Ontario, to be at his dying father's side. Within a few days of his return, he is reported missing, and no trace of him can be found. Shortly after, Nathan's wife arrives in the village. Claiming that she can contact the dead, she begins to hold séances for the villagers. Thaddeus Lewis, a Methodist circuit rider, is outraged, and his ethical objections propel him on a journey to uncover the truth about the Elliotts. Religious conflict and political dissension all play a part in this tale set in 1844 Upper Canada.

47 Sorrows

47 SORROWS
Janet Kellough
A Thaddeus Lewis Mystery

When the bloated corpse of a man dressed in women's clothing washes up on the shore of Lake Ontario, a small scrap of green ribbon is found on the body. The year is 1847, and 100,000 Irish emigrants have fled to Canada to escape starvation in their homeland. But the emigrants bring with them the dreaded "ship's fever," and soon the ports are overflowing with the sick and dying. Itinerant preacher Thaddeus Lewis's son Luke, an aspiring doctor, volunteers in the fever sheds in Kingston. When he finds a green ribbon on the lifeless body of a patient, he is intrigued by the strange coincidence. Young Luke enlists his father's help to uncover the mystery, a tale of enmity that began back in Ireland.